SHIFTS

T0021640

PARTHIAN

LIBRARY OF WALES

Christopher Meredith is a poet, novelist and translator. He was born in Tredegar and brought up on the Cefn Golau housing estate. One of three brothers, his father was a steelworker and former collier, his mother a home help who had been a factory worker and a maid. He was educated at Aberystwyth and Swansea universities. He has been a steelworker, a schoolteacher, and a university lecturer. He lives in Brecon.

Poetry
This
Snaring Heaven
The Meaning of Flight
Air Histories
Still

Fiction
Shifts
Griffri
Sidereal Time
The Book of Idiots
Brief Lives – six fictions
Please

For children
Nadolig bob Dydd
Christmas Every Day

Translation from Welsh
Melog by Mihangel Morgan

As editor
Five Essays on Translation (with Katja Krebs)
Moment of Earth

SHIFTS

CHRISTOPHER MEREDITH

PARTHIAN

LIBRARY OF WALES

Parthian, Cardigan SA43 1ED
www.parthianbooks.com
The Library of Wales is a Welsh Government initiative which highlights and celebrates Wales'
literary heritage in the English language.
Published with the financial support of the Welsh Books Council.
© Christopher Meredith 1988, 2023
First published by Seren Books in 1988
Library of Wales edition published 2023
Series Editor: Kirsti Bohata
Foreword © Diana Wallace 2023
Cover design by Marc Jennings
Cover image: Detail from Hot Strip Mill by Norman Hepple (1908–1994), c.1952, courtesy
of Ebbw Vale Works Archival Trust
All Rights Reserved
ISBN 978-1-913640-79-8
Typeset by Elaine Sharples
Printed by 4Edge Limited

Foreword

Widely acknowledged as the classic novel of de-industrialisation in Wales, *Shifts* is a far funnier, and stranger, book than that rather dry description might suggest. From the unsettling opening sentence – 'O clocked off at exactly half past three' – we are in a novel which combines closely-observed realism with a tightly-woven, but lightly-worn, pattern of imagery and symbolism. Christopher Meredith is an accomplished poet as well as a novelist and one of the great pleasures of *Shifts* is his playful dexterity with language. Just one of an exceptional range of linguistic registers in the novel, the south Wales valleys dialect spoken by his characters ('Hiya butt. How be? A'right butty. Owzigoin? No' bâd mun') becomes a rhythmic, even poetic, expression of the specificity of a people and a place. When he began writing *Shifts*, Meredith has said that he 'wasn't even entirely sure if it was a novel at first'. One way of thinking about this impressively assured debut novel is to regard it as a kind of big 'poem' where the textures of language itself are part of the world Meredith is (re)making.

Published in 1988 but set a decade earlier in 1977, *Shifts* is a novel concerned with history (rather than a historical novel) which looks back at a moment of radical change in south Wales. Set over just nine months, it follows the fortunes of four characters linked by their association with a steelworks, the closure of which will irrevocably alter their lives and the landscape they inhabit. Jack Priday is the returning 'native', back from Lancashire to find work and lodgings two valleys over from his old home and using his facility for puns and anecdotes to integrate himself into, and distance himself from, the community. His former schoolfriend, Keith Watkins, is employed at the steel-plant but increasingly obsessed by local history. Judith, Keith's wife, is bored by their marriage but unable to commit to either becoming pregnant or finding employment herself. And, finally, the strangely named 'O', or Rob (nicknamed 'Snobs' in school), is a marginalised figure at the steelworks, obsessive about routines such as counting the number of times he can re-use a Sunblest plastic bag for his lunch. His name suggests both clock time ('o'clock') and nothingness ('zero'). Weaving together the personal and the political, the novel shifts deftly between these four points of view, engaging our sympathies even as it turns a sharp eye on the characters' weaknesses. Each of them, like everyone else in the novel, is 'just looking for a bearable way of living' in a town where the options are narrowing.

The title itself is multi-layered. Most obviously, it refers to the shift-work which has dominated the lives of the steelworkers. Monotonous and often at odds with the workers' own natural rhythms (working night shifts has 'Put [Keith's] body-clock wrong'), these shifts nevertheless structured a way of life which is being lost as the men are laid off. '"They'm on'y fucking rolling one shift mind, days regular five days a bastard week,"' one steelworker expostulates, '"Three shifts a day it used to be. Three shifts a fucking day seven days a week [...] End of a shift you 'ouldn' know whether you was coming or bastard going."' This mixture of resentment and loss reflects the ambivalent status of work in our lives: 'the psychology of the thing's complex, built on a paradox,' Meredith has said of *Shifts*, 'that your job is both what you are and what destroys you'. On a macro-level, the title also indicates the major historical 'shifts' taking place, which the characters for the most part only dimly recognise. The process of de-industrialisation, over which they have no control, up-ends traditional gender roles (the new jobs opening up in the marshmallow factory are primarily for women) and leaves the community in a state of limbo and paralysis.

The history of Welsh culture, Raymond Williams has argued, is marked by 'a broken series of *radical shifts*' within which there are 'certain social and linguistic continuities'. It is these 'shifts', as well as the continuities, which Meredith is tracing in the novel. While Jack presents himself as driven by the 'biological imperative', and Judith seems to look to the men around her for meaning, Keith turns to local history to try to make sense of his place in the world. From traces such as place names and old buildings, he tries to re-imagine how the landscape was transformed when the English Samuel Moonlow built the first furnaces in the then densely wooded valley and kickstarted the processes of industrialisation. Thus Meredith connects the 'shifts' which mark the beginning and end of this particular historical cycle. Language is crucial here too. Unable to read or speak Welsh, Keith cannot interpret his own history although it is marked on the landscape in names like 'Henfelin' or 'Ty Mister'. Listening to a university professor explain how the town has existed on many 'frontiers' – of rural and industrial, farmland and desert, moorland and dense forest – Keith recognises that these are 'Huge ideas'. Likewise, Meredith's novel deals with 'huge ideas' but expressed through language, symbolism and imagery grounded in the ordinary details of ordinary lives.

If Richard Llewellyn's 1939 novel *How Green Was My Valley* is what Raymond Williams called the 'export version of the Welsh industrial experience', *Shifts* is an insider's version. Born in Tredegar to a father who was a steelworker and former collier, and a mother who had been a domestic servant, Meredith grew up on the Cefn Golau estate. Newly built in the mid-1950s, this estate looks down on the town from the edge of the open mountain which separates Tredegar from Rhymney. This landscape with its paradoxical combination of industrial and rural, tame and wild, was formative for the young Meredith and the setting of *Shifts* is in part a re-imagined version of this distinctive locale. As a child Meredith could go up onto the mountain, to where the nineteenth-century cholera graveyard which Keith explores in the novel is situated, or look, as Jack does, down into the town with its park and its rows of terraced houses, the factories to the north and the reclaimed pits to the south, and know that over the mountain to the east lay the 'two miles tangle of steelworks'. Benefitting from the introduction of comprehensive education, Meredith went to Tredegar Comprehensive School and then on to University of Wales, Aberystwyth where he studied English and Philosophy. There he also learned to speak Welsh which he has described as 'one of the most important things I've ever done.'

Before going to university Meredith had worked for three months at the British Steel Corporation's Ebbw Vale steelworks where his father had worked in the coke ovens, later becoming a foreman and then a tinplate inspector. Meredith worked in the open hearth and enjoyed the sense of having a proper job, finding the place 'anarchic'. But when, after graduating in 1976, he returned there as a shift worker in the hot mill, he found it very different. The steelworks was in the process of closing down and, as he put it, the job 'doesn't seem the same when you realise this is the rest of your life'. He left the steelworks to complete a Postgraduate Certificate in Education at University of Wales, Swansea, and then took up a post teaching English at Brecon High School.

It was while he was teaching that Meredith wrote and published his first two collections of poetry, *This* (1984) and *Snaring Heaven* (1990), as well as *Shifts* and his second novel, *Griffri* (1991). Written in spare moments over a period of four years, *Shifts* took shape against the background of the difficult political climate of the 1980s, including the aftermath of the 1979 referendum in which 79.74% voted against devolution for Wales, the right-wing government which came to power under Mrs Thatcher in May 1979, the now-forgotten steel strike of 1980, the Cardiff conspiracy trials of 1983, and the miners' strike of 1984-5. This added up to what many felt was a climate of political fear and eroded civil liberties. The novel gave Meredith a way of addressing the history of his *bro* (region or country), broadening out from the more personal concerns of his poetry to the wider social and political processes which shape individuals, communities and countries.

Given his versatility as both poet and novelist and the ambitious breadth of his concerns, it is extraordinary that Meredith's work is not yet better known outside Wales. He is a major writer whose work speaks directly, and urgently, to universal themes and concerns precisely because it is grounded in the specificity of a particular time and place. *Shifts* is a novel which helps us to know where we are now, and *why*, in relation to many complex issues: history, time, work, politics, love, betrayal and grief. It is also witty, compassionate, and brilliantly readable. If you don't know Meredith's writing yet, this is a good place to start.

Diana Wallace

Diana Wallace is Professor of English Literature at the University of South Wales. She is the author of *Christopher Meredith* (University of Wales Press, 2018), *Female Gothic Histories: Gender, History and the Gothic* (University of Wales Press, 2013), *The Woman's Historical Novel: British Women Writers, 1900-2000* (Palgrave Macmillan, 2005) and *Sisters and Rivals in British Women's Fiction, 1914-39* (Macmillan, 2000). She has published widely on Welsh Writing in English and edited Margiad Evans's *Autobiography* (1943) for Honno's Welsh Women's Classics series.

SHIFTS

1977

ONE

O clocked off at exactly half past three. He had stood with his card in the timeclock, his palm poised above the punchlever, and waited till the second hand jerked up to the twelve. It was quiet around the clocks on that gate, as usual, and the security man, the spotter, in his glass and brick office, had stood looking away from the timecard racks, out over the crumbling carparks and vaguely at the hills.

O stood, as usual, near the litter basket with Sully, Wayne and a few others waiting for their bus outside the gate. He looked across at the bank of colourless grass and its few blackened, unidentifiable trees. They looked dead but were only January dead. In the spring, as always, they would put out just a few leaves, only enough to show that somewhere in each of them meagre life was continuing.

A car pulled up. A black Viva with a loose exhaust. The driver, darkhaired and wearing platform shoes, got out and walked into the time offices. He left his engine running. O's bus arrived and as he boarded he saw the darkhaired man come out of the time offices, get in his car and drive away.

O sat on his own on the bus and focused his eyes on space a few feet outside the window. His hands were stuck into the pockets of his frayed blue quilted anorak. In his right pocket, as usual, he held his bus ticket. The man in the seat in front of him, he noticed, had not been given a ticket and the driver had not charged him the full fare. In the left pocket, as usual, he fingered the carefully folded plastic Sunblest bag from which he had earlier eaten his sandwiches. He could feel the hard breadcrumbs through the bag, and soft yielding bits. Those were the small lumps of corned beef. He could feel the meat spreading between his thumb and finger and sticking

3

to the bag. But he would not break the plastic with his nail. He would shake the crumbs out and use the bag again the next day.

The bus had climbed away from the steelworks and over the hill down into the next valley, homeward. Past where they were building a new estate and the road was widened. Momentarily on the downward hill O could see, over some rooftops to the north, some tumbled rocks on some rough yellow grass in a hollow. It was fenced around.

O got off the bus by the town clock. He checked it against his watch because the town clock was often wrong. But no. Nearly four. It was quite right. O walked up a hill towards his house. He kept his hands in his pockets, even when he looked at his watch. He had a scarf on because of January. He also had gloves but did not wear them because they were big and ridiculous. They were suede and lined with wool and had been his father's, but they felt huge and stupid on his small hands.

His breath formed on the air. He puffed, pretending he was smoking a cigar, though unlike his father he had never smoked, blowing the warmed air up over his nose and going crosseyed trying to see it. He stumbled doing this, crossing the waste ground where some houses had been demolished in Buchan Row. He looked around in case anybody had seen him. A man was standing on the steep bank behind the row, looking down into the backyards of some empty houses. He recognised the glasses and the heavy figure in the hooded coat.

'How be, O' the man called, and turned to walk away.

'A' right, Keith' O said.

O slowly walked up the bank, following the rutted narrow track, to his house in a short terrace. He skirted round the small front garden and went in through the gate in the back lane. When he opened the door, his mother called from upstairs.

She said, 'Robert. It's all ready in the oven, love.'

Robert took off his anorak and scarf and hung them on the door. He took out the sandwich bag and, going into the back garden again, he shook the crumbs into the dustbin. Inside, he smoothed the bag flat on top of the fridge in front of the bread bin. There he left it for his mother to attend to later. He took his shoes off and pushed them under the usual chair. He opened the door of the oven and looked at his warming dinner. He would go into the middle room, sit down, and read the paper, looking mainly at the television page, for fifteen minutes. Then he would take out his dinner, by that time a pleasant crusty lump, and eat it while watching whatever television programmes there were.

* * *

Like standing in a pisshouse, Jack thought.

He stood in the personnel office's waiting room. It was very small and tiled and eight men were crammed in it. Five sat on a short bench, all with their arms folded or hands together to avoid contacting their neighbours. One man had stood leaning against the wall, gradually slipping down the white porcelain till he was sitting on the floor. Another stood awkwardly in the angle of the inner and outer doors, moving his weight from one foot to the other. Jack stood at the other end of the room, cluttered against the coatstand. No one spoke. Nobody looked at anybody else in case anybody else was looking at him.

Jack thought, I could have more fun having all my teeth out.

He looked through a pair of feet at the white tiles.

Like standing in a. Waiting for the trickle. Or waiting for the doctor. Doctor, I've got this pain in my. Everybody wondering what everybody's got. He's flu. He's back trouble. He's acne, definitely. VD. Dust. After a sicknote to go to the match. And him by the door is piles. Nice to be back in mine own countree.

Jack thought, elaborating his theme, I could have more fun on Brynmawr bus station. I could have more fun smalltalking with the landlady, she too old to be young and too young to be old, while she attempts to extract the rent.

Some of the men were young – a couple were teenagers, some, like Jack, were about in their late twenties. Most, like his landlady, were in an indeterminate middle age. Easiest to date them by their clothes or hairstyle. One of the benchmen was actually wearing a suit, old, dark, and well preserved. Eyes doing the round of feet would occasionally come to rest on his highly polished brown shoes with leather laces. They looked absurd among the oilsmudged suedes and split trainers.

Every now and then the man would stretch out his chin as people are supposed to when wearing an uncomfortable collar.

Serve him right, Jack thought. The pretence of selfrespect showed that the man did not understand what was happening to him. Definitely dust. The old hardworking good timekeeping type who didn't know that in the end that makes no difference. Up the road, pal. This is a new one on him.

The man had false teeth and they seemed uncomfortable too, as he constantly levered at them with his tongue. Jack was reminded of his father. The man shifted on the bench, moving the pressure from one hunker to the other. His lips moved slightly, as in some imagined or remembered conversation, and his eyes moved as though following words written.

Trying to work out how he got here, Jack thought. Years on end in some chronic job and then wham bam here's your cards and thirty pee, why don't you go and take a flying leap at yourself. Good company man just like the old man. Every shift leaving the house with his sandwiches in the old Oxo tin. Except they kept him on long enough to see him off altogether.

The lips worked almost imperceptibly.

Yes. The speech you should have given the manager.

He remembered the curtain whirring shut at the crematorium and the hymns his father would have hated.

Serves you right you old fools.

He wondered how the man in the suit had done in the tests. That was the delay, of course. They were marking the tests. Logical, numeral, visual. If lever A is depressed in the direction shown, in which direction will cog B revolve: (a) clockwise? (b) anti-clockwise? The gingerhaired man with the torn snorkel coat had sweated in there.

The redhaired man sat on the bench, leaning forward, an elbow on one knee and a huge hand clamped over one side of his head. He breathed noisily and sniffed.

Flu, definitely.

The inner door opened and the personnel officer's secretary, a woman also in indeterminate middle age, appeared with a list.

'Mr Janes' she said.

The redhaired man started.

'Would you like to come through, Mr Janes?'

As Mr Janes went through, there were indistinct sighs, shuffles, and even exchanged glances in the waiting room, by which means the men signalled that they thought something significant was happening.

Jack noticed the secretary's accent. It was good to hear his own accent again all around him. While he'd been in England he'd lost some of it. Everything seemed very Welsh. Although, he told himself, no, it was only itself.

How did they get the results of the test to the office? Too complicated to phone. Must be a back door. One of those tube things like they used to have in the Co-op for sending receipts and change. A man in a Zorro outfit leaves the hot results under heavy seal pinned by a dagger to the windowframe.

The inner door was opened quickly and Janes came out flustered and red. He went through the outer door, bumping into the pilesman. The secretary hung out on the jamb and called in the next on her list.

Acne. Piles. Each came out carrying a slip of paper, smiling and smug.

'Mr Riley.'

The man in the suit jumped up and went in, stumbling at the

threshold. Jack caught at his elbow. Riley said a voiceless thanks without looking up.

He came out a few minutes later, carrying his slip of paper. He brandished it and looked around at the remaining men.

'I got it' he said. 'Twenty-eight weeks.'

Jack looked at Riley's form and against the printed word 'Department' glimpsed 'OPEN HEARTH (SCRAP BAY)' scrawled on the dotted line.

'You should be all right boys' Riley said. 'They'm giving em out like smarties today.'

'Mr Priday?'

Jack followed the secretary.

Of course, he thought. Janes didn't get anything. In which direction will cog B revolve? I'm sorry to have to tell you, Mr Janes. Poor bastard.

The personnel officer was a large bleak man in indeterminate middle age. The walls of his office were a sickly urine green which even on a dull January day cast a sick tinge on his pale face. His desk seemed unnecessarily large and some leaves of paper and a few pens were scattered remotely across it.

Jack saw the pad of forms and the man's poised ballpoint. 'Department'.

They exchanged greetings. Jack sat. There was a job.

Doctor I've got this boil on my bum from not doing anything.

'It's a thirty-six week contract. Can you start Monday?' the man asked.

Jack said that he could and the man filled in the form, the prescription. Doctor I've got this third leg growing out of my navel. Are you Manx? No it's the way I'm sitting. Try aspirin.

'Can you come in tomorrow morning?'

'Yes.'

'Okay. Go straight to the department on this note tomorrow morning at eight. Your union rep will meet you at the timeclock and show you round. Have you worked in steel before?'

'No. My father used to work here though.'

'Oh?'

'Elvet P—'

'Wouldn' know him. It's a very big place. Well it was. Your contract expires on the date I'm noting for you. If the plant is still working in your department you'll be laid off and if you've been a good boy we'll take you on for another contract. Okay?'

Doctor, I've got this unmentionable disease and the only known cure for it is gainful employment.

The personnel officer tore out the form in a practised way and handed it to Jack. Against 'Department' was written 'HOT STRIP MILL'.

'Your father's department?' the man asked.

'He might have worked there.'

'Don't you know?'

'He moved around.' Mainly open hearth. The old furnace clogs in the coal cot and those dark goggles that you couldn't see through in ordinary daylight. 'He was here a long time.'

'Well, how long things continue is a matter for conjecture. Anyway, here's thirty-six weeks for you.'

Wham bam thank you, butty.

Jack felt a great relief and was vaguely irritated because he wanted to feel angry.

Here's thirty-six weeks. Here's a strawberry for a donkey. Here's a bottle of aspirin. Nice to be not quite home again, even with the three months of indignity and the weekly signature. The landlady can frig off for a start. We'll keep a welcome in the pillside, or how green was my valium. Only no. The green didn't really fit, unless you count the pisscolour walls.

He stepped out into the waiting room and waved his note to the three remaining men.

'Piss in our time' he said.

'Got your smartie then' backtrouble said.

'Aye' Jack said, 'but I'd prefer real food.'

* * *

Judith waited at the back of the crowd in the butcher's shop. She knew that it was always a mistake to come out this late, even on a Thursday. Sprightly pensioners and smartly dressed plump women in hats were at the counter where they elbowed one another for position and pursed their lips sceptically when the butcher or his assistant held up a prime cut for inspection. Judith couldn't stomach all that pretending and haggling. She preferred to walk to several windows and find something good on display, but this shop was the nearest and it was too late now to go to the others, the January afternoon already growing murky. She would have to stand and transact with the shopkeeper. She usually got reasonable value like this, but mostly because she stood ineffectually silent until the butcher sensed criticism and produced better goods. Some shopkeepers interpreted her stare as an unsettling kind of guile. Judith sometimes sensed this, but mostly felt uneasy herself and was always miserable when shopping. Especially when it came to the awkward bits like meat. So she would hang back, draw out and thin the discomfort, while the others carried away their trophies pleasantly, their little acts of bargaining quickly finished.

She stared up at the white tiled walls, listening to the hum of the black refrigeration machine on top of the coldroom.

As the crowd shuffled forwards towards the counter, she realised that someone who had been in front of her was now behind her. She looked round. The figure was familiar, with the crinkled green raincoat that wouldn't keep a sneeze out, the frizzy browntinted hair, the hare eyes and the thin face.

'Hello, Judith, my love.'

'Hiya, Maudie' Judith said. 'How's Arthur?'

Maudie reported that Arthur was all right. The morphine was doing a lot for him with his leg and his stomach. And how was Keith? Judith reported on her husband's good health.

They got to the counter and were the only customers left in the shop.

'Go on, Maudie. You go first.'

'No no. You were first.'

As they haggled over who should go last, Judith thought that she was putting herself at the end, after the dealmakers, the pensioners, after Maudie with the colour washed out of the elbows of her green coat, her nicotine fingernails, her cancerous husband.

Finally Maudie put a bony hand on the glass counter and looked nervously at the assistant.

'Have you got any scraps, love?'

The assistant looked at the butcher and the butcher sighed, looking at the floor. He scraped together a few bones and some dripping for Maudie. She gushed thanks and traipsed her thin body away.

As Judith chose her cuts, she realised why Maudie had kept at the back.

She walked the mile or so back to the estate. It was very cold, but she would get colder still if she waited for the bus. The estate was near the top of the mountain on the western side of the valley. They had been lucky to get the council house so soon after getting married, three years before, and although it was a cold place for most of the year she liked the view across the valley to the pine plantations and terraces, and she had begun to tame a small corner of the tussocky back garden. In the spring there would be crocuses and daffodils and before then she would try to do something with the grass. You couldn't call it a lawn yet. The previous summer in the heatwave, the scorched grass had been matted with deeprooted weeds, their straggling stems intricate with tiny leaves. And Keith of course barely knew that the garden existed.

At home, she put the meat in the fridge and a pie in the oven for her husband. A pie could always be relied on. He liked things overcooked and safely tasteless. He had said that he would be gone all afternoon 'preparing'. She didn't like the way he used that word, as if he was about to die. He made such a drama out of such unimportant things. Why didn't he just say 'getting ready'?

She went into the livingroom and looked at herself in the long mirror. She pouted her lips. Her face was not thin. She turned three quarters and ran her hand over the fly of her jeans to feel how much her womb stuck out. A pleasant, shaped bulge. Enough to be attractive. No more. She liked her longish, smooth hair because it was very dark, almost black. And her eyes did not bulge at all. She put her hands under her breasts and ran them down so that they followed the flare of her hips. If anything she would become fat – not thin and bony and frightened.

Keith was on the heavy side, but that wasn't attractive in a man. If they ever had children she would ask him to lose weight so that the kids would have a better model.

But there didn't seem much chance of children. One, perhaps, she thought, might be all right to try out. She stood sideways and imagined the new bulge. That part wouldn't be very nice, but it would go. The going wouldn't be very nice either. And it changed you.

Maudie had had children. It amazed Judith to think this. It frightened her to think how much Maudie must have changed.

She switched on the light and sat close to the coal fire. It was quite dark already and through the window she could see the faint glow of the steelworks town lights from the next valley on the clouds above the mountain. She drew the curtains.

There was a choice. While Keith's pie shrivelled, either television or a book. Probably it would be television and a halfscanned book at the same time. One day, she thought as she switched on the set, she would make herself choose the book. One day she would haggle with the butcher.

* * *

With some blank paper and a pen in his pocket, Keith spent the afternoon walking the length of the town. He didn't much care for the northern end with its estates and feeling of flatness as the hills and valley thinned away into high moorland, but this was where he went first. He walked out along the straight wide road that some people still called the Dram Road, though there were no longer any rails, and doubled back southward along a curving route that followed some of the older streets and skirted the industrial estates.

He huddled into the thick coat and pulled the hood closer round his head.

At a place where several streets met, he paused. A stony reddish stream was piped under the road and along the back of a terrace. He looked around at the houses. Behind him, two bungalows. Modern. At the left, a terrace of fairsized houses. About 1910ish? And the stream terrace? Those houses were very small and all the building at the back was haphazard. Before the 1850s anyway, he thought. Down a lane on his right, too narrow for a car, he could see the ruin of some shops on a raised pavement. Two smashed up. One lived in but no longer a shop. After the 1850s, those. Something about them. Just a bit too grand. The yellow brickwork round the windows. And in front of him, climbing the slope of the mountain, some modern houses. A cluster of pensioners' bungalows and three rows of lowrise flats. He remembered the original Three Rows, the condemned tenements. And then on the left past the 1910 terrace, the Lion. Hard to place. Pubs get so mucked about. A house set back, the other side of the pub, on its own patch of land. Old. Farm perhaps. He could see its name on the gate at the side of the Lion. Henfelin. And up there, up behind the new three rows, a flat wide patch running north to south along the hill. He followed it with his eye north to the moor and thought of the limestone quarries, and then south where it disappeared round the curve of the mountain.

Keith took off his glasses so the picture blurred slightly, and tried to focus his mind back through time. Turn of the century was easy enough. Before that he had to replace the lefthand terrace. Houses there? Perhaps nothing. 1850s. No street pumps. Streamwater dammed further up for scouring the iron. On the path above Three Rows, horsedrawn drams taking limestone from the quarries to the furnaces. The rough path at the back of the stream terrace would probably not be there because it was made of iron waste. The women would walk up to the hill where the spring was with jugs or buckets for the water. The spring had a Welsh name that he couldn't remember. He focused back further, mentally removing a piece of land that he thought was an old tip. And finally 1800. No Three Rows, no terraces, no shops. Henfelin, probably. The pub perhaps. No dramlines. A donkey team on the path with baskets of limestone. The man driving them blowing his hands. Wrapped in sacking perhaps. Christ. Doing that in a blizzard.

Keith shivered. He rested a hand on a gatepost. There was no one near, so he risked muttering to himself:

'A storm was brewing in January 1800, when a small gang of men started—'

No good.

'A blizzard was raging in January 1800, when the first hard won iron was tapped from the first furnace—'

Worse. He didn't want to lay it on too thick. The cool factual approach might be better.

'On January 12 1800, after much careful preparation, Samuel Moonlow, an English businessman, personally supervised the lighting—'

No. Wordy.

He put on his glasses and the present jumped back into place.

Knowing how to start was the problem, he thought, as he worked his way up onto the track above Three Rows and began to walk southward along it. The cold wind sliced through his coat. Rounding the curve of the hill, he saw below him the partly excavated remains of the furnace arches – they were later of course – and the few tumbled blocks that were left of the first furnace. It stood in a little horseshoe gap in the grasscovered coaltip, a few dozen yards from another row of houses. He could see in a hollow near the river several hundred yards away the big house Moonlow had built for himself, Ty Mister.

14

Keith focused back again and tried to imagine the supplies arriving at the new little works. Limestone, yes, and the ore of course, and charcoal.

'Idiot.'

The loudness of his own voice surprised him.

Trees. Naturally, there would be trees everywhere, even here. Old deciduous forest. Just a patch cleared around the furnace for the smelting. Patches here and there cleared by the charcoal burners. He closed his eyes and imagined how they would slaughter him if he made such a blind simple mistake. He tried to picture the trees, and everything changed. Sound would carry differently. The snow would be different. The light would be different. And of course a lot of the hill would be different because no tips.

He walked on feeling, hopelessly, that he would have to start all over again.

He tramped down to the ruin and stared at it, conscious of his looking, like a viewer at an art gallery wondering what to think. It was like repeating a word till it becomes meaningless. He ran a hand over the stone and crumbling mortar, trying to concentrate. There was still an overhanging plug of iron slag where some stonework had fallen away. The remains of the last tapping. He moved around the ruin running his hand under the overhang and spoke again to himself.

'If you go to the site of the ironworks today, you can still see the remains of the very first furnace. There's even a great lump of iron still in it from the last tap. But it is not the last tap that interests us toni—'

There was the sound of a throat being cleared.

'Oh. I'm. I'm.' Keith tried to apologise to the young couple lying in the lee of the stonework under the iron plug. He looked away awkwardly and then glanced back again. The woman had pulled a coat lapel quickly over her naked breast and the man had rolled tight to her to hide his flies.

Keith stumbled away towards the fence and the houses. The sound of a woman laughing.

He had done his courting like that. Only not so much there, but on the tip behind the dog track and in the plantations up the mountain. More in the new upstart forest than where the old one had been. First up the mountain with Glenda, then Anne, then Jude. And once with Anne a man with a dog had come by. That was in the forest. They might as well have had nothing on. But that was high summer. And then a man with a dog came by and he was very polite, or shy, because he never even looked round. The dog wasn't so polite though. And then once with Anne on the pine needles under the low trees. Then. That too had become history of sorts.

Never in January though. It occurred to him that he could have laughed, or said something witty like watch out for brass monkeys, or stoking the furnace I see. But perhaps that would have been too obscure.

He couldn't imagine himself rolling round on the earth now. Not that he was fat, but he had thickened out a little prematurely. It would be comical like that, though warmer in this weather.

His concentration was broken. As he walked home through the town he mused that he had plenty of time. It was over twelve weeks, and he needn't prepare much anyway. There would be other speakers. His mind turned to other projects. A survey of early nineteenth century gravestones to check for numbers of immigrants and where they came from. And that derelict house Emlyn in work had told him about where there were papers left in the cupboard. You never knew. He made for that street now, a mile or more to the south and climbed onto the banking behind a row of condemned houses.

And there had been that time with Anne in a derelict building after school. Then. Exploring like kids in a story. And it had been the end house – quite big and posh, and on the top floor in all the fallen plaster and dirt. Anne was doing Economics and the teacher had given her a pile of *Economists* to study, and that was how they had sex, spreading the copies of the magazine over all the dust like a sheet. She always was brainy. Still enough to churn the guts after – how many? – ten years.

Keith stooped and looked down into the backs of the old houses. The grey light was waning. Too late.

He caught sight of a figure crossing a gap in the row, a man who was unselfconsciously walking with his head tilted back and puffing his steaming breath upwards as though he was trying to blow smoke rings. He tripped and nearly fell. As he regained his balance he saw Keith watching him. They exchanged greetings.

It was O, coming off days regular, which meant it was about four o'clock. Home to mammy.

Keith decided to turn for home himself. Jude would have some food ready for him and he liked an evening in before starting on the dayshift.

He felt that some more history had fallen and gathered like snow on a drift, and as he walked he thrust his knuckles against the blank page in his pocket.

TWO

The electric wallheaters in the day labourers' cabin on the hot mill had been left on over the weekend. O thought of the waste, but was glad, when he got there on the frozen Monday morning, that the room was so warm. He had taken more than twenty minutes to change into his working clothes in the bathhouse. Lew Hamer the chargehand never came to give the jobs out much before half past eight these days, so that left a whole hour to kill after clocking on.

O had laid out his overalls on the locker bench and changed into his old trousers and shirt. Then the pullover. Then the overalls which had that day new patches on the frayed cuffs. Then socks. Then the workboots with steel toecaps. He would pause after the first boot and wipe the worst of the black oily dirt from his fingers with a rag he kept specially in his locker. Then wipe again after the second boot. Then wipe again after tying his laces. Then he would sit for a while and stare at the floor. Tidy everything back into the locker. Safety helmet on. Lock up. Few of the lockers still had keys and he had been lucky to get one. Then the walk to the cabin.

Inside, Ken Francis was in his usual position, lying at full stretch on the bench in front of the heater. As usual, O inspected the tray of rat poison. There were a couple of large blackbrown cockroaches near it. O bent forward and looked at them closely. A stifled laugh came from the other two benches where the remaining half dozen or so of the day gang were sitting. O did not look round.

'Hard luck, O.' It was Sullivan's voice. 'No ratmeat for your sandwiches again today.'

'Not to worry, Sully' Kelvin Edwards said. 'His mammy will have got him something, you know.'

'That's right' O said awkwardly.

He sat on the end of a bench – the one with its back to the wall so that he wouldn't have to look at the pinups – next to Kelv.

Some of them were playing cards on the stained long table between the two benches. O watched the cards for a while and then pulled his helmet down over his face. He folded his arms so that he wouldn't touch the oily bench, and leant his head back against the wall. It would be all right so long as Wayne concentrated on the cards and didn't pick on him.

As if on cue, Wayne spoke.

'Fucking bastard hell. I've got a fucking hand like a bastard foot.' His voice whistled through a gap where his front teeth had been. 'Why don' you get to bastard bed earlier on a Sunday night?'

O said nothing although he knew Wayne was talking to him. No one else was trying to sleep except for Ken, and no one talked to him unless they had to.

'Oy you' Wayne called. 'Well fuck me. Oy. Spunkarse.'

O felt some playing cards rap against his helmet and flutter down, some into his lap and others to the floor.

'Shit' Kelv said. 'It must have been a bad hand.'

O sensed Kelv picking the cards from the floor.

'Easy now, O.' His Ulster accent softened. 'You'll enjoy this bit.'

Kelv started to gather the cards from O's lap. O's body became rigid.

'Ah, he's excited' Kelv whined.

He slid his hand along O's thigh and made a grab for his testicles.

'Ha' Kelv yelled. 'Well he's got one at least.'

'Fuck me' Sully said. 'Can anybody join in or are you strictly one to one bum chums?'

O sat as still as he could. Kelv was all right. He was only fooling. Now if it was Wayne who had been doing this it could have been very painful. In a minute Lew Hamer would come in with the jobs and everything would be all right.

Jack tut tutted theatrically as he pulled on his old shoes in the empty bathhouse.

Late on your first day, Priday. Hope you're not starting as you intend to continue.

He pictured a severe foreman with a toothbrush moustache, consulting his pocketwatch, tapping his foot.

The previous Friday, Willy the union man had shown him round, and somehow it seemed to Jack that foottapping timesticklers wouldn't survive long there.

After showing him the timeclocks, Willy had taken him on the mill.

The bathhouse, time office and canteen were on a steep bank – the mountainside really – on the east side of the mill. Near the canteen, which was of dirty redbrick, was another single storey building of redbrick which, Willy told him, was the hot mill offices.

Jack followed Willy over a covered footbridge which joined the bank to the mill. They emerged on a catwalk high above the mill floor and went down a steel staircase. Some welders were burning new grips on the last few steps. Instead of just making patterns, they wrote nicknames in the metal:

FAT MAGGOT
TOMMY TACKLER
IANTO FULL-PELT

Jack asked what went on and Willy explained succinctly:

'A fucking great ingot do come in that end' – he pointed south – 'and two fucking great coils of sheet steel do go out that end.' He pointed north.

The mill was big, dark and dirty. An overhead crane went by with its siren wailing, dragging a piece of blackened metal an inch thick, a yard wide and several dozen yards long, northward up the mill. Willy tugged Jack's arm and led him to cover. Jack panicked momentarily and after the crane had passed was struck by the silence. There was no production work going on, evidently.

'Friday see' Willy said. 'Mill's down every Thursday and Friday. Only maintenance and that working.'

He led Jack on a grand tour of the mill and environs. First south to the soaking pits, large circular furnaces where ingots were heated to rolling temperature; then the slabbing or blooming mill, a huge steel mangle where, Willy said, ingots were bashed into slabs; then northwards past huge derelict looking chunks of machinery, including one which sheared each rolled ingot into two slabs, to a series of furnaces with doors that opened onto the endless row of steel rollers that formed a conveyor belt for the hot metal.

'These are the reheating furnaces' Willy said. Jack looked up at their varicose web of green and red painted cooling pipes. They reminded him of those colourcoded pictures in textbooks on human biology. 'Slabs in the slabyard next door are pushed in the other side and heated up to be rolled into coil. Them doors do open up with them chains and slabs do drop out. These rolls where they do drop out is called the delivery table, just like in the maternity ward.'

Jack remembered his father using the term 'tapping off' when a neighbour's wife was about to give birth. But that was a metaphor taken from the open hearth furnaces, where the metal was actually molten, not just soft hot as it was in this department.

More derelict looking chunks of machinery. The mill stands: more big mangles, though not as big as the slabbing mill. First four squat green ones, 'roughing mills' Willy said. These drew out the slabs into long tongues of steel like the one they had seen craned down the mill. Then a long gap. Then six more mill stands, tall and silverpainted. 'Finishing' Willy said. These drew the strip of hot steel faster and thinner over the rolls. Then showers to cool the metal as it travelled very fast into the coiler. This was two drums that wound the strip steel at high speed into neat blackhot bogrolls of metal and unloaded them into a bay called the coilpit, which was below the level of the mill floor.

Jack was shown the slabyard, the boneyard, the roll shop, part of a labyrinth of cellars, and the generator room.

Although no machinery seemed to be working, in the generator room high banks of electrical equipment were crackling and sparking like an old Frankenstein film. The very large room was cream tiled and comparatively clean, with black rubber mats rolled out in long strips, red carpet fashion, in the areas where you could walk. There were big fire extinguishers here and there, mounted in pairs on elegant spoked carriage wheels with solid rubber tyres.

'If you're working cleaning a machine' Willy said, 'you got to come in here to sign it off.'

He led Jack into a glass office containing long rows of large switches and dials. A greyhaired man wearing a sports jacket and tie was seated at a desk and reading the Daily Mail. Willy and the man exchanged greetings.

'Here's the book see' Willy said, swivelling a great open ledger on the desk so that Jack could see it.

There were lists of signatures and notes in ruled columns.

'Say you got to work on the squeezer' Willy said. 'You got to sign the book and then it's isolated, like that.' He pointed to one of the large switches. A sign hanging on it read: 'MEN AT WORK. MACHINE ISOLATED.' 'And make sure you do sign off anything you'm working on. Otherwise you might get bastard killed.'

Jack nodded, trying to look intelligent, though he couldn't remember where or what the squeezer was.

'And if you do sign it off' Willy tapped the ledger, 'you got to sign it back on again after, or nobody can put the machine on.'

'Even if—' the greyhaired man said.

'Even if' Willy said, 'you've fucked off home, somebody'll come and get you so's you can sign it back on so's the mill can get rolling.'

Jack remembered his father turning down a corporation telephone. You'd never have any peace then, he had said.

They stepped through a doorway into the mill again and the light, stylish space gave way to a dark, clammy cold. Jack followed Willy over the blackened, slippery floor. They were now on the west side of the strip. In this area the mill floor was littered with bits of machinery, huge broken cogs, spindles, rusted craneskips of various shapes. Without looking down, Willy sidestepped a pool of slime in which a mangled steel cranesling lay contorted like a writhing snake. Suddenly he stopped, turned, and raised a warning finger.

'Mind' he said inexplicably. 'Look here.' He pointed into the gloom. 'Know what these are?'

Jack strained his eyes and saw a bank of filthmantled metal boxes fixed along the wall.

'Fuseboxes' he said wondering if it was a trick question.

'Thassright' Willy said. His face relaxed for a moment but then the earnestness returned. 'So be careful where you do piss. It 'ouldn' be a nice way to go.'

Jack accepted this advice in respectful silence and followed Willy to a shed inside the mill where they had a cup of tea. In the brightly lit cabin Jack could see that Willy, in his doctorish green coat, had somehow managed to remain immaculate at the end of tour. His own clothes were dusty, the bottoms of his trouser legs smirched with grease, and his hands were sticky and black.

As he tied the laces of his old shoes on his first Monday, he realised that he would need a boilersuit and boots.

He ran to the day labourers' cabin which Willy had pointed out to him. It was a brick building with a garage housing a dumper truck, and stood high on the bank above the south end of the mill, several hundred yards from the bathhouse. Down below he could see the straggling shanty of sheds and outbuildings that had grown out of the east wall of the mill, square concrete walled ponds into which waste metal was sluiced, and the railway track along which hopper wagons of scrap and metal scale were shunted.

In the cabin, Jack pushed open a door which led off the garage.

The door was dirty and a piece of wire was twisted into the hole where the handle had been.

The door knocked against a slatted bench. On this was sprawled a man in overalls, apparently asleep, with one arm shading his eyes from the striplight. There was a window, but a rusted sheet of steel had been fixed over it. On the other side of the room, underneath some geriatric pinups, about half a dozen men dressed in boilersuits or dirty working clothes were playing cards at a long table. One of them, sitting beneath a woman selfconsciously baring firm breasts which in reality would by now be withered and fallen, pushed up his plastic helmet, which had been pulled down over his eyes. At the sound of the door opening the man looked up keenly, but his face glazed when he saw Jack, then brightened again. One or two of the others glanced up and then carried on with their game. Jack stood awkwardly and finally announced himself.

'New boy?' A middle-aged man in a soiled corduroy cap squinted up through thick glasses. He shifted on the bench. 'Sit by here, butty. The chargehand will be in in a minute.'

Jack perched on the edge of the bench and watched the card game.

A redhaired man with a Belfast accent was picking up cards from the floor and apparently groping the man with the helmet.

'Excuse that Irish git, butty' a blond young man with no front teeth said. 'He've got no manners, apart from which he's fucking mental.'

'Aye, Wayne' a youngish man with sandy hair said. 'They taught him to be an arse bandit in the army.' He gave Wayne, the toothless man, a hard look, and the game resumed.

Jack recognised the game, which he knew by the name of 'Joker', but these boys called it 'Nerky'.

'Not talking are you, Jack?' the man with the helmet said. Jack looked at him again, surprised. Through slightly heavy jowls and short dark sideburns, he recognised someone from his schooldays.

'Hello, Rob. Howbe?' he said.

'Oh my gawd' the blond man said to the Ulsterman. 'Sorry, Kelv,

24

your lover have found another. Notice that? Not just "O" but "Rob". "Rob" mind.'

The card game went on and Jack observed. This was the first time he'd met an old acquaintance. There had been occasional familiar faces, but no one he knew positively till now.

Rob sat looking at Jack expectantly and Jack realised they had nothing to say to one another.

Snobs he had been called, Jack thought. The runniest nose in the school. Now, evidently, called O, signifying nothing. And the best collection of Superman comics, later on. A connoisseur of caped crimefighters. Always to be seen by the market stall on Saturday mornings looking for a new Green Lantern or Wonder Woman. Were they a shilling then or tenpence? Most of us graduated onto the soft porn on the same stall. Snobs probably still drooling, or snotting, over Lois Lane. Or one and three perhaps.

Rob asked him some questions about where he'd been and what he'd done. Accrington. The name was repeated round the table. Accrington. Meaningless. Almost the same word.

And then the sandyhaired cardplayer, whose name was Sully, and who had bloodshot eyes and quivering hands, asked the inevitable question:

'What the fuck are you doing back here then?'

Good question.

'It's the old salmon leaping up the river you know' the Ulsterman, Kelv said.

'To spawn and die' Rob said.

'Fuck off you twat' the blond man, Wayne, said.

'Charming' Rob said feebly, looking to Jack for an ally.

'You'll have a fucking job coping here, butt' Sully said. He looked with deep seriousness into Jack's face. 'Can you be a Man of Steel?'

The man in the corduroy cap won the game and collected his money, laughing, as the chargehand came in. He wore overalls and a flat cap pushed back so that a tuft of grey forelock poked out.

'Yes, you fuckers' he said. 'Giving your money to our Clarry again.'

He leant an elbow on the table and farted laboriously.

'You the new fucker?' he said to Jack.

'Aye.'

'You got to watch these fuckers, mind.' He indicated the others with a nod. 'There's some rum fuckers by here.'

'What's the jobs today, Lew?' Rob said.

'See' the chargehand said. 'They're all keen like that. Especially him.' He nodded to the figure still sprawled motionless on the bench by the door. 'Look at him.' Lew paused and they all looked. The figure remained perfectly still. 'Action Man.'

'Want a game, Lewie baby?' Kelv said, shuffling the two packs of cards.

'Go on then' Lew said.

Rob looked disappointed.

'Deal me in' Jack said.

Jack learned quickly that except for the sleeping man, Lew Hamer, the foreman, and Rob, all the men on the day gang were on short contracts like him, some for the fourth or fifth time, some hoping to be re-signed shortly. They explained that the short contracts were intended to save the corporation making big redundancy payments when the department eventually closed. A couple of them had been lorry drivers and talked about their old trade. Kelv was one of these. Sully had worked on building sites before this. He said he was the first man to fly from Monmouthshire to Glamorgan in a dumper truck, having launched it and himself, Jack assumed unintentionally, over the river Rhymney from the stub of an unfinished bridge. Kelv had hit a car in his lorry. Unluckily, it was Kelv who had been on the wrong side of the road when this had happened. Another man had had assorted jobs in various parts of the steel and coal industries, and had constantly kept moving away from closing plants. Yet another man had been a schoolteacher.

'Why should I live in fucking poverty all my life' he said, 'when I can get in here with all these fucking villains?'

For Wayne, unemployed a year, this was his second job. In that other life he'd stacked boxes in a supermarket, now shut. Clarry, the man with thick glasses, had been steward of a workingmen's club, but said he had given it up when he felt the beer getting to him.

Their questions of Jack stirred the weight of useless memories. The upstairs flat on that busy road in Accrington. The market and shopping in Blackburn. The clapped out Cortina and the telly from Tasker's warehouse.

And Rob's face. Snobs. Rob. O was just a deeper layer of the excavation. Not a recognition, but a prising at the edge of cold, hardened events.

They were sent onto the mill about an hour after clocking on. Lew issued each of them with a pair of rag gloves. Jack was paired with Wayne to hose down the finishing mill floor with a steam gun.

Yawning, Wayne explained the job to Jack. They paid out the hose, which, Jack learned, was always called a bag, and Wayne switched on the cocks. First the water and then the steam, because if you did it the other way round the steam blew the bag and you scalded yourself to fuck, he explained. As they played the jet of water and steam across the greasecaked floor, Jack watched the processes Willy had described. In the distance he could hear a clanking as red hot slabs, which Wayne called bars, dropped out of the reheating furnaces. By the time the slabs reached the finishing mill stands they were inchthick, long tongues like the one he had seen on the crane, only red hot on the rolls. Each was stopped before the first finishing mill stand and its curved front edge was snipped square in a shears. Each glowing cropped edge was carried in long tongs to a small skip by the crop shears operator.

'Nice number, that one. Crop shears' Wayne said mechanically. 'Only trouble is you're stuck there all fucking day long.'

When the steel went through the six silver mill stands there was a thunder of mixed noises as it gathered speed. It would tear out of the final stand at its target thickness and cooling under the sprinklers would rattle and hiss into the coiler. The air filled with teacoloured clouds. Jack enjoyed the warmth of the hot metal as it went by them, and the glow it made on the stands.

As they worked, Wayne explained that he was in the territorials and that if the mill did shut he was contemplating going into the regulars. He sprayed the steam gun back and forth across the floor, firing from the hip.

They knocked off and brewed tea which they drank in one of the cabins that blistered the east side of the building. Jack noticed that they were always called cabins, even when, like this one, they were brickbuilt and incorporated into the main building. Most of the day gang boys were there, some huddled on two benches and the others sitting on the floor. Again there was a harsh striplight, again the window was glassless and sheeted over with rusted steel. Beneath the window was a radiator, dirtblackened and built on the spot out of two inch pipes and right angle joints, serpenting down the wall. It hissed and gave a little steam. An empty Tate and Lyle syrup tin was shoved under the leak. Jack noticed how startlingly pure the dripping water seemed inside the silvered can.

The rightful occupant of this cabin was a small, thin old man called Ben. He wore an oily cap and works safety glasses. He sat on the end of a bench with his feet tucked up like a gargoyle and rested an elbow on a locker knocked up rough out of welded steel plates. His equivalent of a nervous tic was an involuntary raspberry sound, often emitted midword, out of one side of his mouth. He got to know Jack quickly with a series of economical questions. The room fell quiet then. Jack sipped from a borrowed mug.

'Know when was the last time I got a leg over, butty?' Ben said, looking at Jack.

VE Day, Jack thought. He wondered why he should know and said that he didn't.

'Two years ago this February' Ben said to everybody. 'My missis in hospital see. Aye. Two years ago the last time I went fishing.'

The salmon leaping up the river.

This opened a recounting of recent sex. Kelv's account of himself

28

was the most lurid. The debate went on to a discussion of preferences as to time of day and conditions.

Unpleasantly, Jack felt his penis stir and stiffen a little.

Liz, he thought. Then, anybody. I could just do with.

On the mill again, he warmed himself for a while at one of the tall coke braziers and then went back to plying the steam gun. Wayne put a few buckets of an industrial detergent into the tank, and this, with the jet of steam and water, started to blast some of the lumps of muck away.

Jack cut away some of the solidified dirt with the heel of his shoe. Play the jet along the clean edge and it would work its way under the plated grease, lifting it, breaking and tumbling it away in bits, like umbrellas in a storm.

'Fucking waste of time' Wayne said. 'They're going to shut it anyway.'

Although the leaky bag soaked his gloves and his armpits, Jack enjoyed prising at the dirt with the steam gun. It was, he thought, pleasurable, like picking scabs.

THREE

Judith dreamt that she was swimming in a huge lake surrounded by mountains. The water was superbly clear and light prismed in the ripples over her belly as she scissored along on her back. She had the sensation that the lake was immensely deep. Turning onto her face she duckdived and felt the weight of her legs driving her down. As she fell, she spread her arms and legs so that she cartwheeled through the hard greens barred with shafts of light. She felt herself revolve on an axis through her left arm and right leg, and then spin forward end over end. Her hair spread in a cloud round her head as the motion became more complicated. She tucked into a ball and then spreadeagled and repeated this, so that the movement became a pulse. When she tucked, she closed her face against her knees. Opening out, she stretched her fingers and toes to feel the spaces between them. The water grew cooler around her, and darker. She was falling towards a dark, indistinct place. Suddenly she realised she needed to breathe. She looked for the light and tried to claw towards it. A straining feeling moved up her throat and into her mouth, pressing against her teeth, trying to blow her lips open.

Her face breaking the surface, her eyes opened on a blackness. Her mouth burst open and she gasped the air.

Ticking.

She relaxed, mildly confused by the warm bed. Keith was moving around downstairs. She heard the rising note of the kettle being filled. It was still dark and the clock had by now lost its luminosity. About seven. He got in off nights about ten to; by ten past he'd be in bed. This she did not have to think; her body vaguely remembered the pattern.

Feet on the stairs. Door opening.

Drifting onto her shoulder, Judith started a slow sidestroke keeping on the surface. Through the water she could hear her own breathing, deep and rhythmic with the stroke. She swam for a long time, until fronds in the water began to brush under her. A quickening panic filled her and she tried to kick away. Suddenly she was standing ankledeep on the edge of the lake and she was covered in small leaves, meshed with the fine shoots they grew on. She started to walk. Ashore, and then across a moor toward a mountain.

The bed jerked and Judith rocked back.

She was aware of her real face frowning, the eyebrows drawn down as she dragged herself back to the dream.

There was a strong sun, but her body did not become dry. There was heather and a breeze. She walked down into a wide depression and the sun struck her strongly as she dropped into shelter from the wind. She stretched out on the heather and picked at the small leaves sticking to her. Skies drifted over, the clouds at many altitudes and of various shapes, suggesting great space. She watched them without thinking. Arms slackened first, then neck, then back, then legs. She seemed to flow over the prickly, springy plants.

The bed jerked again. Judith knew she was being woken.

The frown on her dream-forehead unknotted itself. Her front seemed to open up to the warmth, to bask. It was a long time with the sun shining on her closed eyes before she became aware of the voices. There was a restrained babble of talk, as in a restaurant. She opened her eyes and the sky was still randomly there. She shifted her head and looked around the depression. Many people, all wearing hats, were sitting at tables covered in gingham cloths. They were all clothed and holding books and looking at her. She spread her hands over her naked trunk, felt cold. At one table, a fat man in a morning suit stared at her over the edge of his book.

Keith had got into bed. Judith wrestled with her waking mind, trying to put it back to sleep. She was aware of the shift in balance on the mattress, the new wrinkles in the bottom sheet radiating from the places where Keith's body pinned it. There was a sensation too of cold, and tension, his body being awake and taut. There was the awake sound of his breathing, sudden movements as he sought a position to settle in.

She felt her dream ebbing. The fat man stared, but her picture of him had the transparency of her waking imagination. She knew that if anything else was to happen she would have to contrive it consciously.

Her real frown melted and she opened her eyes again onto the grainy dark.

Keith rolled close to her and pressed himself along her back. He was cold. She tugged down her ruckled nightie before he could get his freezing fingers on her hips. Instead, his hand found her breast. She could smell swarfega and soap and that smell of oiled metal that reminded her of passing the metalwork room in school years before.

Not now please, she thought. Hardly ever, and then only when I don't want to and then not very well.

He pressed harder. She kept still.

She guessed it was about half past. Today would be Tuesday. Stupid bloody Tuesday. She felt herself smile as she sang the song in her mind. Stupid bloody Tuesday man you've been a naughty girl you've let your. Goo goo gajoo.

Keith kissed her on the back of her neck. She kept still. He bit her and her head turned and moved back so that it touched his face. Of course he had forgotten.

'Glasses' she said.

He sat up suddenly, letting more cold air in, took off his glasses and put them on the floor. Dimly she could see the swag of his belly.

He tucked back down and turned her on her back, pushed a cold knee between her thighs. One hand gathered up her nightie like a cinema curtain.

Vaguely she thought it would be good to have a telephone. Why had she thought that?

Keith lay heavily on her. They were travelling opposite ways. He towards sleep, she waking.

He fidgeted into position, pushing his pants down to his knees. She didn't like the way he slept in his pants. The white braided elastic nipped in his flab, which felt and looked ugly. He shouldn't have swapped that afternoon for a nightshift. Put his bodyclock wrong.

Not in now. Kiss me a bit first.

'Oh Keith' she said.

It didn't occur to her until after she'd said it that it might sound like encouragement.

With a phone she could call up the cinema to find out what was on. That was if there had still been a cinema in town.

She wondered what he thought about while they did it. Probably he was still mentally 'preparing'. Perhaps that was why he was so bad at it. Or perhaps he was like the men in that article she'd read, pretending she was some film star. Perhaps that was why he got all excited and did it too fast. She wouldn't mind, if he could learn to time it better. But probably he was still 'preparing'.

He got as fully into her as he ever did and she felt mild pleasure. That always took her by surprise. The subsequent usual disappointment, she supposed, made her forget every time. He started slowly. She liked that and caressed his shoulders.

Yes, come on, Eggman, she thought.

His movement became frantic spasms and she groaned inwardly. She caught hold of the rolls of fat under his shoulderblades and dug her nails in, but it only made him go faster.

He was holding himself up from her on his palms, as if he was doing pressups, and she felt his belly slap on hers with every shove.

That song. He is the Eggman, I am the Walrus, or something like that. Thinking of herself as an onlooker, even though it was dark, she thought of Keith becoming the Walrus. She was being made love to only that was the wrong way of saying it by a small walrus preoccupied with local history. The thought made her laugh and listening to it, she thought it was a very wicked laugh.

She drew her nails down his back to his hips. This was no good. She wanted the Eggman.

Keith slowed and nibbled at her neck. She relaxed her hands and pressed her palms against his buttocks.

Better.

His movement became a sort of snuggling. His breathing was deep and measured and she could hear the clock again. She felt his ribcage bell out as he breathed and his weight deadened on her. His face was greased with sweat against hers, and so relaxed that the mouth was hanging open distorted.

She kept quite still. Quietly, inside her, he deflated like a balloon near twelfth night.

The dark was thinning, becoming greyish. Judith liked mornings. Her nose felt cold. There was probably a frost. She liked that. But Keith had spoiled this morning. She could partly cure it with tea and toast and the newspaper, when it came. It would be nice, too, to be able to sit at a newly lighted fire – but there was that to do, and the dry heat from the electric fire and crumpled flex to the plug depressed her with its feeling of seedy impermanence. And the dead ashes in the grate. The ruin of one day to rake out before you set another.

Keith, fast asleep, pinned her, with her nightie uncomfortably doubled across her breasts. She didn't like to move. It was easiest to do nothing.

He nuzzled her in his sleep. As he unconsciously slobbered at her ear, she remembered that the man in the morning suit was someone she'd seen in an old film. He had been in a restaurant and a waiter had brought him a telephone. And so the telephone. She felt the satisfaction of solving an irrelevant puzzle.

The thought pleased her as she felt a coolish, sticky dribbling in her crotch, eased out from under her husband, and reached shivering for the kleenex.

* * *

That day Keith went back into work on the half past one bus, so doubling back onto his normal shift.

There was a frost which had only partly thawed when he got up at twelve. Clouds were clamped across the valley and the ridges of the mountains were obscured. It would be one of those days with the lights on all afternoon.

The maintenance shop, which opened off the east side of the finishing mill, had, in any case, no windows. The smirched striplights were perpetually on for the endless rotas of maintenance shifts, although continuous production had stopped years before.

The mill itself, Keith thought, could be like a cathedral on brighter days, especially when it was smoky or there was the brown steam that rose when alphasil was being rolled, and when the sun struck in shafts through the high skylights. Or even in winter, like today, with the great pedestalled braziers of burning coke strategically placed on the mill floor, it could impress him unexpectedly. Especially when the overhead cranes might start to roll without warning, or the bogeys near the slab shears start to shunt out, or a dumper pull in at a derelict looking bay. Then everything would seem mysteriously purposeful and unsafe.

But the maintenance shop, with its low ceiling, with its concrete floor so dirty that it looked like beaten black earth, raglittered, with a few decrepit abrasive wheels and drills and a workbench, the clutter of lockers improvised from welded plate painted green, this was just the numb space where much of his worktime was spent.

Afternoons were the worst. He had been glad of the chance to swap one of his afternoons for a nightshift, even though it had meant doing a turn with B shift. B was about right, Keith thought. And doubling back. B shift's fitter-foreman always found a dirty, awkward job somewhere on the mill. It was probably wise to keep that lot occupied, but they still got restless towards the end of their turn. And they had that night.

On afternoons the mill went down at half four or so these days and then there was just the long slide towards ten and clocking off. Unless someone clocked you. Emlyn, the fitter for whom Keith was mate, had never had his card clocked by someone else in his life and he told Keith this sometimes when they were working together. It was like a private point of honour with him. So Keith always felt obliged to stay to the end too, and in any case no longer knew anyone who might have clocked his card.

Keith and Emlyn stood in the maintenance shop, hands in their boilersuit pockets, looking down at the pattern of one inch pipes and joints laid speculatively on the floor like a map of the underground. Keith yawned and Emlyn scratched his balding head.

'There must be some way of doing it' Emlyn said. 'Even if there's no flaming point in doing it.'

'They ought to make up their bloody minds now' Keith said, 'and shut the bloody place right away if they're going to.'

'That's the words of a man who've doubled back off nights onto afternoons.' Emlyn went down on his knees and tentatively tried a different arrangement of the pipes. 'If they stay open till open till September' he said, without looking up, 'them grease pipes'll have to be replaced and there's no two ways about it.' His nervous repetitions, a kind of extended stutter, and very slightly Anglicised accent – he pronounced 'maid' and 'made' the same way when concentrating – gave him a stage professor sound. His frizz of thinning grey hair and sharp eyes added to this. Walking his dog on the hill, he could be taken for an academic working on the next chapter or an intellectual labour politician.

'Next September?' Keith said.

'That's the latest latest word anyhow.' Emlyn's face had reddened as he squatted. Keith noticed his fingers were still white with cold.

'How many latest words is that?' Keith said. It was the conventional cynicism.

Emlyn looked up, as if to deliver the final comment on the matter and saw Keith yawning.

'Dai Rutter and them playing up again last night?' Emlyn asked.

Rutter had played up. The job was replacing some bearings on the rollers in front of the roughing mills. When it was finished, at about half past two in the morning, men drifted away to quiet corners to wait for clocking off at six, but Rutter trapped Keith in a cabin off the shop and talked for two and a half hours about his time in the army and his deepsea fishing exploits. It was cold in the cabin – the heater was broken – but Rutter didn't mind the cold. Keith remembered the story about him hitting a man clear over the big abrasive wheel – probably not true – but he sat still and grew numb, just in case. Finally Keith dozed off, so Rutter smashed the windows to wake him up. There were six or eight panes, painted rather than covered with metal, so the glass mostly fell outside as Rutter swung at it with a spanner.

'Yes you fucker' he said. 'Sack for sleeping on the job here.' And he slammed the spanner on the table.

At school, Keith had thought that only children behaved like that. Rutter was nearly sixty. Emlyn called Rutter mad. Others coped with him by saying he was a 'character' and his behaviour could then seem like self-parody. But on your own at half four in the morning and him playing the weight of a spanner in his palm. He was unpredictable. Keith almost admired his impulsiveness. He could not imagine himself like that, any more than he could imagine his fat self rolling around on the earth with a girl.

But then, only that morning he'd surprised himself. The need for Jude had come over him after Rutter had walked out, leaving him looking at the blackness through the broken windows.

He thought of inexplicable incidents of violence. A fight in the pub that had simply started. Some silly bugger thinking he was John Wayne probably. Nothing was inexplicable. It couldn't be. The Enniskillen soldier in the Merthyr Riots in 1831 who strolling in a quiet street decapitated a dog with his sword. Perhaps he was a middle-aged man. More likely young. The blooding of the young. And Jack Priday, his old best friend that was, smashing the milk bottles on their way home after stoptap.

'He smashed the windows in the cabin' Keith said.

'That was him was it?' Emlyn said. 'Christ it'll be Christ it'll be cold in there now.'

He stood up and looked at the new permutation on the grease pipes.

'That Rutter' he started, looking at Keith, and paused as steel roared through the finishing mill next door. He was red and sweating, Keith noticed, although it was cold. 'That Rutter' he said when the noise died, 'is a bloody luny. The man's not safe, mun.'

'I put a bit of board across the window' Keith said.

'No bugger'll come and glaze that now.'

Keith looked down at the new pipes. 'They'd want to know how it happened anyway' he said.

'Who in his right mind would voluntarily do a permanent nightshift?' Emlyn looked at his watch. 'Mill won' be down for an hour yet. We may as well have a wiff now and do the job then.'

They brewed tea and sat in the cold cabin. The striplight buzzed and fluttered so that Emlyn couldn't concentrate on his crossword. He took the Telegraph, although he called it fascist, specially for the crossword, which he usually filled in about half an hour. The sheet of plywood which Keith had leant against the window left gaps where the draught drew in. Finally a gust caught it and toppled it onto an empty bench. Emlyn threw down his paper and shoved the board back into place. He went out cursing incoherently.

Keith liked Emlyn. It was odd that Em was less popular than, say, Rutter with the rest of the maintenance crew. Emlyn had some interest in local history, and also lived near Scwrfa where the old furnaces were, had told him about the house in Buchan Row where, he'd heard, there might be some old papers left. Keith still had that to check. So Keith could talk his ideas through with Emlyn. It was useful to have someone to listen. Not that Emlyn would be a good historian. His thinking was endlessly convoluted. He would be obsessed by the origin of a placename or sidetracked by a reminiscence, or sometimes he would lock into some speech he had made before, which would become more and more generalised, become a truism on the hopelessness of things and end in a snort or a shrug.

38

Keith wondered whether he would be like Em by the time he was in his late fifties. Not like Rutter, anyway. I'll be like Em perhaps, he thought. Jack, if he was still alive, might become Rutter. Except Keith would never earn as much as Em, being only a mate. But then, if it was right what Em said about September, all this would melt away and what then? What would happen to Rutter? It was hard to imagine him surviving anywhere else. Perhaps it would be a good thing.

He looked at the crusts and chewed bacon rinds still on the floor after the last shift, and up at the broken window.

Shut it down before it falls down.

He took off his safety glasses and his vision smudged. Yes, shut. Otherwise in thirty years he might be another Em. But then even if it did shut.

He tried to think of something else. 'One hundred and seventy-seven years ago, Samuel Moonlow's men commissioned the first furnace in the Gwedog Valley.'

It was too cold to think. The donkey team and panniers of lime. The teamdriver blowing his hands. Trees. (Idiot.) But there were twelve weeks yet for him to prepare the talk. He shouldn't get worked up about it like Emlyn worrying about the new pipes. It would be coming into the warm time of the year then. Hard to conjure up a blizzard. Never mind atmosphere, though. Get the details right. That was what they always tried to catch you out on. Six or seven years before, he might have had a couple of pints before the talk. But that was another habit he'd left behind, like having it off out of doors. Or, he almost thought, like having it off anywhere. He remembered mwtshing school, with Jack one Friday, thumbing to Cardiff and drinking flagons of cider on the national museum steps. But the day with Anne in the derelict house. Then. And all the other days with her.

He remembered again, then, how he'd surprised himself that morning. And after such a rotten nightshift too. It may not be often, he thought, but it's good when it happens.

*

After the mill went down, Emlyn and Keith fitted the new grease pipes near the blooming mill stand.

Keith always found the mill pleasant when there was no rolling. By now it was dark outside. The strip was still hot from the slabs, so that he warmed up quite quickly. In the quiet, he always noticed the constant hiss of escaping steam and the small noises of men whistling, boots clanking on catwalks. And without the twelve-tonne ingots being rammed through the blooming mill, it was easier to notice the tangle of blackened pipes and gearboxes and spindles on the other side of the strip, and the huge dusty signs recording the dates when production records were broken, from the days of continuous rolling. Astronomic figures in tonnes. Keith looked up at the big mill stand and its massive rolls, the mangles that squashed the ingots down to six inches or so thick. What would they do with a thing like that if they closed? Melt it perhaps. The business gorging on its own tail.

'Em' he said as they worked, 'what do you reckon'll happen to Rutter when they shut this place?'

Emlyn stopped and stared at Keith as if he'd just farted in front of his wife. 'You're worried about Rutter?' he said. 'That bloody maniac can go and.' The conflict between Emlyn's belief in moderate speech and his desire to describe a suitable activity for Rutter caused a choking silence, like different lightwaves making darkness. The veins bulged in his neck and finally he spluttered, 'he can go and take a running jump at himself for all I care.'

'It's just that' Keith said, 'he's such an odd bugger, I can't see him getting on outside. He'd be a fish out of water.'

Em faced Keith. 'He'll survive. You watch. The question is, will we?'

When the job was finished they stood by a brazier for a while and watched some of the other fitters and a welder working on the mill stand. Emlyn's comment gnawed at Keith. He tried to blot it out by seeing the welder as a knight in armour. The visor, boots and long suede gauntlets had always struck him like that.

He took off his glasses and thought back to that morning again. The best for ages. She was half toasted with sleep. And she had actually given that laugh of pleasure, and when she really got going her nails had gone deep and she had drawn them down his back. Actually drew blood. He would be careful in the bathhouse tonight, face out in the shower and put the towel over his shoulders as soon as he came out.

When Emlyn had finished a diatribe which started by condemning management practices and ended by condemning everything, Keith wandered towards the opening in the mill wall where the bogeys were shunted in to the slab shears.

Outside it was starless and silent. There were flecks of ice on the wind, which was raw and hurt the throat. Keith shivered, put on his glasses and turned back.

Emlyn by the fire and the figures clambering on the mill stand. It could hardly be cool enough to work up there.

The hot cokes dropping through the grille of the brazier and oxyacetylene flaring on the welder's mask seemed comforting. Keith put his hands in his boilersuit pockets and there were the scrap of paper and the ballpoint he carried like charms. Perhaps he would get in half an hour on his talk before the end of the shift.

FOUR

Home is a place where you can crap with the bog door wide open.

The thought struck Jack like a revelation when he saw his landlady's face drop as she mounted the stairs and caught sight of him enthroned, with his trousers round his ankles. He gave his open smile and raised his eyebrows slightly before he pushed the door to.

It was a bad area for furnished digs. No colleges. No tourists. The few people likely to stay, travellers on exes splashing out in the few hotels, or the odd stranded motorist putting up in the most rundown pub. Worse than Accrington. Much.

In the couple of weeks he'd been working, Mrs Williams, the landlady, had changed remarkably.

Not that she was a real landlady like the Blackpool postcards. In fact, she wasn't bad for her age, which must have been the early forties. She wore rollers to excess and clasped her wrists in the appropriate Mona Lisa way while talking, but still, she was all right. He suspected that probably most roller wearing wrist claspers were really averagely human.

She was a widow, and worked in a factory from eight to half past four. The factory made electrical components, she told him, but she didn't know what they were for.

At first she had shown a kind of reserved sympathy for Jack's being unemployed but this had worn away to lack of faith as he failed to get a job. This turned to something like friendship when he got work and started setting the alarm clock. But he'd changed his attitude to her too. It was 'Connie' and 'John' now. And that uncertainty you get between owner and tenant when neither is quite sure how to play the part. No meter in the bathroom, an amateur fumbling of the money when it fell due on Fridays.

She ought to call him Jack. It was only because of seeing his signature she called him John. His father had called him John and then Jack had read somewhere Jack was short for John and adopted it. His mother had called him Shwn or Shwna after the local fashion, or rather old fashion, which at least was better than John, but as a kid he'd liked Jack best of all. She should call him it. After all, he called her Connie, which was short for something. Constance probably. The virtue of being stable and reliable. 'Call me Jack: Everybody does.' He practised saying it. Slipping fully back into the patois it was 'everybody do' – except nobody do, or did when he should have said it, because then he hadn't known anybody, having no job.

He was not yet, after all, back in his home town. After nearly two hundred miles, he had stopped exactly two valleys short. Over the mountain to the west of his digs was the steelworks, and over the mountain to the west of that, home. The end of the salmon ladder, where the bog door had no bolt. Except there was no bog door that was his there now, and hence.

But still, even here things had a familiarity he was constantly catching out of the corner of his eye. The moor between Accrington and Blackburn, he'd thought, had been close, and the colour of the light on a trip to Howarth with Liz had almost rung home bells, but here there was. He wasn't sure what it was. Places remembered from childhood. Dead, grassed tips that only a practised eye could spot. And the true clichés: sheep that vandalised housing estates, shitten ponies gone feral, men like Ben sitting around the bilingual war memorial wearing their flat caps when the weather picked up. And something else. Or nothing. Landlady stories. It's about the ceiling Mrs W. Yes Mr P? Well I'd like to have one. Don't worry, the neighbours don't walk around much. And while I'm at it Mrs W, can I wheel my bike up your back passage? No, put it in the front between the railings. You know, Mrs W, they don't bury people here; they sit them in The Prince of Wales lounge bar with a pint of Albright. Local councillors are going to take measures. Two gills of vodka and a litre of scotch. Et cetera. And then there were the familiar names on the destination boards of buses. That was part of the something. Once, a bus driver he'd recognised, the father of a former friend. A man who'd known his father, worked with him, years and years ago. Before he was born. The bus driver hadn't recognised him. Jack did not let on. He could have done. Hello, Mr Watkins. I'm Jack. I was at school with your son, Keith. Remember? All that excavating. No.

What would she say if he said it this Friday?

There we are, Connie. Eleven pound. Thank you, John love. Oh, call me Jack. Everybody do. Oh right. Jack.

They were both too amateur though. She might think, after all this time, it was an opening move. He would surely have said it sooner if it was innocent.

She was still attractive. And the house ached with the gap left by her husband. There was one photograph, black and white, that froze the unnatural wedding moment, the husband looking as if he'd be happier in winklepickers and a shoelace tie, she looking older than him with a horsetoothed, forced smile. Just that on the stereogram that probably dated from one of their early Christmases. Although the house was well furnished, the central heating adequate, corners of rooms seemed remote and cold. Just too big, he supposed. One of those big terraced houses with a bay window and a stained glass Viking ship in the front door, like the house where an uncle and auntie probably still lived, two valleys away.

Perhaps they would exchange looks. A coy come-on. All right, Jack then, she would say. He would go to the rugby club with her and be shy and young while she introduced him to her friends. The openhearted would say good luck to them. The grown-up daughter living in Newport would find out and be upset, confused. Why, Mam? This isn' like you. Connie would blossom, look younger. If we could give each other a few years. He would shave more often.

44

She would exorcise her husband's ghost and, flouting convention, they'd be perfectly happy. Jack it's been so long, she'd say when they did it, gently, in the early morning. *The Indian Summer of Mrs Williams*. Fade in violins. Roll credits.

And her daughter was all right too. Not much younger than he was. You dog, Priday. Or as Wayne would say, I wouldn't mind hanging out of her guts. The mother more imaginable, though. But she's old enough to be his mother, nearly. Ladies and gentlemen, Jack Priday. Shit anywhere, shag anything.

Surely her thoughts must wander the same way though. The arrangement was too loose, with too few barriers for it to be quite right. Their bedrooms were next door to one another and if she had a lie down after work he had to turn his radio down. The smell on the landing must irritate her when he made food on the Baby Belling. Sometimes he would glimpse her if she left her door ajar. Their milk bills were entangled and the rent book was from Woolworth's. They met awkwardly on the stairs, knew each other's wardrobe and footwear, knew each other's smell, saw each other early in the morning and late at night. Everything except the contact.

Tonight she was going to a concert in the rugby club. That would mean warpaint and beads. Her face was worn and lined in the week when she came home. She explained to him once that if she fitted together twice as many of the little pieces as she was meant to fit together for her basic rate she got a bonus of thirteen pence per hour. It only made you tired, she said, if you thought about it. Some days she thought about it and came home greyer in the face than usual. Concert tonight, no bonus tomorrow, Connie. Just think, he thought, if I went out on binges like that in the week, the economy would crack. I am a Man of Steel. Like Sully and Kelv and Wayne. Except that Sully came in pretty frazzled most mornings and so would Wayne, except that he didn't get hangovers. Still too young.

Jack washed and went to his room.

He could hear Connie moving around next door. It was early evening, dark, and the lights were blazing, though however bright the bulb in Jack's room – he had replaced the sixty with a hundred and fifty watt on his first payday – it never seemed to push the darkness quite out of the far corners. She was probably choosing her dress for the evening and applying the first layers of paint. She hung her nylon housecoat on the front of the wardrobe, he noticed in one of his glimpses, and left her flat shoes by the door. Looking for decent tights, putting her cigarette lighter in her handbag and enough money.

He lay on the bed and tugged at the piece of loose wallpaper. Underneath the floral pattern he could see the grubby Yogi Bear paper. The daughter, Clare, must resent his being there, taking up the spaces that had been hers before she'd married, crowding into her memories. O let me crowd into your mammaries instead. The prospect from the bed of wardrobe, dressing table, window, must be her first memory of waking that all her wakings were compared with. She must resent the Baby Belling, the washing-up bowl and incongruous kitchen cupboard shoved into the middle of that.

Connie was singing softly.

Jack decided that he would go out himself. None of his immediate workmates lived in the same town, except for Ben who sat in The Nag's Head looking at the wall and blowing raspberries between sips of his pint. The rest were scattered around the other dormitory towns, Wayne and Sully and O of course from his home town. He'd been out a few times, had a miserable pint, and come home, or at least back to his room, early. He'd even started looking at the posters in the library for evening classes and clubs, struck up conversations with strangers, some slightly familiar from work. The result was he said hello to everybody and knew nobody. He could imagine people saying: there's a pleasant bloke he is. He do always say hello. A crawl was in order. He could probably say hello to somebody in every pub and club. Hiya butt. How be? A'right butty. Owzigoin? No' bâd mun.

As he put on a clean shirt and changed his socks, he recalled his own bedroom, two valleys away, his own first choice of wallpaper.

In his case it had been Huckleberry Hound. Later, conventional flowers, chosen by his mother just before she died. Except Dad had stripped the cartoons off first. Perhaps Connie's husband had died before they repapered. Perhaps it was to mute the memories that they redecorated in a hurry.

He and his father had papered the room after his mother's death without considering her having chosen it. Simply, the paper was there and should be used. In the years since he had left he had been home once, to his father's funeral five years before, in the Cortina in its better days. Carless now. How that left you helpless, without control over your own destiny. He'd stayed two days with the auntie, uncle and Viking ship. His brother, who got the little house, for what that was worth, would not have him there. Barring his way in the doorframe.

No further than that. Don't speak to me. You broke his heart.
You can talk. You buggered off to Reading when it suited you.
And when it suited him, unlike you.
He bloody threw me out.
Jack shuddered.

As for the rest of the family, they had been full of silent reproach. Anyway, returning, to them, was a sign of failure. Successful sons left with parental blessings and a wad of A levels. They were civil servants in Reading. They never came back but wrote and phoned occasionally from distant English towns where they were deputy headmasters. So pick up your patrimony and piss off.

In those two days he'd seen no one he knew, apart from family, and was glad to get back to Liz. Home. A place where. He remembered at the crematorium those darksuited attendants who looked as if they might be working for the Church of Latter Day Saints, or Special Branch. As they went back to the car one of them came up. Would you mind leaving as quickly as possible, gentlemen. We've got another one coming in a minute.

It was seven o'clock. Indecently early to be going out on a Wednesday. I have taken my clean socks from my little blue rucksack that holds all my possessions and I have put on my best trainers and I will go out now into the little town and get pissed out of my little head.

He bumped into Connie on the landing as he heaved on his coat.

'You're going out too' she said. 'I'm going to a concert down the rugby.'

She could probably smell the Old Spice. It would damp down the smell of the sausages he'd had for tea.

'You said.'

'Some boy on the organ and a girl singing.'

'Sounds nice.' Liar.

'Well, it do make a change.'

No it don't. 'Aye. I suppose it do.'

They stood at the landing banister like lovers on a liner in an old film.

She was wearing a veenecked green dress, far too thin for the time of year, and white high heeled shoes with ankle straps. She shook her head to demonstrate the rollerless hair and the flailing pendant earrings. Eau de Cologne, Old Spice and sausages. She was bound to ask him down for tea one day if only to reduce the niff.

'Where you off to then, John?' She fingered the gold bar on her neckchain, pointing out to him its hallmark, and the vee of flesh it lay in.

Tut. Unprofessional, Connie. A proper landlady would never ask the lodger where he was going. At least, not like that.

'Just out for a drink.' Be cool and aloof under the glad eye. Set her wondering.

He went past her and down the stairs. Not too aloof, though. He glanced up to try to get a look up her skirt. She stood her ground.

'Call me Jack, Connie. Everybody do.'

She said that she would, fingering the gold chain where the bar hung, pointing down between her breasts.

In the first couple of pubs Jack said his hellos, drank his pints, and left. In the third, the only other customer in the bar, a nervous teenager in denims, challenged him to a game of pool. The boy made telegraphic conversations as he darted round the table, his eyes constantly on the baize. Jack learnt that he'd been out of work since he left school eighteen months before. Jack suggested that he should try the steelworks. The boy snorted and smirked arbitrarily as he concentrated on chalking his cue. He dropped the chalk, tried unsuccessfully to balance his cigarette on the edge of the table, and frequently miscued.

After potting the black, Jack drained his pint and promised a return match the next time he was in. He did not feel especially pleased with himself for winning.

Outside, the evening had become mild and damp. There would at most be only a light frost. More pleasant for getting up in the morning, or for that matter in the middle of the night to go to the toilet. He nestled down into his collar. Have to get a scarf, he thought, and he remembered the wardrobe full of clothes he'd left in Accrington.

In The Nag's Head, he had a pint with Ben, asked after his wife, and moved on.

I'll sing you five-o. The fifth pub was the first smoothypub lounge complete with horsebrasses and indirect lighting – i.e. tinted striplights behind a sort of hardboard pelmet that ran round the room like a picture rail. Also no outsize colour television, but smooth music, just loud enough to hear, not loud enough to recognise. There were a few young couples in far corners, mostly holding hands and not talking as they sat at the low tables topped with stippled copper.

Jack sat on a tall stool and hunched over the bar, like in an American film, as he sipped his pint.

The yoozooal, Mr Priday?

The yoozooal, Joe. An the racks.

Sherr thing, Mr Priday.

Except there should be a bowl of salted peanuts which he would eat without ever wiping his fingers.

Through the bar he could see in the saloon bar the regulars, the movement of dart and pool players. The row of bottles on the optic behind the bar, the clutter of plastic ice buckets and cards of nuts and pork scratchings were beginning to look unnaturally garish.

He had just reached the end of his fifth pint when Kelv and his wife came in. Jack greeted Kelv like an old friend, then Kelv snatched up his glass and bought him another before he had time to pretend to protest.

'Jack, this is my wife, Jane. Jane Jack. Jack works with me.'

Jane was small and dark and had an Ulster accent.

'You're both from Belfast?' Jack said. So what the hell are you doing here?

Jane laughed.

'No' she said. 'I'm from Belfast but Kelvin isn't.'

Man and wife observed his puzzlement.

'I'm from round here' Kelv said. 'I was in Belfast four years, you know.'

There was something funny about somebody from round there sounding like Ian Paisley. But then he, Jack, possibly sounded like George Formby. He heard himself laughing, distantly.

'We were going to this concert in the rugby club' Jane said, 'but we were too late to get in. The place is crammed.'

Kelv looked surprisingly respectable and ordinary in his clean best clothes. Jack had only really seen him in his superannuated patched blue boilersuit and sometimes an old cap to keep his ginger hair clean. He would turn his cap back to front and beat his thigh with his rag gloves, making clicking noises like a jockey urging on his horse as he jogged down the mill. In the pub, in a rugby club sweater complete with discreet logo, a beautifully ironed shirt, grey slacks and shiny shoes, he looked like a collage of photos from the menswear section of a mail order catalogue. He also had a car, of sorts. Easy to tell he was into his second contract.

'My landlady's going to that. Some bloke singing and a girl on the organ. Or is it the other way round. By eck, Jane. You do look after your husband. We don' see any of this Pierre Cardin stuff in work.' By eck. Lancashire that.

Kelv drained his pint with relish.

'Ah she looks after me, Jack. Best thing I ever did was get married.'

Jack stood his round and they talked. Kelv and Jane and their daughter lived with Kelv's mother. Jack described his digs, suitably fantasticating them with anecdotes about his attempts at cooking and the landlady jokes. He was aware that he was speaking more loudly than he needed and that his gestures and head movements were impulsively jerky and exaggerated, but he seemed unable to do anything about this. A young couple sitting nearby laughed and groaned obligingly at his jokes.

Glug. I'll sing you eight-o.

'So how's the mother-in-law, Jane?'

Jane and Kelv exchanged nervous looks as if telepathically trying to agree on a halftruth.

Jack heard, muffled by the smoothypub carpet tiles, the proverbial ballock thudding to the floor.

'Have another, Kelv, Jane.' Be professional. Change subject.

This time only Kelv looked nervously at Jane.

'All right' Jane said. 'Go on you two. I'll drive.'

Wait a minute. Whose round?

The rows of bottles and the faces of men in the saloon bar looked glazed like toffee apples and voices now were tinny and distant. Kelv was buying the round before Jack could collect his thoughts.

'Sorry Kelv. I meant—'

'That's all right, Jack. You'll not run away.'

Through in the saloon bar, Jack could see the boy in denims, playing pool. He was circling the table like a caged jaguar, as before, his eyes fixed on the constellation of poolballs. Poor sod. Probably did a crawl of the pool tables every night. Probably losing.

'That's true' Jack said. 'I can hardly bloody stand up.' He ran a hand over the temporary beerpot straining against his shirt like a ghost pregnancy. 'I'm out of practice.'

51

They drank, discussing the drinking feats of yesteryear. Kelv told some squaddie stories. Hence Ulster hence Jane – Catholic, he discovered – hence accent.

At last Jack was aware of Kelv patting his shoulder saying something like: 'Well my old butty, we'd better be going.'

He watched uncomprehendingly as they pulled on their coats. 'Aye. See you morning, Kelv' he said, when he understood.

'Aye, maybe' Kelv said as they went.

They've gone. Must be stoptap, Jack reasoned. End of evening. Collapse. Wake up with headache at six. Go to work.

He climbed down from his stool, smiled inanely at the couple who had laughed at his jokes, who smiled inanely back, and did a fair imitation of a sober man leaving a pub.

It was drizzling. He walked back through the town trying to spit the thick feeling out of his mouth.

It puzzled him that the pubs seemed still open. Their lights were on and there was movement behind the sandblasted windows. In the square, by the bilingual war memorial where old men sat when the weather picked up, he looked up and felt the cool drizzle on his face. Good. At the top of the market hall the white disc of the market clock looked indifferently across the tops of the drizzlesmudged streetlamps. In the distance there was a rhythmic bump and a voice distorted through an amplifier. Concert. He stared at the clock for a long time before he realised that it was only half past ten.

Thirty more minutes, he thought. Pint. Two. Chips. Then collapse wake up six headache work. There's civilised for you. Leaving early. Best thing ever did get married. And Mam disgruntled babysitting. Restraint. Fuck restraint.

He went into a pub in view of the rugby club, at the end of the town. The long, low prefabricated rugby club building, looking like a converted advance factory, was throbbing like a headache and the lighted windows were running with condensation.

The pub was quiet. Jack was confusedly aware of young women playing darts and glancing at him suspiciously as he watched their buttocks when they went to collect their arrows. Sort of place where you watch the dartboard and throw darts at the telly. File that one away. There will come a moment for such words. Must look a sight. Drizzle sodden sot.

Suddenly he was outside the rugby club, wolfing at a bag of lukewarm chips. The club stood on the edge of the rugby field. Old tip levelled off. Takes a practised eye. He threw away the chip papers and scrambled up onto a bank at one end of the building to try to get a look in. Bump bump. The girl was singing 'My Way' though it was hard to tell if the boy on the organ was playing the same tune. Down through the steamy windows he could see the laps of men and women, tables littered with empty glasses, handbags and fans. As the song reached its final drawnout crescendo, hands moved to the ready for applause. There were shouts and whistles of appreciation.

Jack lost his footing on the damp grass and slid down the bank, slithering over thawed mud into the base of the wall. One hand and arm and one side of his coat were smeared thickly with mud.

The music had stopped. He heard people talking, saying goodbyes and car doors slamming.

He got up and ran. He seemed to be able to run without getting out of breath, feeling the damp and the deep lungfuls of air sobering him a little.

He stopped outside the house and went down the two yards of front garden path. Viking ship almost invisible. Almost no panting.

Also no key. He went through all his pockets twice, and then looked for an open window. One of the sash windows of Connie's bedroom was open a fraction of an inch. He planned a route up via the downstairs baywindow sill and the downpipe next to it.

He had one knee on the baywindow guttering and both hands on the drainpipe when something broke and he toppled back into the garden.

He sat up and looked at his hands. Dimly he could see on his right palm blood welling through the muck. It showed black under the orange streetlights.

Tapped shoes tapping and voices. Connie was approaching the house with some friends. Jack scrambled into the doorway and as they got nearer, walked out to the gate. She was wearing a thick duffelcoat and looked unsteady on her white strapped high heels.

'Jack' she said. 'There's a surprise.'

Jack stood with his muddy, bloody side to the gatepost.

'Here we are, Maureen' Connie said. 'This is my fancyman they do all talk about down the rugby.'

The friends were a couple about Connie's age. They laughed, said, 'G'night, Ceinwen' and walked on.

Jack leant against the post. 'I lost my key' he said.

She took his arm and they went in.

In the lighted hallway, she registered her surprise at his wet, dirty, bloody condition.

'Sorry I'm a bit pissed' he said.

She took his coat, gave him coffee, sponged his hand, applied a plaster.

He was sitting in her kitchen while she stood in front of him, rubbing his head with a towel. Where did her coat go?

'My father was a landlady' he said.

'What?'

'I mean a widower.'

'You *are* half cut en you.'

The gold bar jiggled in the vee of flesh, pointing up mammary valley to the end of the salmon ladder.

'Less face it, Connie' he heard himself saying, 'we fancy each other rotten.'

'Don' get any cute ideas. We both got to get up early in the morning.'

He made to kiss her. She pushed him away, then let him peck her on the cheek, then pushed him away.

'Right. That's enough. Off we go. Up the wooden hill.'

She steered him along and they floated up the stairs.

'Don't worry. There's nothing I haven't seen before' she said as she undressed him. 'In fact I saw it this evening. My my, you *are* excited.'

She spoke with the practised indifference of a district nurse taking a sample.

Jack started to sing 'My Way'.

'You're not going to do it any way, Jack love. Now come on.'

'Why not? Doggy fashion is the best.'

'Come on, I'm old enough to be your mother. Nearly. You ought to find a nice girl your own age.' She pushed him down on the bed and went to the door.

'Why should we stay masturbation fodder for one another?' he said.

Her expression froze. She lifted a hand, pulled out her false teeth and gave a grotesque collapsed smile.

'This is why' she said. 'Now leave it there, there's a good boy. And next time you're on the toilet, shut the door.'

She slammed the door.

The room was dark and spinning.

It doesn't matter, Jack thought. Like those primitive farmers using up the earth and moving on. Say sorry tomorrow. All over. Why not go back to auntie uncle and Viking ship, two ridges away? Dignity, that's why. Dignity pissed and covered in mud with a stonker on. No. The whirr of a curtain, that's why.

FIVE

It must have been obvious to everybody on the bus that Sully had a very bad hangover. O had never seen him quite this bad before. He groaned and rubbed his chest and made lapping noises as if he was trying to bring moisture to his dry mouth. His fairish hair was dry like straw and uncombed, his cheeks sunken. Odds on too, he hadn't brought any sandwiches – he seldom did anyway, even though, like O, he lived with his mother. So he would eat in the canteen and have chips with something, which would upset his stomach more.

O held with satisfaction the Sunblest bag of sandwiches in his lefthand anorak pocket. The bag had lasted now for a number of weeks. If he needed a new one, he decided he would keep a record of its endurance, perhaps by pencilling a tally like a cricket score inside the door of his locker.

In work, O completed the changing ritual and, wiping the grease from his fingers after drawing on his right boot, stared at the bathhouse floor. Sully had stopped at every other step on the path down from the time offices, hanging on to the handrail and retching. He was a bit younger than O, and O thought charitably that Sully might grow out of it.

When O went to his Uncle Dennis's sometimes at the weekends, they drank his homebrew and sometimes went to help his mother and auntie with the sherry and the place would fill with a warm certainty. But he would never drink on an evening before work, and never like Sully did. But then, Sully was a Catholic and lived in the rough end of that estate at the north end of town. He would probably expect the others to cover for him now.

As O left the bathhouse he saw Kelv standing anxiously outside one of the toilet cubicles, where Sully was installed still retching.

'Sully my old butty' Kelv said. 'Are you all right?'

In the day gang's cabin that morning Ken Francis was asleep in the usual place. There were some dead cockroaches around the tray of rat poison. Wayne shuffled the cards. Of the others, only Clarry looked up, offered a greeting and commented on the mildness of the weather. Jack was sitting with his face cradled in his hands.

O sat so he wouldn't have to look at the pinups.

He wondered, as he had wondered every morning for the past few weeks, where Jack lived. He didn't have a car – he talked to Kelv about cars – and he was never on the bus. Strange that he hadn't come home. He couldn't exactly come home, but he still had relatives. Perhaps it was suspicious that he was, almost, home. Jack reminded him of schooldays, which on the whole he had enjoyed. There were friendships and enmities then which seemed more real in his mind after ten years than anything happening now. It was suspicious. Perhaps O should ask Jack about these things. His big friend had been Keith Watkins. A great chunk of their contemporaries had left at the same time to go to colleges and universities, or away to work. O saw some of them like ghosts in the town sometimes, presumably visiting parents. Of course, Jack couldn't do that any more. It was odd that Jack seemed not to remember school in the way that O did. That common thing should have been the basis of a friendship, but Jack seemed dead to it. It was unfair. Kelv and Sully could clown like children, as if they were schoolboys. They would sit huddled together talking about women like perverts, and Jack would join in as if they were all just little boys. And Kelv was at least thirty-four. Jack had nothing in common with O because Jack was immature still, still only experiencing things, so he recognised nothing familiar, no common ground, when he looked at O. Jack didn't look very lively this morning though. And he had a large plaster on one hand.

Kelv came in, followed by Lew Hamer.

'Yes, you fuckers' Lew said. His usual greeting.

'Steady on, Lew' Clarry said. 'It's a bit early yet.'

'I've come to stop you taking any more money from these young fellas. Come on. It's Thursday.' Lew kicked Ken Francis's bench so that he actually woke up. 'Mill's down. I've got some work for you for a change. Hang on.' He looked round the gang. 'Where's our Irish friend?'

'Here I am, Lew' Kelv said.

'Not you you silly fucker. Sullivan mun.'

'He's an Irish one all right' Kelv said. 'About as Irish as Max Boyce. I just saw him in the bathhouse, Lew. He's on his way.' He winked secretly at O.

Lew looked doubtfully at Kelv for a moment, then sent some of the gang to hose down the roughing and finishing mill stands. The rest – Clarry, O, Jack, Kelv and Sully – he arranged to meet in the slabyard in ten minutes.

The slabyard was quiet. On production days it was full of noise, with the greensuited slingers hitching and unhitching the steel slings on the six tonne slabs for the overhead cranes, the charging machines pushing slabs into reheating furnaces which formed part of the wall between the yard and the mill, so that they could be heated and dropped out ready to roll on the delivery tables nextdoor. Now there was almost no movement. The cold slabs were stacked in their fourcornered crisscross piles. The cranes were still.

Kelv fetched Sully round to the yard. Looking a little better, he propped himself against a wall, pulled a face that went with a nasty taste, and looked blearily around. The net of blood vessels showing in the whites of his eyes reminded O of the crazing on an old plate at home. It sometimes upset him when mopping his gravy to discover he was eating from that plate.

Lew arrived with five pairs of rubber gloves and explained the job. A generator sunk in a concrete pit about five feet deep had been hit by a slab which had somehow fallen from the rollers by the furnaces. The slab was slung out, but the generator was smashed and the pit had flooded with grease and oil.

They looked at the greenish black mess as Lew told them to empty it, using a bucket, some ropes, and shovels.

'It do look like I feel' Jack said, when Lew had gone.

'It do look like I fucking look as well as feel' Sully said.

Nobody disagreed.

Clarry fetched some shovels which the gang kept hidden behind a disused control box on the mill. Kelv knocked the tops out of some empty forty-five gallon drums with a hammer and chisel. O dredged the bucket through the grease. Jack dug a shovel into it and inverted it over a drum. Very slowly the dollop of grease elongated and part of it finally flopped away into the bottom.

'This is going to be a pleasant little job' he said.

O was glad that the gang was split. No Wayne.

By half past two they had filled the first couple of drums and the grease level had fallen by a foot. While they worked, a man in a suit and hard hat came up and watched them for a few minutes without comment.

'Who's that nosy get?' Sully said when he'd gone.

'I don' know' Kelv said. 'Must be a manager.'

Later another stranger approached. He carried a spanner and had thinning, grizzled hair. O had seen him round the mill before and knew he came from somewhere in Scwrfa.

'When will you be when will you be finished, boys? he said.

Lew came back and looked into the pit.

'Fuck me. Haven' you finished yet?' he said, and dodged a glove aimed at him by Sully. 'All right. How do you fancy some overtime on this?'

The grizzleheaded man went away muttering.

Overtime was rare. They were all willing to stay, though O looked doubtfully at Sully. He had done some work, but he'd stopped frequently and lit a shaky cigarette, and since coming back after dinner he'd sat nursing his stomach for most of the time.

'Right then' Lew said. 'The five of you stay on till the end of the afternoon shift and clock off at ten, right? Time and a quarter from half past three mind.' He noted their names and went.

O was happy to do the overtime, though he would have to phone home to warn his mother he'd be late. He would perhaps have a chance to talk to Jack.

* * *

That morning Judith talked with her neighbour, Beryl. If Beryl had been a little less open and only a little older – say in her sixties instead of fifty-five – Judith would probably have called her Mrs Phillips and the whole tenor of their conversations would have been different. There would have been more reminiscence, less gossip, more deference on Judith's part. As it was, the two met in a kind of no-woman's-land where Beryl would talk as if to an equal and Judith would feel herself initiated into the full mystery of woman/mother/housekeeperhood.

Judith had been thinking of getting a job. The new possible lay-off date was in September, Keith had said, so she had to plan. She had worked in a factory and hated it. In a shop you met people but it was all transaction and you had to be nice to them. An office perhaps, or a bank would be better. 'A hard day at the office' they always said on television, but not really all that many people worked in offices. And then the home help was another possibility. All those old people, all those reminiscences, all that deference.

Not that Beryl was really a gossip. She told amazing stories but Judith never caught her out on a single fact. Their talks were calendars of disasters: breach births, widowers gassing themselves, murders and nervous breakdowns, together with the standard pregnancies and affairs. Crossreference to conversations with others always showed Beryl's version of the world to be the least hurtful and most plausible, if morbid in its selection of important facts.

They would sit in Judith's livingroom drinking tea. Judith would provide a cracked saucer for Beryl as an ashtray.

'It's looking bad, love, en it?' Beryl said, flicking ash into the grate. Keith had lit the fire before going out. 'Nice little job in a factory would do you good. Get you out a bit.'

Beryl had recently taken voluntary redundancy from the chicken factory where she had been working for twelve years. During the war she had worked in a munitions factory and before that she'd briefly been in service. She had two grownup children. Her grey hair was tinted variegated improbable shades from red to auburn to blonde. At first, hers seemed an expressive face, the laughter lines suggesting friendliness, but it soon became clear that it had hardened in only one expression somewhere between a smile and an expressionless stare. The wrinkles had set like wax so that what at first seemed animated came to seem wooden, like the faces of some animals or a puppet.

Judith agreed that things were bad.

Beryl talked about her friend from a neighbouring street, a regular visitor, who had called in the previous day. Bron was from west Wales and her clipped, unfamiliar accent singled her out as much as if she were, say, Italian, though she had been in this area, so Beryl said, for all her adult life. She would call on Beryl, sometimes to touch her gently for a fiver, sometimes to go shopping. Judith would see her trailing a few paces behind Beryl like a Chinese wife, bearing bulging plastic bags, looking at the ground. The two would sit in the Olympia Cafe waiting for the bus up to the estate, extravagantly drinking espresso coffee, Beryl smoking. Beryl had laughed telling Judith about Bron's furtive trial of smoking, holding the cigarette like a pencil and hiding it under the table when anyone resembling her husband had passed the window. She had described too how Bron had taken to accepting a glass of sherry in the morning in Beryl's kitchen. After a sip her face would redden and she would giggle. Unlike Beryl, Bron was dumpy and smoothskinned and, sherry apart, pallid, as though the colour had been washed out of her. She had four children, the oldest grown up and married, the youngest not yet in school. It occurred to Judith that Bron had always seemed too old ever to have had children. It seemed impossible to guess her age from her appearance, except to say that she wasn't young. She was not good at practicalities and her husband was worse. Beryl usually talked of her with the kind of affectionate condescension reserved for small backward nephews. Still it was hard to fault Beryl's approach. It seemed to Judith both just and kindly. Today Beryl was not laughing.

'She've had a hard life mind' she said.

Judith agreed. It was clear that something was grieving Beryl.

'You haven' heard anything have you?' Beryl said.

'How do you mean?'

'About Bron.'

'No. Nothing special.'

'Poor dab. She can't cope see.'

'What's happened?'

Beryl looked up from the cigarette she was stubbing out.

There was a ritual of diffidence and coaxing in some conversations which would prelude the passing on of a story. Beryl never bothered with that ceremony. Whatever was in her thoughts, Judith believed, would soon come out unbidden.

'It's about her boy' Beryl said. She hesitated. This was untypical. She actually needed a prompt.

'The eldest?' Judith said.

'Aye.'

'Have he had an accident?'

'Not exactly.'

Judith waited.

Beryl avoided her eyes. She looked into space as if at someone a little to one side of Judith as she spoke:

'He've attacked a man over Rhymney' she said. 'His wife told him she'd been having an – affair with this bloke and he went and attacked him. Since his car have been off the road he caught the bus over one night last week and walked into this man's house and this man was playing with a train set with his little boy and he just went up and attacked him with a pickhandle. They were friends apparently. And then he walked all the way back and walked into the police station and give hisself up. Just walked in with the pickhandle in his hand and soaking wet like that.'

'Is this man all right?'

'Not dead thank god. He's down the hospital. God, what's his poor mother going through now? And Bron's boy was doing so well. He'd settled down proper and then this do go and happen. The stupid girl. She ought to have known better.'

Bron's eldest son was younger than Judith. She remembered him at school, gawky and bigeyed. Judith had been surprised when he married early. First the council had housed him and his wife temporarily in a condemned house and then in one of the new lowrise blocks of flats by the church.

Beryl was looking away, her face frozen into its usual half smile. They're all a bit simple love em, Judith remembered her saying of Bron's family. She imagined the scene in the flat and then him catching the bus. Standing outside the lover's house in the rain and the door opening. The hall light showing his hair plastered with rain, his fingers white with cold on the club. There was a television switched on probably, and the aftersmell of supper. Bron's boy probably in tears, shouting something. The sluggish responses of the man's family.

Proper kitchen sink drama, Judith thought. She imagined the gawky schoolboy and then the man like a character in a story with his head in his hands in a police cell. Only this was real. She thought that, in making her think this much, the story had moved her a little. It would make the registration of the expected responses that much easier.

She looked at Beryl as she prepared to speak and saw that from the smiling, hard mask tears were swelling.

* * *

Keith took off his glasses and studied the papers spread before him on the table. At last some photocopies he'd ordered from the county library twenty miles away had come, and he had all the relevant books from the 'Local' shelf stacked in a tower to one side.

It had been a struggle. The first assistant had refused to get the copies. We en allowed to photocopy anything over a hundred years old, she said frostily, bureaucratically. The next assistant had said the same, though unfrostily and after a pause had said that she'd see what she could do.

So before him were copies of pages from an account book and a letter from Samuel Moonlow to his wife recording the day of the lighting of the first furnace. Of course the letter had been published in journals, but to see that handwriting was to taste something of the day.

The *D* of *Dearest* was inflated taut as a full sail. It pushed your eye positively along through the letter.

The content was disappointing, giving little detail of the furnace work, but it did mention the weather.

The snow has not been so heavy as to impede our Progress badly and none falls at the Moment – There is Wind but I do not Mind this as it prevents the freezing Mists unpleasant and frequent here.

Keith remembered the words from journals. Frosty and bureaucratic. One thing the journals had not shown was a crossing-out after *The snow has been*. There was a *c* with a swift stroke through it. What had he decided not to write? Catastrophic. Calamitous. Causing problems. Cast in drifts. Perhaps it was an unwelcome truth he decided to water down or cut altogether. He might have been avoiding a lie or choosing one. The moment of choice caught on the page. All the time from all the possibilities running through his head he had been selecting, shaping, rejecting. The quick stroke trimmed the sail suddenly so that the letter cut logically through all the choices to the signature at the end. For an instant you heard the machine working, the rigging creak.

There had been terrific snow. The books showed the hire of extra men to clear it. Keith imagined it flung against gable ends, against the backs of men and the flanks of animals. And the trees. Snow etching the bare trees black and white like oriental script. It was hardest to imagine Moonlow. Leave your wife and family, move to a remote frozen place at the beginning of a new century and put all your money into lighting a fire. There were others already there in neighbouring valleys of course. Having a vision or being a pioneer didn't quite ring true. Greed then. That wouldn't do, though for Moonlow's son and grandson it might. Madness might come closer. A kind of fever. A random infection with the preoccupations of a new age. Except that when you looked at the letter Moonlow called it *our Business* in a way that cooled all thought of burning fevers. It was not a cosy *our Business* nor had it much exclusive hint. *Our Business proceeds quite well. Our* could include the labourers and the mules. It was hard to see what Moonlow meant, let alone see his character. He would live in the big house, even have his own money minted. Perhaps he just didn't get on with his wife. The letter was formal enough for Keith to believe that. There was such an ocean to chart, even in one day in one man's life, that Keith was amazed that historians would try to grasp and explain whole civilisations. It was hard to imagine anyone with that much nerve. Or perhaps they were greedy or mad.

He thought of the mules with snow on their flanks. Surely for a moment Moonlow must have sat in his room and had no more idea what he was doing there than the animals. No more understanding than Keith had of himself sitting in the library reference room poring over the letter. The snow must have made him doubt.

The snow. Keith looked up, remembered, put his glasses on and looked up again. The wall facing him was all window. And no snow. The weather was disappointingly mild. A freeze might help him to work. That was why he wanted to get as much done as he could before the spring. Drizzle, mist. Unpleasant and frequent. Dim in the mist he could see the hill curving away. It was an old tip, landscaped and grassed, the old Number Seven, but you'd never guess it, looking through the huge picture window out over the new police station roof. The anonymity suited the library, especially the reference room, not so much flooded as sponged through with the weak grey light. It was roomy and carpeted but that didn't make up for the small number of reference books and a colourlessness that made it seem cold even when it was warm.

He knew he had had enough there. He was afternoons and had told Jude he would not go home but would have something from the chip shop and go straight to work. He whiled away the last minutes by leafing through part of the tower of books. One was about the Workmen's Welfare Institute. He came across a photograph of the Workmen's Library Foundation Committee. Three rows of moustached faces from the 1890s. The library they had founded no longer existed. The collection they'd started had been broken up when the new building went up. As he looked at the photo, he thought that libraries, like museums, stultified what they tried to keep. There, looking at the picture, he found it harder to imagine those men in their stiff collars and squeaky boots, or Moonlow in his room, or the remains of tracks and drams under the collapsed layers of mud and shale of the landscaped tip, harder, probably, than he would when he stood in the queue for his chips. And he promised himself again that he would look at the old house in Buchan Row that Emlyn had told him about.

In work that afternoon Keith discovered that there was a job on in the slabyard. In the windowless cabin, Emlyn explained about a smashed generator in a pit flooded with oil and grease. He had been over to see the job, but some labourers were cleaning up and looked as if they'd be a long time. They'd even been given overtime.

The mill was down and it was very quiet. Most of the rest of the maintenance crew were doing small jobs or had vanished into various boltholes. Some would have flyers. They both disliked the unnatural silence. It let you hear the hiss of steam from a pipe outside and sometimes the scuffling of a rat.

The plywood board in the window fell over again. Keith watched as its top edge swung, hung in the air for a moment, and then toppled. This time Emlyn was sitting underneath it. The board thumped onto his head, piledriving his neck two inches into his shoulders. He snatched up the plywood and shoved it out through the window as though posting a huge letter. Veins stood out on his neck and his face darkened with blood as he went out growling.

A few seconds later Keith saw him pass the window outside. Em stooped and picked up the board. Keith rose to watch him, the fitter's body quivering like a couple of armwrestlers, as he chose a place, wedged the board between the ground and a wall and leapt onto it, snapping it in two.

If others had been there to watch there would have been laughter, but there was only Keith. Em's rage seemed strangely distant and small, though not funny, as he replaced the wood time after time and smashed it again under the high wall of the mill. Behind him were the tall ruststreaked hopper wagons motionless on the railtrack, and to the left the steep, tussocky bank where the labourers' cabin was. Keith's eyes moved up and took in the wedge of sky, spongy grey, suggesting the coming dark.

* * *

Jack stood halfway down the steps that led into the pit. He had borrowed wellingtons from the waterman's cabin on the blooming mill and was standing over the ankles in sludge. It was impossible to shovel the stuff in a mechanical rhythm because of the thickness. As they got deeper, too, the mouth of the forty-five gallon drum got further away. Clarry was hauling up the bucket and trying to persuade the grease out of it. He laughed.

'Fucking great this is' he said. 'They on'y want to stick a pump in and they'd clear this in five minutes.'

He pulled off a glove and rubbed his hand across his forehead, smirching it the colour of liquorice.

'If you're going to be fucking cheerful' Sully said, 'I think I'll join the foreign legion.'

'Why bother' Jack said, 'when you can stay here and bury yourself in your work?'

Bury yourself, he thought. At the end of this I'll have to go back to Mrs W. Sorry. No burying. In the end you have to surface.

Inside the boots, his feet were beginning to feel sticky. Somehow the grease had got through his gloves too and he sensed that the canvas plaster was sodden black.

She wouldn't ask me to leave, probably. But. The nice young lodger no longer. Rugby club gossip will raise blush instead of laugh or rebuff. I have been found out. Move on. With a contract till September? Not on your. Brother in Reading. A surprised look as his door opens. Instead of a Viking ship he'll have aluminium framed double glazing. A little balder – thirty-four now – and the newspaper dropped by a chair. Come in, we never expected. Perhaps a fortnight and then a discreet word. He moves his glasses back onto the bridge of his nose as he comes to the delicate matter. You see, I wouldn't mind but my wife.

Like those farmers. Zulu was it? You stay till a patch of earth is exhausted then find another patch. Except that people don't recover like land, though brother in Reading might vestigially be still fruitful. Every phase like that, your progress chiefly recorded in a trail of bruised people.

He tried to work faster, but slime, leisurely rolling off the shovel into the drum, would not let him.

They took a break in the early evening and went to Ben's cabin, which was deserted. Kelv fetched food from the boiler shop canteen in greasy bags, paying for it with the grubnotes they got on overtime.

Jack's hangover told, and leaving his food unfinished he slumped over the table.

'What happened to your hand, Jack?'

It was Rob. Snobs. O.

Jack told him. In the pause that followed, Jack did not ask where O lived or how his family was. He could hear the water leaking from the radiator into the silvered tin.

'En you going to bother coming back home?' O asked.

Jack said nothing.

Drip.

'Didn't you hear me? I said: en you going to bother coming back home.'

Jack sat up and pressed his back and head to the wall.

'Aye I heard.'

O waited.

Jack listened to the dripping. The gap between each sound was quite long so it was hard to anticipate exactly. That way you couldn't get used to it and ignore it, not like the ticking of a clock.

'Well' O said, shuffling on his bench and looking away.

It was quiet until Sully said, 'Right. Who's going to clock me off?'

They decided that Sully and O should go and the others work to the end of the shift. O said he didn' mind staying, but Kelv told him he'd have to wait his turn. O looked put out, but went. Jack smiled to think of O and Sully together, squeezing through the gap in the railings.

The three remaining went back to work. The man with the spanner who had appeared at the beginning of the shift came back several times and went away cursing. Clarry and Kelv worked quickly, so that after an hour Jack could actually see that the grease had fallen a little.

A bit of graft, he thought, and this could be cleared in another shift.

The blade of his shovel started turning up rubbish in the bottom of the pit. There were empty plastic milk cartons, mysterious, functional looking lumps of scrap, some gloves fleshed with the sludge as if mummified.

Good therapy, playing in the mud. Like picking scabs. This oozing satisfyingly like a squeezed pimple. Though O probed and it hurt. Not therapeutic at all.

The slimepit became all-absorbing. Jack even started scraping his shovel down the revealed walls to make them cleaner. And the drowned machine began to appear.

He was standing in the bottom, the grease nearly flooding his boots and his eyes fixed down on his work when Clarry called:

'Oi. That's it, butty. Half past nine. Time to bath.'

The jolting, nearly empty bus. Connie breathing nextdoor and the stale fat smell of the Baby Belling. No let me work on.

In the bathhouse Jack undressed, discarded the blackened plaster that had come loose from his stinging palm, and smeared his body with swarfega. The oil had seeped into some inexplicable places. The wellingtons had leaked badly and his feet were black. Harder to understand the tidemarks at his knees, crutch and elbows.

Daubed with the green jelly, carrying his soap and shampoo, he went under the shower.

There were few men there, not like the bustle of days regular. As he turned to face out, someone in the opposite cubicle did the same. It was like turning to face a mirror.

Jack recognised his old friend at once, although he was a little fatter and without his usual glasses. The nose studs had left their lozenge depressions. Keith Watkins stared into a blur.

My old butty my old mate straight out of prehistory and not fossilised not mummified but alive, like myself in a mirror.

Jack stepped forward.

'Excuse me' he said. 'Are you Keith Watkins, mild-mannered reporter of the Daily Planet, or are you a Man of Steel?'

Keith looked at the blackened face, greensmeared and running wet.

'Good god. Jack!'

Drying themselves, they talked.

'Married?' Jack asked.

'Aye.'

'Anne was it?'

Keith covered his head with his towel and rubbed.

'No' he said. 'Remember Judith?'

Jack remembered. 'You did well' he said.

'Not really. I've been stuck here ever since school and you've been globetrotting.'

'I wouldn' call Lancashire the ends of the earth.' He paused. 'Although, I don' know.'

And Keith asked where Jack was staying and inevitably why he was back. Keith's marriage as yet not blessed with children and his council house roomy.

'When can you come over' Keith said, 'so we can go out for a pint?'

'Funny you should say that' Jack said.

SIX

It was freezing again. The sky was a hard blue that scarcely softened even on the horizons. There were high, ribbed clouds sometimes, and higher still, swirling wisps that seemed frozen into place like the scoremarks left by an iceskater.

Jack, near the top of the mountain, looked up as at the underside of a frozen lake. It was so clear that temporarily he thought that he had no hangover. Which was how it ought to have been, because this was journey's end, sort of. His eyes shifted from the sky to the frozen grass at his feet to the western horizon. A sense of space. The next mountain ridge cut against the sky with absolute starkness. He opened his mouth and the cold air hurt his throat.

Below him, to the north east, his home town lay. A cushion of trees where the park was. A tumble of grey slated oblongs where the shopping streets followed the hill. The terraces opposite contouring the valley side. Gaps of demolition and the ageing-new estates. Far to the north where the valley disappeared into moorland were the factories. At the southern end, a tip, startling black in the hard light, in the process of being reclaimed. It was clear enough for him to see windowframes and doorsteps and the patterns of tiles on roofs. There was the sound of traffic distantly, dogs barking. Above the terraces and a few posher houses on the eastern side of the valley were the pine plantations, much bigger than the Christmas trees he remembered, and above them the open mountain, frostwhitened. As a child he'd thought of the sea on the other side, or an endless tundra spiked with castles, but there was beyond the mountain the two miles' tangle of steelworks.

To the west slightly, saddled in a curve of the mountain he stood on, was the Grib pond, sheeted with a lens of white-grey ice. Grib pronounced grebe, like the bird. He remembered swimming there when he was about twelve. His father standing on the stone breastwork that made the steep far bank of the pond, wearing those heavy, coarse blue trunks they used to have and a picture of a helmeted diver in mid flight stitched near the leg. His father had dived. The body a flattened arc running the rim of an invisible circle knifed the water.

He shuddered with cold.

The pond had been changed, he noticed. Cut into a new shape, stocked by an angling club. Fish leaping up the. Fish under the ice.

Near the pond were the cemeteries. There was some reason for having the cemeteries on the mountains. He couldn't remember. Something only in that area. Keith would know. Jack would ask him. Funny that Keith had become a kind of expert on these things. And below us we see, ladies and gentlemen. Though nowadays most people choose the flames rather than this sodden, frozen acre. He had a bit of iron rail from the early nineteenth century as an ornament. A paperweight eighteen inches long, speckling its rust on windowsills, shelves.

Jack rocked back his head and looked at the sky.

A sense of space. Journey's end. The two sounded at odds, yet he felt them both. He felt, too, the blood move in his head. A dull throb in his temples and pain in the eyeballs. Too much beer making a cramp in the skull.

Because of Keith's shifts, Jack had had to wait over a week for a coincident free night when they could meet for a pint. Connie had been not so bad as he'd expected – almost as though on the brink of apologising herself, though she had no reason to. The words had choked in his own throat once and her eyelids had dropped in a kind of understanding exclusion. Exhausted.

Before leaving to catch the bus to meet Keith, he had automatically pushed his few possessions into the bashed blue nylon rucksack and left it on the bed, pushing to the back of his mind thoughts of coming back to that room.

*

The night was clear and moonless with stars like hard iceneedles, the freezing pavements glinting. Jack got off the bus in the town square in the tumble of oblongs where his own street was somewhere, with no sense of anticipation, except for his first drink. He noticed that where a sweetshop had been there was now a betting office. The barber's nextdoor was unchanged from his earliest memories of the square.

Keith, sitting in the lounge of the King, wearing his hooded coat, sipped over frequently from his pint and looked around without seeing anything. An unaccustomed drinker on his own. Unlike.

'Been here long?' Jack said, as if they met there every Saturday. He put down his drink and sat. The rough pub he remembered had been smoothied up to the point of being a different place.

Keith measured the amount gone from his pint between index finger and thumb in a forgotten-familiar way.

'This long' he said.

'They've done this place out.'

'Have they?'

'Last Chance Saloon this used to be.' This used to be. There's Welsh you speak. Back into the rut, butty.

'That was years ago.'

Keith had got fat. Fatface. Jowls and glasses. Eyes pigged under fat behind the spectacles.

'You've gone thin to what you used to be' Keith said.

'It's the executive strain of the job.'

Pause.

'So what's new?' Jack asked.

Keith smiled and looked away.

'Sorry I asked.'

'The time do go don' it?'

'It do aye.'

And other halfbaked platitudes. They ought to say, once they would have said, this is a shitting waste of time – forget it. Except.

Oddly nervous, Keith drank quickly. Jack warmed with their second pint.

'Can't imagine you married, mun' he heard himself saying. 'You've gone all respectable. It do make me feel old.'

Keith shrugged. Always hard work, Keith, like a pond where stones plopped almost without rippling the surface. And then sometimes suddenly talking, urgently explaining. But that was years ago.

'Judith too' Jack said. 'You did well.'

'They haven' caught you though, Jack.'

Jack shrugged. 'Just charm, I suppose.'

And other halfbaked clichés. There was nothing to catch up on so next would come I remember I remember. All that sickly stuff.

'So you've been in the works ever since school' Jack said.

'Aye. I went over not long after you left. I was too old to get took on with an apprenticeship by then.'

'What will you do if they get shut in September?'

'Don' know.'

'Lucky you haven' got a mortgage.'

'There'd be redundancy money anyway.'

'Much?'

'Probably not a lot for me. I on'y been there nine years.'

Only nine years. Wham bam thank you, butty.

The I remembers started in the course of the third pint. The King had started to fill with young and youngish people dressed in their best thin shortsleeved shirts under heavy coats, tight jeans painstakingly faded, labels prominent. Keith, flushed with beer and still in his hooded coat, leant over to Jack and talked just audibly through the newly started muzak:

'I remember us mwtshing off school one Friday afternoon and thumbing to Cardiff. Do you remember that?'

Jack vaguely remembered, though the memory blurred with many similar days.

'We got flagons of cider' Keith said, 'and drank them on the museum steps. I don' know how we didn' get nicked.'

'Those were the days.'

And other halfbaked.

The memory grew in Jack's mind, and with it the certainty of what Keith had been like. Somehow straight always. When they had lifts, Jack would instinctively lie to the driver. Thanks for the lift. Our van broke down and we had to leave all the group's equipment locked in the back. But Keith, lean and earnest, had never been able to join in.

He looked at Keith's reddened, puffy face. He had taken his glasses off and was squinting at Jack as if waiting for him to say something.

'Sorry?' Jack said.

'I said so what brings you back home.'

Home.

He had avoided the question in the bathhouse.

'Desperation' Jack said. Too quick. The truth turned into a joke but said too quickly.

Keith pursed his lips and squinted down the barrel of his pint. 'That's not a good reason' he said.

'There isn't any other.'

'What about the ones who stay?'

'I don' know. Same reason for them staying I suppose.'

Keith looked away and then into Jack's face. It was a steady stare held a little too long. If Keith had not looked so smalleyed without his glasses it might have been disconcerting.

He's puzzled, Jack thought. Don' know what I'm talking about. Or no. He knows perfectly well. Truth hurts. No more of that tonight.

But Keith spoke. Slowly, as though he wasn't using readymade phrases.

'Desperation for coming back perhaps' he said. 'I can understand that. But not for staying. That don' make sense to me.'

And the stare that wasn't quite disconcerting continued for a few seconds before he turned back to his pint.

'Anyway' Jack said, 'shall we move on?' He drained his glass. 'You're the native guide. Show me the sights.' He looked at his watch as Keith forced down the rest of his beer.

Half past eight, nearly. Should have checked the last bus back just in case. Say six miles, two mountains one valley. Hour and a half or two walking drunk. Hello Connie. Me. Pissed again. How about a quick.

They went to a social club where the beer was cheaper. The bar was much as it had been when Jack had seen it last, nine years before. A long room with a low ceiling, originally cream but umbered now by tobacco smoke. Cast iron pillars supported the umber, above which, in the upstairs hall, wives sometimes with husbands in tow might be playing bingo or tripping the light fantastic to the thump of the organ. No women in here though, except behind the bar, reassuringly marked off from the rest of the room by the heavy wooden framework holding the metal grille that came down at stoptap. The large colour television on a high shelf in a corner irrelevantly and mutely gave out an inane game show, sometimes scoffed at but mostly ignored by the men sitting at the long rows of tables, playing cards and drinking steadily. Most of the men were in late middle age or older. There was a group of young men, mostly teenagers, playing cards and loudly, clumsily copying the talk and legpulling of the others. Their new clothes, wispy, selfconscious moustaches and earrings stood out among the dark jackets of the older men.

Keith and Jack sat on the upholstered bench that ran the length of one wall, under the stopped pendulum clock and the framed certificate of affiliation to the association of working men's clubs and institutes. Keith wasn't a member but had signed a visitors' ticket and put twenty pence in the box at the door, presided over by an old man with a flat cap and a pint. It was warm, noisy and startlingly overlit with striplights after the dark, smooth King and the freezing streets.

Keith took off his coat and at last seemed to begin to relax.

'I had a feeling this place wouldn' change' Jack said.

'Proper thing too' Keith said. He rubbed a palm on the belly of a cast iron Britannia on the table leg. 'God, I do hardly ever have a drink these days, 'cept with Jude on my long weekend. Can' take it like I used to.' He shook his head, blinking theatrically, as if to clear his mind. 'You're still in practice though.' He grinned at Jack.

At last a smile. Still hope.

'Not really. I was pretty dry when I was out of work. I used to put it away when I was in Norfolk though. And then Lancashire.'

'I bet.'

Anybody else would have had the whole story by this time.

'I had a job' Jack said, 'driving a van with a frozen food firm for a bit in Norwich.'

And gradually he volunteered information, even mentioned Liz. Finally Connie and the comfortless digs. Except a cartoon strip version. Why not? Blow the dust off the landlady stories.

'Do you know' Jack heard himself saying, 'she do work for this factory making electrical components and she don' even know what they're for. The pubs round there are the sort of place where they watch the dartboard and throw darts at the telly.'

Keith, who had almost finished his fourth pint, laughed unexpectedly loud.

'Speaking of my landlady' Jack said, 'why did Golda Meir ban miniskirts in Tel Aviv?'

Pause. Catch him in mid swallow.

Keith shook his head as he drank.

'Because' Jack said, 'her clitoris hung down below her knee.'

Keith choked and sprayed a mouthful of beer back into the glass.

'These old ones are the best' Jack said as Keith wiped his eyes. 'I'll get a fresh one.' He took Keith's glass.

The phases were familiar. Hilarity would last a long time. And then, after stoptap perhaps, the earnest talking. But that was.

'Speaking of lowdown twats' Jack said as he returned with fresh pints, 'where do the cunt hang out in this town these days?'

'Out of touch with all that' Keith said.

'Oh aye, I forgot. Married. No sex please, I'm married.'

'Don' think I can take much more anyway.' He meant beer.

'Got to return to the breeding grounds mun.' Jack stared at the polished, brassplated cribbage boards displayed on a shelf and then at the television sending its frantic signals over the unheeding heads of the club members. The colours seemed both distant and right against the eyeball and the voicefilled air seemed both loud and muffled. The slow start of the whirligig. The teenagers were leaving, noisily making farewells. Filled with cheap beer now making for places with women. Become men for the night by public ritual and now making for assignations and private provings, failures. 'Like them.' He nodded towards the boys at the door and Keith blankly followed the direction of his look.

'The old salmon leaping up the river' Jack said. 'You know. The fucking biological imperative.'

'Or the biological fucking imperative' Keith said. The forbidden word sounded odd on his lips. 'Or just the fucking imperative. *Fucking* implies *biological*.' He paused, evidently surprised by his own cleverness.

'And they said fitters' mates was stupid' Jack said. 'Dare British Steel lay this man off? The intellectual power unleashed could cause undreamt of changes in the world. Did you hear about the fitter who asked his mate for a half inch spanner? "Gi's the half inch spanner" he said. Gormless mate hands it over. Don' fit. "No good" he says, "le's try the three quarter inch." Gormless mate hands over the three quarter inch. Still no good. "Five eighths?" says the fitter, and the mate says "Forty."' He used the conventional deep voice of the stock moron and found himself, unpleasantly, trying to adopt Keith's blank expression.

Keith smiled.

'Yeah I've heard it' he said.

'Don' let school interfere with your education.'

And other. Get on and out, Dad said, like your brother, but remember where you came from. Ballocks.

'They're trying to get us to go to Scunthorpe before the layoff' Keith said.

He explained to Jack how some of the men had been taken expenses paid to see the English steel plant. He giggled pointlessly as he talked. Whirligiggle.

'They heard rumours while they were there' Keith said, 'about female mates in the hot mill.'

''Ckin' hell' Jack said. 'Best kind of mate to have. You'd be all right up there down the cellars on a nightshift.' Keith was still rubbing the cast iron belly on the table leg. 'Will you go?'

'They haven' asked me' Keith said. 'Even if they did I 'ouldn't.' And again the stare that wasn't quite. He shrugged and looked away. 'Some of us'll go I expect.'

Black streets tilted at crazy angles, glittering with frost. Dirty children, one on a bike, in the spill of warm light outside a sweetshop open late. Discarded chiptrays in the oily gutter. And into the smooth places. The King again. And the full lounge of the one star hotel with warmth, and alcoves, and people drinking shorts. Music from somewhere. Exposed brickwork. Done out, of course.

Keith was swaying in front of him. Wearing his glasses now but the plastic studs not sitting in their beds, pulled slightly forwards on his nose. As they stood in the little available floorspace Keith tried to roll up his coat and put it between his feet while still holding his pint. Some beer slopped on the floor. Then Keith was talking with somebody at the bar. People on tall stools. A man on his own, out of place here. Oldish. Familiar.

Their voices, Keith's and the man's, were very far away. Keith seeming nearer to sober, better spoken now. The man obviously very sober. Striking bored poses as he smoked. Familiar. Wait. Daily Mail. The man in the generator room. Thinks he's a cut above.

Jack looked around the bays and alcoves. Groping grottos. File that one away. There were a few half remembered faces. Mostly unknown. Young. All in brand new clothes. He became aware of his own clothes.

Jeans baggy in the crutch. Trainers split. Have to buy. Must enrobe for the ritual. Clothe me in my manhood. They talked across the low, stippled copper tabletops, the big plastic ashtrays almost buried under empty crisp bags, hemmed around with foamscummed empty glasses. All these best clothes, stifflabelled, scarcely wrinkled, straight out of Marshall Ward, sitting in a pile of rubbish.

And Keith next to him again.

'Nice bloke Ray' Keith said. His voice slurring. The hilarity leaving him like a tide going out. Soon the next stage of urgent talking. 'Interested in local history he is, a bit. You seen him on the mill?'

'Seen him around. That's your thing now is it? Local history?'

Keith cocked his head on one side like a shortsighted parrot and looked surprised, as if he'd been told something new.

'Aye. I suppose it is.'

'You got to have an hobby in this fucking hole I suppose.'

'It's not an hobby.'

The not quite stare clouded by beer. Keith's eyes looking a little bigger through the glasses as he tilted his head back to look at Jack.

'See this pub' Keith said. 'One of the oldest pubs in the town. Pre 1820. In the thirties the chartists used to meet here.' He looked round the room, having pulled off his glasses, probably not seeing anything. 'And now it's the meeting place for all the plastic gnomes in the universe.'

Like a tide going out. And next the deeply meaningful stage. What was washed up after the swirling waves. Thoughts ground smooth as quartz pebbles. Ideas immaculate and shapely as driftwood. Or seeming to be. Oh yes, and all the shit that should have been swept away.

Keith talked about the history of the building. Gabbling detail as though it was profound knowledge. Jack watched his mouth working, not listening, making neutral grunts and swigging his pint rhythmically. Betweenwhiles he looked over Keith's shoulder for a likely conclusion to his biologically imperative quest.

A woman at a table looked at him and smiled. Held the look a little too long. She moved her eyes away without blinking. Always awkward that. Always blink as you look away, otherwise it looks as if you're tearing yourself away against your own will.

Jack pretended to make some comment to Keith and tried to make himself look sober by carefully focusing his eyes, adopting what felt like an intelligent expression. Not that Keith noticed. He just talked on.

Then she got up and was coming towards them. She smiled again and raised her hands, a small empty glass in each, to squeeze between Jack and another standing drinker to the bar. Jack craned his neck to see, over Keith's shoulder, the table she had just left. Another girl, looking uncomfortable on her own. And words lit up in neon inside him as he looked back to Keith. *She's got a friend.*

She came back from the bar carrying fresh drinks. Jack stepped back so that she would have to pass between him and Keith. The smile again and the nod and almost a word, an invitation to talk. Jack made his 'Hello.'

'Hello, Jack' she said.

He looked again as she moved her head from side to side. A hint of both profiles, challenging him to recognise her. A chubby face. Wide mouth. Short dark hair with a sideparting. Gold droplet earrings. Smartly dressed. Not trendy.

'You don' remember me do you?'

'Have I got a good reason to?' He loaded 'reason' with innuendo.

'Well no. I suppose not.'

'We must put that right.'

Keith was looking over her shoulder at Jack, his mouth open, squinting. The three were pushed unnaturally close together. An odd pause and Jack and the woman laughed.

'Kath Thomas' she said.

'Ah yes, of course. Well. Kath Thomas.' Who? School? Fair bet. 'After all these years. I remember you in school.'

He put a hand on her hip and kissed her on the cheek. She started but then pressed the cheek forward.

'I'd shake hands' he said, 'but your hands are full.'

He looked at her face once more but could find her in no layer of his memory.

'I was in the fourth form when you were in lower sixth. Well, you weren't really in lower sixth, not for long, but you know, when you were that age. Lorraine said it was you. You look just the same.'

'Is she the other glass?'

She was. Why didn' Kath call Lorraine over? Kath was very keen to. She waved to her friend and theatrically mouthed the invitation.

A single loud chime rang through the bar. Jack automatically looked at his watch. Last orders. Say six miles. Hour and a half or two. Hello Connie.

'My god' he said clutching his heart. 'The ball's nearly over. Soon I'll have to go back to the ugly sister. My landlady.'

'My round' Keith said. He took Jack's drained glass and swayed off towards the bar.

'See' Jack said, 'Keith there en really a handsome coachman. He's Buttons my humble friend.'

Lorraine had arrived. Thin and bored looking. Jack dimly remembered her. Much fancied by his contemporaries in the rugby team. Once more he looked at Kath, who looked hugely pleased with herself and snuggled up to him as she talked. She could conceivably have been a fat and spotty sidekick of the then luscious Lorraine. They always had ugly friends. Sod's law. This was all wrong. The returned native should be successful, well-off, and the Women Left Behind should be prematurely aged by childbearing, cruel drunken husbands and bad dentistry. He was half drunk and baggy crutched and she was clearskinned, had good teeth and a mouth big enough to allow her to prove it.

'I remember two things about you' she was saying. 'Well, three things really. I remember you coming to the youth club in the vestry but never coming to the chapel. I remember you playing rugby—' she pronounced 'rugby' breathily, as if the word were nicely pornographic, '—and I remember you spending all day in the

83

Olympia Cafe playing the flipper machine and drinking Vimto instead of going to school.'

Jack winced. She didn't notice and talked on.

Keith swayed back with the last beers, smiling and shaking his head at Jack over Kath's shoulder. Lorraine stood awkwardly, shifting her weight from one foot to the other.

'You did that for days on end didn' you?' Kath's eyes swung on him like searchlights. 'For ages in the cafe every day. We used to come in after school and sit in the front window and you'd be in that little back place with the partition with the boys and older girls. We were always too afraid to go in that little back place, weren't we, Lorraine. Very sophisticated I thought you were, then.'

Her eyes flickered away, unblinking, as she began to realise that she had stared too long. She asked him what he was doing now and he found out that she and Lorraine worked in a bank. Lorraine meanwhile made halfhearted attempts to engage Keith in some aimless talk.

Ray, the man from the generator room, was coming around gathering empty glasses and chivvying the drinkers, who were beginning to pull on coats and straggle out into the cold street.

Jack made a show of looking at his watch again.

'Look I'll have to go, Keith. You know. Last bus and all that. I used to go to a pub in Norwich where the local Hell's Angels went. You know. Leathers. Chains. Helmets. And they all used to go at quarter to eleven to catch the last bus.'

Easier than improvising a time. Might check up, his Dad being a bus driver.

Keith was looking as thoughtful as a drunken man can. Still hope.

'You know' Jack prompted. 'Landlady and all that.'

'No, no' Keith was pawing his shoulder. 'Look, doss down in our house tonight. Jude won' mind. You come.'

Thank you, oh lord.

Keith looked thoughtful-drunkenly at Kath and Lorraine.

'See this man?' Pawing the shoulder again, 'This is a friend from the morning of my life. And you've got to know, it's—' the words coagulated and he paused, searching for some mental lesion for a fresh flow. 'Well, you know. We're butties. That's all.'

Jack made his thanks for the invitation, ritually checking that it was truly all right.

'Can we give you a lift somewhere?' Kath said.

Ray came up to them and began to take their glasses. He apologised perfunctorily as he waited for Keith to bolt the rest of his drink.

'Officious bugger your friend' Jack said when he'd gone back to the bar. 'He do think he's a cut above the rest of us.'

'He's all right' Keith said. 'He's only trying to help the staff.'

Kath repeated her question, quickly.

'Yes' Jack said, quickly. 'You can drop us off—' he hesitated as he wasn't sure where Keith lived '—on the way to Keith's house. Thanks. That'll be very nice.'

In the gents', Keith leant his head against the wall, and, propped out like a flying buttress, had difficulty in aiming.

Jack examined his teeth in the mirror and straightened his hair.

'By god, Keith boy. She's begging for it. Ruhugby she said. Ruhugby. Imagine. While I was on the flipper machine I was being lusted after from afar. What did you go and mention Judith for?'

Keith giggled.

'Damn me Jack. I'm pissed. I'm pissed assoles. Time was you 'ouldn' have looked at her. Don' you remember what she looked like in school?'

'You're living in the past, mun. Look at her now. Or call me compassionate. I do hate to see a nice lump of minge go by neglected.'

Kath's car, a new Fiesta, was comfortable and upholstered in dark cloth. The orange streetlights and figures lurching home on the pavements slid by across the windscreen, which was still partly skinned with ice. Keith and Lorraine sat in the back in silence. Jack, in the front passenger seat, was listening drunkenly to Kath as she drove more efficiently than seemed possible and talked about car accidents she'd had.

He spread his knees and waited for her to change gear. As the stick slapped into second she let her hand stay on his thigh momentarily before changing up. He turned and massaged her left earlobe between finger and thumb.

'Like your earrings' he said, and slid his hand across her neck onto her shoulder. She gently moved her head from side to side against his arm.

In his half turned position, he saw Lorraine rolling her eyes to heaven. She folded her arms and looked out through the iced window.

Jack snuggled to Kath's ear.

'Listen' he said.

'Hm.'

'Don' you think we should ask Keith where we're going?'

'Aren't you coming for coffee?'

Just like a script. Come up and see my.

'That will do nicely, Miss Thomas.'

'I don' think he's very well' Lorraine said.

Jack turned. Keith's head was lolling with the movement of the car. He moaned something about the missis.

'We could drop you off, if you like, Keith. Jack could catch you up later. And I could drop you off in town, Lorraine.'

Lorraine's jaw tightened and so did her folded arms. She looked a few daggers into the back of her friend's head.

'See, it's him it is' Keith said, suddenly loud. 'On the frigging steps of the flaming national museum, it's a wonder—'

He retched noisily and sat forward. Jack and Lorraine fidgeted ineffectually. Kath twiddled her mirror to see the back seat.

The car skidded to a halt on the gritted road.

'Get him out get him out' Kath said.

Jack tumbled out onto the pavement and started to drag Keith out by his shoulders over the tipped-forward seat.

'Quick' Kath said, 'before—'

With an obscure visceral whoop, Keith threw up over the cloth back of the seat and rubbed it in with his knee as he fell out onto the icy pavement on top of Jack.

'Shit' Kath said. 'You dirty bastard. Look at that. My father'll kill me.'

Jack got from under Keith quickly before the second burst. He grabbed the edge of the door as Kath, reaching across the empty seat, tried to pull it shut.

'Sorry, Kath' he said. 'He've had a few. I'd better get him home.'

'I'm sorry too, but he's not coming back in here. The dirty bugger. He was a slob in school.' She paused and looked at Jack for a moment. 'I work in Lloyds' she added.

He let the door go. It slammed and the car drove away.

Keith was sitting under a lamppost in the empty street, rubbing the vomit off his chin with his coat cuff. Jack clapped his fists to the top of his head and howled.

'You stupid git. What did you go and puke up for?'

He kicked the lamppost and looked down at his friend. Keith was muttering under his hood, which he had plucked over his head. Something about a blizzard and the moon. Jack lowered his arms slowly.

'Come on then' he said, helping Keith to his feet. 'What's the address?'

They staggered up a hill. Keith stopped by a tree and stared up through its branches at a streetlight.

'See' he said. 'Trees. Now think of that. Place was hardwood forest once. Just didn' think of it at first.'

Jack glanced up into the orange light fretted with black twigs and dragged Keith on.

* * *

It was cold in the spare bedroom where Keith sat. The nylon sleeping bag lay rumpled on the unmade bed where Jack had slept and the room smelt of stale beer and socks.

Keith looked over the neatly arranged papers, the stacks of books and magazines on the table. The unmarked A4 notepad. Morgan's *Early Years of The Gwedog Valley* open at chapter two. He had almost no hangover, just a certain lightheadedness, as if he was still a bit drunk, but he did not think that he would do any serious preparation this morning. He should try, but the night before had set off other thoughts. There was a need for endless calm. The dip into drunkenness was offputting, like looking through different eyes, or speaking a different language perhaps. There was time needed for refocusing, for relearning an old tongue. The night had corroded a hole that would spread some way through the days that followed. But it wasn't a hangover exactly.

He looked out onto the back garden which was enclosed by the gardens of neighbours. The concrete clothesline posts hanging at drunken angles; the chickenwire fencing arched into neat passages here and there where cats made their entrances; the bit in the corner he had seen Jude digging up. The grass was still frozen, which disguised its dirty yellow under a beautiful steel grey.

It could not have been a wasted evening to see Jack again. He had always seemed purposeful. By hanging onto his coat, Keith had been led through much of his adolescence.

Suddenly Moonlow, seeking his fortune, came into his mind. Leaving his family and setting up in the frozen stump of an almost uninhabited foreign valley. That decisive hand sweeping the curves of the letters that led to Keith himself, sitting shivering at the cold window.

The same thought had come to him the night before. But chunks of the evening had disappeared from his mind. He struggled to bring back the piece when Moonlow had come to him, but it was not there.

He crossed his forearms over his stomach at the thought of the night before. There was a certain queasiness still. He had noticed, getting up, the dried vomit on his shirt cuff and, mysteriously, the crusted patch on one knee of his trousers, where they hung folded on a chair.

Jude had laughed when he went down and hovered into the kitchen. She was drinking coffee, the newspaper on the table open at the television page. 'You big swci' she said. 'Do you think I'm going to tell you off?'

She described how they had come in and stood in front of the television, smelling of frost, seeming to fill the room, Keith making a confused speech about Jack's virtues and Jack, his eyes half shut, nodding mutely, raking the phlegm from the back of his throat occasionally with a glottal snort. She imitated the noise and laughed again.

'He've gone up the mountain for a walk to sober up' she said. 'He said his shrivelled up braincells were rasping against one another. You all right?' And again she laughed.

After having some breakfast and lighting the fire, which Jude had cleared out, he had come to the spare room, the latest issue of *Gwedog Historian* under his arm.

Being in a car and Lorraine Tranter, whom he remembered at school, and Jack hauling him to his feet all whirled in his mind. The queasiness passed.

He felt an inexplicable remorse. He had done nothing wrong. Perhaps it was some residue of nonconformist temperance surfacing. He smiled at the thought, imagined Jack saying 'Ballocks'. It was more likely to be something physiological. A doctor or a toxicologist or somebody would know. And with the remorse came a gush of love for Jude, uncomplicated, downstairs keeping an eye on the newly set fire, laughing at him. He wanted to buy her something.

In Cefn Social Club Jack had mentioned a girl. It was what held most clearly in Keith's mind. Keith had said that he hardly ever drank.

'I used to put a bit away when I was in Norfolk' Jack said. 'I had a job driving a van for a frozen food firm in Norwich for a bit.'

Keith was interested in the cast ironwork of the table legs. It was ornate late Victorian with catclaw feet and at the top the helmeted figure of a woman holding a shield over her belly, a swelled oval, full and sure as the D in Moonlow's letter, making her look pregnant.

'Then I went north' Jack said.

'What, north Wales?'

'No.' Jack sounded impatient. '*The* north. I met a girl on a run up there a couple of times and I managed to cop a job near where she lived. Working for the firm I delivered to. I mean she was working for them. I got a job in a furniture warehouse. And behind a bar in the evenings.'

Jack was thinner. Not from being out of work, surely. People didn't starve of that any more. Or at least, Keith thought they didn't. And he thought of September. Jack's faint dark stubble showed the hollow of his cheeks when he clenched his jaw, as he did occasionally when he paused and looked away.

'Liz. We had a flat then. Four rooms. All the upstairs of a biggish terraced house. Got decent furniture on the cheap with my job see.'

Keith rubbed the ironwork with his hand. All the legs, frame and stretcher, had been cast in four pieces.

'It all got on my nerves in the end, so I just blew.'

Blew. A word from the past, Keith thought. A bit like freaked out and man, only not so obvious.

'So you came back.'

'Aye. Desperate. Well not quite. Not quite back I mean. By Christ, Keith, you ought to see my digs.'

And Jack went into detail. Keith could feel him accelerating the talk away from the north and the flat and the all that had got on his nerves. He told jokes which made Keith giggle. It was strange to hear himself laughing like this. He listened to his own laughter uncomprehendingly.

'But then see' Jack was saying, 'I haven' got any family left here 'cept an auntie up Scwrfa. My brother's still in Reading. Boring old fart. Dad would have been proud of him.' He glanced away as he drank.

Jack had become untidy too. The affected casualness of

adolescence had worn into a habit. Keith could imagine it becoming selfneglect and he remembered vividly their sitting on the museum steps in Cardiff drinking flagons of cider like two tramps. Jack had offered his bottle to a passerby. Want a swig, butty? He thought of the spare room at home, a table spread with books letting it pretend to be a study, and the spare bed never used. Under the big statues and the fluted columns, in front of the house of relics they had sat. And that also had become history of sorts.

In the distance he heard himself laughing again.

Later in the crowded lounge of the posh hotel. It was a swirl of copper light and faces too close. He saw Ray in his usual place by the bar and asked him how his daughter was. Too loud, too drunk asking. Ray answered leaning close to him but Keith could not catch the words.

It was uncomfortable. Keith preferred the bar of the Cefn. It could not have been so posh when the chartists had met there. People's clothes almost glowed in the dim alcoves. Without his glasses on, he saw their drinks catching the few lights as auburn or amber flares, people arranged in shifting groups around the shining circular tables like figures contorting around unreal fires. The cigarette smoke stung his weak eyes and the noise confused him.

He sweated in the press of standing people with Jack. There was an unnecessary arch made of old firebrick. Keith looked at brickwork, old and cracked and roughly pointed, and built perhaps two years before to the brief of some consultant, no doubt with some concept like 'characterfulness' in his notes. The name of the hotel was the only recognisable survival of its first days.

Suddenly, Jack was kissing Katherine Thomas. Keith saw her occasionally in town, seeming to look better groomed and better heeled at every appearance. He realised that he was talking to her friend, Lorraine. He could hear his own voice faintly, seeming vehement and saying something important. He felt its urgency inside him, but he couldn't quite catch the words.

He imagined himself having sex with Lorraine on the lounge-bar floor. A posh house amid the fallen plaster and dust. Ludicrous. That was more in Jack's line, surely. He couldn't imagine himself any more and saw only Jack and Katherine Thomas rolling round in the cigarette ends. Purposeful.

He looked at Jack and saw him looking at his watch and saying something about buses.

The spare room and the spare bed never used.

Keith felt himself lean heavily on Jack's shoulder and knew that he was inviting him to stay at his house, though he wasn't sure how the words were coming out. And Jack smiling and nodding.

People putting coats on and Katherine smiling a false smile. How Jack went to seek his fortune. Keith remembered the fairy tale. How Moonlow went. No more unpeopled places, valleys, except perhaps. He looked at Katherine and Jack.

And then being in the car and then his cheek pressed against the ice and then bare branches against the orange light bars across flames and then seeming to float into the living room and Jude and Jack laughing, working at the buttons on his shirt.

The remorse did not ease and the queasiness returned. Keith wondered if the two wore off together would it mean they were connected. The intestines as the seat of the emotions. He hoped not, though he could imagine the idea appealing to Jack. I love you with all my bowels.

Feeling the cold, he pressed his forearms against his belly. Fat men then would be more emotional. He seemed to be living disproof.

His breath formed on the air. Jude wanted central heating. Sensible, though it would put the rent up. And a telephone. Now those would be good things to give her as he didn't particularly want either. They would be truly selfless gifts. She liked useful things.

He thought of her sitting in the warmth downstairs, he in the cold bedroom. It was as if she had a firmer grip on things, but without any consciousness of this. He would buy her a present before September came.

He stared at the blank page and pulled out a sheet of plans for his talk, hacked with corrections and worried with tiny notes he could not remember making and could hardly read. He had this now to show Jack. Jack would see the town with fresh eyes. It might help.

Keith imagined himself showing off his papers and relics to Jack. The L shaped rail on the windowsill, the token coin from Moonlow's company shop. Jack could perhaps solve Moonlow for him.

He remembered Jack clenching his jaw in the Cefn, mentioning the girl in the north of England. Nervous jokes about the landlady. He had lost weight and his parents were dead and his brother had been away for years and there was the spare bed that was never used.

Keith shivered. Jack must be freezing on the mountain, weakened by his hangover. A figure with sacks over his shoulders. Jack had a knack of saying things simply. Desperation, he had said, and he had been Keith's best friend.

Shoving the tortured page of plans back among his papers, Keith got up. He would have a cup of tea, talk to Jude about Jack. It was too cold for preparation that day.

* * *

Judith felt a cold hand rub the back of her neck. She jumped and looked round. Keith pushed his hand under her teeshirt and leaned over to kiss her where she sat in the livingroom. For a moment she had thought it was Jack, come back from his walk. She pushed his hand away.

'You're freezing' she said, and let him kiss her. 'What's up with you? You'll have to get drunk more often.'

He sat down on the arm of her chair and nursed his stomach.

'That Jack's a bugger' he said. 'He haven' changed at all.'

'Perhaps he'll do you some good' Judith said.

She had watched for outward signs of the suppressed drama of

Keith's 'preparation' for weeks now, and seen him grow quieter, more distracted, often not hearing when she talked to him. It irritated her. It had been funny to see him rolling drunk and noisy, with a few layers of pretension peeled away.

'He was like death warmed up when I saw him' she said.

Jack had looked and sounded fairly sober the night before, though his eyes were glassy and his face flushed. This morning he had looked drawn and bloodless. He was thinner than she remembered him, and he had talked shyly with her while she made him a cup of tea. The shyness surprised her when she thought about how he had been before, though she had never known him well.

'He looked thin and ill' she said.

'He looked thin and ill when I met him last night.'

'I thought it was just the beer.'

'He've been out of work a long time' Keith said. 'He haven' got anybody. He don' look after himself I don' think.'

'He's the sort who'll always manage' she said.

That was how she remembered him. Cocksure.

'What do you mean "the sort"?' Keith said. 'You hardly know him. Besides, he do hardly look like he's managing now.' He stared at the fire.

'You know what I mean' she said. 'I didn' know him well, but you know what he seemed like to us.' She meant herself and her friends, disappeared into jobs and marriages in other towns.

There was a pause.

'Perhaps we ought to get central heating' Keith said. 'If you want. Before September.'

He looked at her with an uncertain smile.

Judith was pleased and told him so, they discussed it further. He was unusually talkative. Jack's being there seemed to have woken him. Keith laced the talk with mentions of Jack, who seemed to be continuously under the surface of his mind. He squeezed into the armchair next to her, put his arm round her.

94

'I'd say he's in a right mess' Keith said. 'He've had trouble with his landlady.'

Keith was too slow and perhaps even too honest to be devious. She considered for a moment. A lifetime of slow maudification, of the living face hardening into a mask.

'He could stay here if you like' she said.

Keith was concerned that Judith was sure that this was okay. He asked her several times and talked of how awkward it could be having a stranger there, even though he wasn't really a stranger.

She said, 'Well, if you en keen—'

'No no. I'm just thinking about you that's all.'

'I—'

Love the idea, she almost said. She was bored enough to look forward to having central heating, bored enough to look forward to trying to find a job. She leant against the pile of Keith's body, felt him already to be a little changed. She pictured him soaked with rain, carrying a pick helve.

'I don' mind' she said. 'If it's what you do want.'

* * *

Keith pushed his glasses back up onto the bridge of his nose.

They do the married couple act very well, Jack thought. The modest but comfortable furniture. Nicely finished wallpaper. That smartarse salesman in the warehouse with the green couples. I know just what you want, sir. Understanding the sexual politics. Nominally addressing the husband, aiming the patter at the wife. What you want, sir: a nice three piece suite in the early matrimonial style. Big smile and polite laughter. Prick.

Jack sat by the recently lighted fire, not having taken off his coat after the walk. He held his head very still. He felt his brain shifting like a load of wet cement when he tried to move.

Nylon fitted carpet. Big colour telly. Won' catch me settling for this. Sort of place where they watch the goldfish bowl and sprinkle ants' eggs on the tv set. Except no goldfish. Must be some way of working that one in.

He looked at Keith.

Good company man. They might take him on somewhere else. Keep him and his better half in the anaesthesia to which they are accustomed. And then wham bam and curtains.

They had insisted that he should stay and have dinner. Clattering in the kitchen. Keith tried to help, stating the obvious, getting in her way. She seemed cheerful, though Jack could imagine her getting irritated if there was no audience. The marital act.

Jack could see that they would need no prompting. Just sit and wait. Minimise head pain.

He looked sideways down into the fire. The paper and firewood had burnt away to nothing at the centre and the blocks of glowing coal had settled and welded into a pierced vault over the space they had left. The backs of some blocks were still wet with recently melted frost. A new fire was full of caves. Alive with heat. The hearth. A roof over my headache.

He gingerly stood up and pulled off his coat.

'By god' he said, looking through the window and across the valley. 'You've got a cracking view from this place.' Terraces, pine plantation, mountain. His own tumble of slated oblongs tucked below, out of sight.

'We en far off the top of the mountain' Keith said.

As they sat down to eat, Jack asked, 'Why did they put the cemeteries up on the tops then, Keith?'

'That was after the cholera epidemics in the forties. The eighteen-forties. They thought it was safer to bury em away from the town. Stopped burying in the chapel graveyards beginning of the fifties. That's why some chapels haven' got graveyards even though they've got the land. Opened after the new rules.'

Keith struggled to eat but Jack found himself unexpectedly hungry. Judith ate slowly, having sat down last of all after preparing the food. Her face was blank. While her jaw worked on the food the rest of her head contrived to be still, giving nothing away. She looked at Jack occasionally but without communicating anything, while Keith seemed totally preoccupied by his struggle against the food. Until he looked up suddenly, pushing his glasses back onto the bridge of his nose.

'Listen' he said. 'We've been thinking.'

Corporate thought. Not the royal but the marital we.

'If –if' he waved his knife vaguely, 'if you want to you could – if there's nothing keeping you over there you could – look, we've got a spare bedroom we never use – if you wanted to you could'

Jack was tempted to save the floundering and finish the sentence himself. So prepared for Keith's speech, he was surprised, when the sentence tailed away unfinished, that he had no words of his own ready.

'That sounds very nice' he said at last. 'Thanks. I'd like that.' And he continued eating.

Keith almost laughed. 'That's great' he said.

Judith didn't react, continued eating without looking up.

'That is' Jack manufactured a thoughtful voice, 'if it's okay with you.'

She didn't look up.

'Judith' Keith said. 'Jack's talking to you.'

She looked up as if surprised.

'Of course' she said. 'It's fine by me. You might do Keith some good.' She smiled. 'He do seem livelier already.'

Keith looked at his wife as if he were trying to understand her words. Jack observed, feeling himself to be an onlooker only.

'I'll have to go back and pick my stuff up' he said.

His head felt much better. Her eyes, this time, had changed their expression, did not seem detached from her smiling mouth, though her face froze over again as she turned back to her food. He looked around. Their home. Won' catch me settling for. But. The diver's body arching into the. The warm vault with the cold outside.

SEVEN

Ken Francis, reclining on a bench in the waterman's cabin on the slabbing mill, talked.

'Haydn Luke, who used to be in this cabin with Ieuan Stoddart' he said to Clarry, O and Kelv, 'had a ballock that was eighteen inches long.'

Clarry and O had been hosing down the floor and sweeping up around the slabbing mill stand. Kelv had been sent on a job down the soaking pits with Jack. The mill was working that day. Clarry and O had stood and watched the crab crane lowering the claw that gave it its name into one of the far soaking pits and long travelling with the red hot ingot, twelve tonnes and shaped like a square shouldered medicine bottle. The ingot would be delivered onto the rolls in front of the slabbing mill stand. Sometimes when an ingot was driven through the closing jaws of the big mill rolls for the first time it would give an explosive boom and spit sparks and shrapnel out over the mill. Men at their work walked back and forth mostly unheeding, though some would duck when the glowing pieces flew.

O loved to watch the slabbing process; the ingot bashed flat then tipped on its side, rolled back and forth through the stand till it was one long smooth slab and then sent on its way up the mill. It was controlled from an enclosed bridge over the strip, which had a large window looking onto the stand. This was the pulpit, where the pulpit operators sat, controlling the mill rolls, the stand and the ingot, thrusting the last in and back. O stood on the catwalk behind the pulpit sometimes, looking in through its back window at the operators working nonstop. This had been his father's job for many years.

Clarry had thrown down his sweeping brush when some hot scale from a new ingot going through the rolls had lodged under his collar. He had turned and ducked instinctively when the bang came. O thought that he was not used to it and should not have taken this job.

'It won' hurt you' O said.

But Clarry would have none of it. 'Fuck this' he said. 'Le's have a wiff till things do go a bit slacker.' And he dived for the cabin.

'What, just the one?' Kelv said.

'How do you mean?' Ken said.

'Did he just have the one ballock?'

'Oh no. He had two. But one of them was about eighteen inches long.' Ken went so far as to measure a length in the air with his index fingers, moving them together and apart judiciously like a fisherman. He pursed his lips and considered. 'Maybe even two feet.'

'You don' mean his prick?' Clarry said.

'No. His one ballock. Honest to god. I saw it myself.' He plucked his peaked cap down over his eyes and replaced his hands beneath his head, settling back as if the matter was closed.

Clarry laughed. The waterman came in, sweating, and collected some leaky looking wellingtons.

'They're busy today' Kelv said as the waterman left without speaking.

'Mill's going full pelt' Ken said from under his cap.

O thought of the pulpit.

'I'd like to be on production' he said.

'You must be fucking mad' Ken said. 'You 'ouldn' have a second to yourself on a day like this.'

Clarry supposed that it would be better for money, and Kelv said he wouldn' mind production work either.

'It's okay sitting round here like this for a while, Ken, you know' he said, 'but after a while it do get on your fucking nerves.'

'You wait' Ken said. 'They're going like mad now. There'll be hot cobbles and busted machines and fuck knows what after this lot. The mill's already clapped out. That fucking stand out there is nearly forty years old. They'm running it into the ground. There'll be plenty of cleaning up for you to do after this.'

'Speaking of work' Kelv said, 'I'd better get back and help my butty Jack. Can't leave him down them soaking pits on his own.'

But he did not seem inclined to leave.

O had noticed that Jack had been travelling on his bus recently. He had come home, evidently, though he had not said anything to O. On the bus, Jack usually sat with Sully, sometimes Wayne. Some mornings he would see Jack and Sully sharing hangovers, eyes glazed, in the back seats. Jack's remoteness disappointed him. He knew Jack had been a bit wild and had heard about his making a mess of his time in the sixth form, but he was goodhearted, O had thought. It was a pity. Now he was only one step better than that pervert Wayne. O thought of working the pulpit and getting away from them.

Jack put his head round the door and pointed a finger at Kelv.

'There you are bastard' he said cheerfully. 'Come on. Get and help me with them drums of grease. That fitter with the red face have just finished fixing them grease pipes. He've been sweating like a cunt down there and you've been sitting here like Lord Treorchy.'

'All right, all right. Sorry my darling' Kelv said. He held his rag gloves in one fist like a Regency dandy and slapped his thigh with them as he rose. 'Hey Jack, Ken here says there was a man here with a ballock two foot long.'

'It's true' Ken said pushing his cap up. 'He used to sit by here like this with his one long ballock hanging out of his boilersuit and dangling over the edge of the bench. Haydn Luke. You ask anybody.'

Clarry laughed.

'And his butty Ieuan' Ken went on, 'used to sit by there where Clarry is with his legs crossed and swing one foot and gently kick the ballock so it swung back and fore like a pendulum.'

Kelv started singing:

'Oom tiddly oom shit or bust
Never let your ballocks dangle in the dust.'

Jack joined in and they linked arms as they sauntered out of the cabin, crooning.

'His wife ran off with another man in the end' Ken said.

* * *

There were eighteen drums of grease, each about a yard deep, cluttered in the hot dry gap between the walls of two of the soaking pit furnaces. The drums had been shoved one after the other under the leaking grease pipes until the maintainers eventually came round to repair them. Lew Hamer had shown Jack and Kelv the job, telling them to manhandle the drums out and chuck them on a spoilheap.

They had sat and looked at the drums for a while. Jack dimly recalled myths about Greeks being set pointless and impossible tasks.

They were two flights of steps below the soaking pit covers where the crab crane took out the ingots. At the other end of the passageway between the pit walls was a barrier perhaps nine feet high. On the other side of it was churned earth, about six feet above their floor level. The spoil heap was on the other side of the building across this earth, over which the crab crane long travelled with the ingots, plates of red hot scale falling from them as they slid past.

The air was hot and stung the throat. The floor seemed to be made of warm brickdust, very dry to touch, and was strewn with brickends and other oddments of scrap. They piled some of this rubbish against the barrier so that they could climb up and look out.

Through the open side of the far mill wall, many of the corrugated metal sheets having disappeared ages before, they could see large flakes of snow falling steadily.

They had taken turns to have a break so the one remaining could cover for the other.

When Jack fetched Kelv back from the waterman's cabin, the older man turned his old cap round the right way and seemed to concentrate.

'How about this, Jack?' he said. 'We walk the drums over to the barrier, one of us sits up on the top, we haul the drums over, both get over the top, pick the drum up between us and leg it for the spoilheap between passes of the crane.'

And they did, except that the drums were too heavy for legging it to be more than a slow waddle.

They sometimes sat teetering on the barrier while an ingot went past seeming close enough to tap them on the heads with only a slight swing. Once Kelv tried picking a drum up on his own and tottered over the broken ground to the spoil, the greenblack grease slopping over his shoulders. Mostly they waddled like penguin Siamese twins, laughing frantically when hot scale dropped near them.

By twenty-five to two they had finished and sat exhausted against the warm wall of one of the pits. Jack could feel that his neck and chest muscles were stretched and hurting.

'Nothing like it to make you feel good' Kelv said.

Jack felt himself agreeing. He said nothing but he knew he was exhilarated.

'You can't beat fucking hard work' Kelv said. 'I only wish it could be some use, you know. Who the fuck cares whether we shifted them or not? Lew won't check. It's all for the chop anyway. And even if it wasn't, them fucking magnificent ingots only get turned into bean tins.'

'It's a few bob' Jack said.

'Still.'

They sat unmoving for minutes.

Kelv rarely talked about Northern Ireland but Jack had learnt gradually that he had stayed on there for some years after leaving the army and marrying Jane. Whether they had left Ireland out of fear or to find work he was uncertain. It couldn't have been easy for a Catholic family to have a British soldier son-in-law. Or perhaps that was all wrong, that was just what the news said. Or perhaps Kelv came home to spawn.

Jack was almost sleeping when Kelv tapped his shoulder.

'Hey, get off home with the two o'clock shift, my old butty. I'll clock your card for you. Just shove it in the slot with mine.'

Jack got up, wearily, automatically. 'Is it my turn?' he asked.

Kelv looked at a hot ingot crossing the gap above the barrier.

'Never you worry about that' he said. 'Get off home now.'

* * *

'See' Keith said, 'I'm giving a talk.'

Jack looked into his face as if he was interested.

'Local history' Keith went on. 'It's the twentieth anniversary of the society and I'm doing an address.'

Keith thought of Jones, picking his moment carefully after the meeting one month. Think you could do it. Specialist knowledge. Be nice if somebody local. Sure you can manage.

'They have a guest lecturer, some professor this year, as the main speaker, but they thought somebody local still in the industry would be good as well. Huw Jones asked me.'

Jack looked blank.

'The physics teacher' Keith said.

'Oh him.'

'History's his real love. He wanted me to do it.'

Jack patted him on the shoulder.

'You're going to be a star, my boy' he said.

'I'm shitting myself' Keith said. 'I think I might back out.'

There was a pause.

'That'd be a shame' Jack said. He picked one of the books from the table and started to leaf through it.

Keith stopped him when he came to the photograph of the ruined furnace he was to talk about. He began to explain how it was commissioned, where the stone was quarried to build it, the tonnages, where the iron was scoured. He felt himself talking too much, the details driving on top of one another like snow gathering. His words gradually stopped and he glanced at the window where real snow was plastered. Cold. He should be working now.

Jack looked at the window too. The reflections from the snow made his face look as though it was lit from all angles, the shadows softened. Keith haltingly started in again on the events he would have to expound and analyse in front of fifty or so local experts. Again he was alarmed to sense that he was talking with feverish urgency but not getting the facts across. The words petered out once more.

Jack looked politely at the poorly reproduced photograph and said, 'It's fascinating en it. I admire you.' He looked at the bookstrewn table and the token penny from the company shop. 'You've. You've got a lot of interesting stuff.'

Keith watched him picking through a few layers of books, not really looking at any of them, and then shuddering theatrically.

'By Christ' Jack said, 'it's cold in here.'

He went out of the spare bedroom leaving his friend holding the open book. Keith put it down and followed him, thinking that he was right.

* * *

Judith shivered and hugged herself in her dressing gown. The dry heat of the two bars of the electric fire made her calves prickle and come up in red blotches, but the warmth hadn't reached her back yet.

It was Saturday and Keith was on days, but he had actually managed to clear the fireplace again this morning. The ashes must still have been quite warm when he raked them out. They smirched the snow on the back garden. It was good of him. Not something he normally did on days. Jack's being there had made him more conscious of the house, of how it looked and felt.

She liked mornings like this, especially when the room was filled with diffused light because of the snow. No dead day to rake out, just the new one to kindle. Paper and sticks and a bucket of coal were laid out on the hearth ready for her. Very proper. It was Keith's equivalent of getting the best china out for a teatime visitor, and he had kept it up every dayshift morning since Jack had arrived.

Her clothes were folded on the settee beside her. Clothes left out in the unheated bedroom became clammy and cold. She and Keith habitually changed in the livingroom in front of the fire or the electric fire. It was a habit difficult to keep up with someone else in the house.

She heard Jack getting up upstairs.

This was the first morning that he was off work when Keith wasn't there. Jack worked days regular seven to half past three Monday to Friday and Keith worked continental shifts.

The toilet flushing and taps running.

She looked at her clothes. Knickers and bra, jeans, a shirt and the long striped cardi. Quickly she pulled on the knickers and contrived to put the bra on without taking either nightie or dressing gown off. She had just pulled up her jeans under her nightdress when Jack came in.

'Morning.'

He was fully dressed. He breathed in sharply and sat in an armchair, rubbing his hands before the electric fire.

'Parky up there this morning' he said.

Judith wrapped the dressing gown around her trunk once more and sat down. She felt him looking at the hems of her jeans and her bare feet next to her empty moccasins. She slipped them back on.

His clothes will be feeling cold and damp, she thought. He ought to change down by here.

He made fresh tea for them both, nervously, she thought, calling in smalltalk about the weather from the kitchen.

'It'd be nice if we could keep the snow and have it a bit warmer' he said.

While he was out of the livingroom she changed the rest of her clothes quickly, even taking time to air her shirt before the two bars as she stood in her bra and jeans.

'Mind, I like the spring as well' he said, coming in carrying cups. He stopped momentarily when he saw that she was fully changed.

'Me too' she said.

It was hard to make conversation. When Keith was there it was easy because he was what they held in common. It was strange for her to think of Keith like that, actually having a kind of importance. Without him they struggled and she would find herself waiting for him to come back. She felt herself now looking for something to fix her eye on rather than look into Jack's face. Keith had hinted that things hadn't been good for Jack, though she wasn't sure how much Keith knew. In any case, Jack might manufacture a tale. That might be a difficult way to lead conversation, starting from the weather. But the fire had to be lit and that would end the awkwardness for a while.

He watched her building the nest of paper, wood and coal. The mild yellow flames licked around the lumps, which settled, nestling down on yesterday's disintegrating newspaper. He seemed happy to watch until the fire was well alight. Finally he stirred, as if waking, saying that he was going down into the town.

'Catch the winter at its best' he said. 'Before it do all go slushy.'

Retreating, she thought.

'I'm the same' she said, moving into the kitchen to wash the coal from her hands. 'I do like it either one way or the other. In between is no good. A thaw is such a messy business.'

* * *

Jack thought it was a pity that the bank would be shut. Hello, remember me? My friend threw up in your car. I'd like to reopen my account. Something like that. Never mind. Time and the hour.

In the pocket of the coat he had bought a few days before he held a satisfyingly crumpled fold of five pound notes.

Having the stuff in a constant and sufficient flow was something to savour, like bare feet on a thick carpet. Take home thirty-five or thereabouts a week, bung eleven to Keith and Jude. Twenty-four. No overheads. Heaven. Bus fares and beer. Buy some more clothes. Trousers without baggy crutches. Enrobe for the ritual. And with a few months' careful husbandry, even an old banger perhaps.

He paused in the high street looking sightlessly into a shop window, amazed to think how money could deliver back into his hands the control of his destiny. He imagined himself driving, taking Keith and Jude out on day trips.

They seemed to him helpless. Not because they didn't have money, though that would come. It was something like a lack of imagination, or will.

But then, that patience. The quiet waiting. It had a quality he could not pin down. It was hard to be close to them, or even just to Keith. The total honesty of nine years before wasn't possible. They were obscured from one another by layers of polite caution. It was impossible to go back to what they had been, the river only running one way.

And his obsession with local history. It was like men on life sentences making models out of matchsticks. Becoming accomplished painters, leading authorities on ornithology. Counting the tiles on a cell wall. It boiled down to the same thing.

Still, they were goodhearted, and there was the patience. Stuck somewhere between easy adolescent closeness and the fussy generosity of middle age. Not quite knowing what form to cast their good intentions in. Not like Keith and Jude's respective parents. He could imagine them chatting, bringing tea and biscuits on a floral plate, asking the selfless questions that the old ask the young. Perhaps they would get like that, learning to twitter in their chains. But that was unfair. He thought of Judith, not resentful as he had expected. Dark eyebrows and evasive eyes. A blank face and no obsessions to betray her frailty. Firm and kind, like a father in a story.

The shop window came into focus.

Cheapish electrical goods. Elements for kettles. Lamps with the names of football teams smudgily printed on the shades. It had been an old fashioned shoe shop before, with a shut in wood-panelled display window. The proprietor, a lame old woman, used to stand on the step endlessly, watching the streams of shoppers. The contiboard shelving and the bright lights and the cheap goods were an improvement.

At the front, its price eleven ninety-nine in black felt on a fluorescent cardboard star, was a digital clock-radio in black plastic. A present for them. Why not. Buy it for Judith. A small token of my.

He came out of the shop with the clock and a three pin plug in a plastic carrier bag.

The town was drab in the aftermath of Christmas. A few windows carried SALE signs and the shreds of rubbish left from the spending. As it was Saturday morning there were many shoppers, mostly women, mostly in indeterminate middle age. Too cold for the young to be on parade. Tucked in cafes if not in adolescent sleeping pits. Occasionally older couples would waddle through the crowd, the husbands carrying the crammed bags selfconsciously, wearing flat caps with nylon panels round the sides and back and thick glasses and false teeth. Half familiar faces loomed and passed him. There were a few he could say hello to.

He paused by the window of the Olympia Cafe. Through the glass running with condensation he could see unchanged the bentwood chairs and tables topped with thick glass, the steam from the coffee machine still taking the silver off the cloudy mirrors. Jaded shoppers with piles of bags and at other tables groups of bored teenagers filled the place. At the back was the partition that marked off his old corner where you could play the single flipper machine and sometimes even buy cannabis. Near the window sat a woman with a wrinkled, simian face. Jack recognised her as a neighbour of Keith's. With her was a flabby-faced woman with strawcoloured hair and pale eyelashes. She seemed to be talking haltingly and simian face had her head tilted forward, listening hard.

He walked on and through the shopping centre, past the plaque announcing its opening in 1966, past the empty shop units and the indoor market, out onto the carpark that stood on high ground above a factory. Here he could see the mountains and snow again. If he took a path along waste ground on a high bank, above the works where pitprops were overhauled, he would come close to the street where he had been brought up. He paused and wrapped the clock-radio tightly under his arm before starting.

His shoes socketed the four inches of snow over the waste ground. At its far side he dropped over a high retaining wall into a lane.

He was well below the level of the high street now, and a network of streets draped the shoulder of land between him and it. He turned downhill at first and then turned up a steep road that would take him back towards the main street.

Familiar territory. The old salmon. A terrace on a raised pavement with a cast iron balustrade.

He walked gingerly to avoid slipping.

Winters with the brother, socks on their hands, making slides. Paran chapel. Unchanged. And then a stretch of terrace with corrugated galv riveted over the windows and doors. Downpipes hanging away from walls where moss and green ooze clung.

Further up, before the hill joined the main road, it crossed the street where he had been brought up, which ran down the slope at another angle. He slowed as he got near the crossroads. There were no people. He could see the traffic passing at the top of the hill, a small slot of movement.

To the right at the crossroads, the small bakery and further up the Ram Inn and then the new police station, the new library. Left – how many doors? – after Monnigan's, Mrs Rees's.

You broke his

Get on and get out but remember

Jesus. No more of this.

He kept his head down and looking at the ground went straight on up the hill. Out of the corner of his left eye was a blur that seemed strangely white, as if there were only snow, but he did not look up.

He almost ran to the top and stumbled over the piled kerb of greyish snow into a doorway where he paused, breathing heavily.

EIGHT

'I had it this morning, Clarry baby' Kelv said.

He skipped round and walked backwards, looking into Clarry's face.

O was walking with them and Wayne, Sully and Jack along the high bank above the mill from the bathhouse to the day gang's cabin. There had been a thaw that had eaten some of the snow away and a refreeze. The coarse grass on the bank below them was badged with islands of dirty snow and stiffened under clean frost.

Kelv turned and put an arm over Clarry's shoulder.

'Just right in the morning see' he said.

'You've got more energy than I have in the mornings then' Clarry said, laughing.

'Shagged it all round the bedroom' Kelv said. O saw him looking up reflectively. 'Better then, you know? Not too fishy. Been stewing quietly all night.'

'Don' do this to me Kelv' Jack said. There was a false whine in his voice.

Sully joined in. 'Aye. It's cruelty to homeless pricks.'

'Well I put mine home this morning right enough.' Kelv pulled his cap round peak forward and then round again so that it was back to front once more. A kind of victory roll.

'You'll be putting some wind in my old boy in a minute' Sully said, 'and then I'll have to go and have a fucking wank.'

'Ah, it's hard on you fellers without a house to put him in' Kelv said, 'but I was just sharing my recent experiences with my mature colleague here.'

Clarry laughed his high pitched laugh.

'I'm so mature I'm going off' he said.

'When was the last time you had it then, Clarry?' Wayne said.

Clarry's laugh stopped.

'Cheeky bugger en he?' he said mildly, looking at O, but went on: 'Oh I don' know. I think it was the night Sunderland won the cup.'

As they drew near the cabin, Wayne came to O and whispered in his ear. His hard fingers gripped O's shoulder and his breath was warm.

'I bet that's more often than you've had it, wanker.'

O nudged him away weakly.

'Don' be cruel now, Wayne' Sully said.

'It's only half cruel. O's not a homeless prick. He've got a home. He's just a prick.'

'Fuck me' Sully said. 'She almost said something witty.'

O felt his cheeks burn, but Wayne moved away from him. Sully was the only person there who could get away with this. No one but he would dare to call Wayne *she* like that. O was glad that none of the others liked Wayne. Not even Jack seemed to like him, although he didn't seem to care who he was with. If they had liked Wayne, O knew that he would have been physically hurt by now. It was for their own selfish reasons that they disliked him no doubt, but it was fortunate for O.

'When was the last time you had it then, wisearse?' Wayne said.

Sully slid open the workshop door.

'Mind you own bastard business or I'll fucking well run you over with the dumper.'

O got into the cabin first. Ken Francis was there sprawled in his usual place, the crook of one arm over his eyes. Some of the other men, the teacher and a couple of others, sat playing nerky.

O stirred the dead cockroaches around the tray of poison with the toe of a boot. No luck. But he heard rats scrutting around the works sometimes. Had seen one a couple of days before. They must nibble the stuff. He wondered where they went to die.

'Ugh' Sully said. 'Don' do that, mun, O. Them bloody black pats do give me the shivers.'

And O could see that Sully meant it. He pitied Sully for being so weak as to fear the pathetic dead insects.

* * *

Later that morning, Norman, who seemed to be the chief welder and was owner of a large number of quiz books, came into Ben's cabin and propped a spouted kettle on the blackened radiator made of two inch pipe. The kettle contained tea complete with milk and a lot of sugar. He had topped it up from a hot water urn on the roughing mill, and Ben's radiator, too hot to touch, would keep it simmering.

'Got your mugs, boys?' Norman said.

Sully ceremoniously took the open padlock off Ben's grimy steel cupboard and distributed the mugs, blackened by divers fingerprints.

'Hear about the urn in the electricians' shop?' Norman said.

Ben made a lipfart as Norman poured the tea. The heater in the welders' cabin nearby was broken and his territory had been invaded.

'They 'ouldn' ever fucking let me in their cabin' he'd said to Jack one day. Now his two benches and blackened floor were parking space for half a dozen of the day gang and a further group of assorted welders. Jack looked at the dirty, boilersuited figures, the welders in their shabby black kneelength boots, then the ruststreaked plates fixed over the window, and he marvelled again at the pure water distilling out of the leaky radiator into the silvered syrup tin.

'Be rolling all day today' Ben said. 'They've been having hot fucking cobbles all morning. Bit of luck there'll be some welding jobs soon.'

Ben was in his gargoyle position, an elbow resting on his cupboard, the hand propping his chin. Norman sat next to him and slurped his tea with a grateful 'Ah.' Ben lipfarted again, annoyed that the welders had missed or ignored his dig.

When hot steel passed on the strip out on the mill its roar filled the little room.

'Almost like the old days with the mill running like this' Norman said.

'What?' Ben was upset, but not so upset as to alter his pose. 'They'm only fucking rolling one shift mind, days regular five days a bastard week. Three shifts a day it used to be. Three shifts a fucking day seven days a week.' Unhappy with this he elaborated his theme. 'Twenty-four hours a day. Six till two, two till ten, ten till ballocking six. Continuous rolling. End of a shift you 'ouldn' know whether you was coming or bastard going.'

Norman had set down his tea and taken from a pocket one of his quiz books, which he now studied. He was about forty, solidly built, with a thick moustache and dark greying hair. His boilersuit was intricate with buttonflapped pockets. There was silence as he studied. Jack expected a round of the insipid quiz game. No score was kept. The object, apparently was only to pass the time. Like lifers making models out of matchsticks.

Kelv, who was sitting on the floor, said, 'So what about it?'

He looked at Norman, who went on reading. Jack could see the welder's eyes following a line to the end of a sentence.

'What?'

'What about the urn in the electricians' shop?'

'Oh. A bloke I do know there was brewing up one day. He drew some water off the urn to make the tea. Water come out a funny colour.' He levered the covers of his book so that the spine cracked, as though he was going to turn back to his reading.

Like a bird's wings giving a lazy movement, Jack thought. An unconscious action of the hands as Norman looked at Kelv. He remembered his father teaching him how to open a book. But that was for hardcovers. Spine on the table. Hold the pages of the book and let the boards drop. Lever them down and open the book a bit at a time, first one side, then the other, till you got to the centre, There. The book do open flat at any page and you won' break the spine. Kiff. That was his word for done, complete, like some people said pat. Having it pat. Kiff like that. And he remembered the cupboard in his and his brother's bedroom that had become a book cupboard by default. Under the layers of Biggles, Dandy and Rupert, his father's books. You could excavate, pick your way through to the brickred spines. Amazed at his recall, he read the titles of the Left Book Club editions: *China Fights Back* by Agnes Smedley, *Justice in England* by a barrister, *An Atlas of Empi*re by Somebody Horrabin. Those and a few battered reference books and a squashed war economy Penguin of *The Iron Heel*. The first piece of science fiction he had read. He had found a Michael Moorcock in the bottom of his dirty clothes locker in the bathhouse. Dirty and thumbed, but still intact. He would bring it on the mill. Like becoming an expert on ornithology or local history, only a less affected way of spending the time. Like Judith. She was less inclined to selfdramatise than Keith. A book or the telly was enough for her. She didn't have Keith's need to make activity purposeful. She could sit and stare without Jack feeling that it was time worse spent than if she kept busy. It was not icy, exactly, though Jack had read it that way at first.

Norman had lapsed back into his book, but before Kelv could pursue him, pointlessly, about the electricians' shop urn, Ken Francis looked in around the door.

He scanned the dozen or so faces as if looking for someone.

'Fuck me' Ben said. 'It's like bastard Piccadilly in here. Enter, Kenneth. Leave your hat and cane with the butler and pull up a chaise longue.'

Ken's eye lighted on Norman.

'The very man' he said. He came in, waited till Norman finished his sentence, evidently familiar with his ways, and said, 'tell these buggers. Haydn Luke. Did he or did he not have a ballock that was eighteen inches long?'

Norman considered this.

'Haydn Luke' he said. 'His wife run off with another bloke didn' she? Well, I've heard people saying it. I don' make a point of measuring the testicles of former workmates.'

'Come on mun' Ken said. 'Everybody knew it.'

'That's what everybody said.' Norman wouldn't be drawn into rash statements.

Ken puffed his cheeks, frustrated.

Baiting time.

'See' Kelv said. 'I told you that story was a load of balls.' He victory-rolled his cap.

'A tissue of falsehoods' Wayne said.

'Where did you hear that from, Wayne?' Sully said. 'The magistrate?'

Ken looked around sheepishly and began to retreat.

'Comical buggers en you?' he said.

There was a brief raspberry and Ben said, 'She didn' fly the nest.' Wings flexing. Escape.

'He caught em at it' Ben said. 'Haydn told me hisself. He came in one day and there she was. Her and Ieuan Stoddart. Banging it away like the war had started.'

There was a silence in the cabin that let you hear the steel being meaninglessly milled outside. Jack imagined himself, Haydn Luke, walking in on them, hard at it like they'd heard the four minute warning. And all of them were imagining that, from Ben to the youngest apprentice welder with pubescent bumfluff on his upper lip.

Kelv broke the communion with words, though they were subdued:

'I'd hit the two of em from arsehole to breakfast time.'

'Would you?' Sully said.

'What would you do?'

'I don' know.'

What would Keith. He's nights tonight. Slimmer about the hunkers than Liz – you can't help noticing these things. No.

'Haydn' Ben said, 'didn' do anything. He walked in and there they was. He told me. He just stopped and looked at them for a bit and they saw him and stopped and he just went downstairs and sat in the kitchen. *Then* she cleared out and left him. Oh, weeks after.'

Jack felt the unbidden thought stir in his crutch.

Ken Francis saw his chance and made his escape while the boys were with Haydn and his wife and Ieuan.

Norman went back to his book and began to prepare the others for a round of questions on The Natural World when Sully reminded him about the urn in the electricians' shop.

'Oh aye' Norman said. 'It's nothing much. They were brewing up and the water came out of the boiler a funny colour and a bit smelly like, so they decided to empty it out.'

Norman was no storyteller. He spoke quietly and expressionlessly, did not embroider.

'They shut the water pipes off and uncoupled the pipes and that, and they turned the urn over on the floor.' He stopped and looked around at them.

'And?' one of the welders said.

'There was a pig's head in it.'

'A pig's head?'

'Aye. On'y a small one mind. Somebody put a pig's head in the urn.'

There was a pause.

'What for?'

'I don' bloody know.'

Some of the boys looked suspiciously into their mugs.

'It was all pretty colours apparently' Norman said. 'Been in there a long time they reckon.'

There was communion of imagining again, though this time it was just relish for the bizarre.

'Some of the bastard maniacs in this fucking hole' Ben said, 'ought to be locked up.'

Keith went out to catch his bus at twenty past nine. There was a film on at twenty-five past. Jack sat in an armchair and Judith sat at one end of the settee. The light was off in the livingroom but the kitchen door was open and the kitchen light on. There was also the fire and the television.

Keith tucked his plastic grub box under one arm – Oxo tin and bit of garter elastic substitutes – and left. Neither Jack nor Judith got up.

She was sitting easily, with her legs folded up on the chair, her head inclined to one side as she looked emptily at the screen. He glanced, trying not to, at the hem of her skirt and her knees, slightly parted, lit with the shifting colours of the television, and the shadows between.

Neither of them reacted to the last item on the news. Vandals had stolen a plastic palm tree from a nightclub and erected it on the middle of a traffic roundabout near Swindon. The newscaster's inane smile and the shuffled papers.

The film was a thriller. The opening had a long scene showing an armed man entering a large house, the silencer on his gun indicating by convention that he was a contracted assassin. There were details of gloved hands on window sashes and curtains billowing in unnatural blue television night. The intruder crossed landings and eased open bedroom doors silently.

Judith snapped on a readinglamp near her seat and picked up a fat paperback. She was less than a quarter of the way through it. Jack could see on its cover a gothic mansion on a stormy promontory against a sunset the colours of childbirth. He recognised the title.

'I saw the film of that' he said.

She looked up.

'It's one of them ones where she do marry the rich older man en it?'

'Yes.'

'They go back to his big house but he've got a secret.'

She looked levelly into his eyes. He looked away and talked on.

'It's usually a mad wife in the attic and the film strings you along like that for a bit, but it do turn out he's just a drug addict.'

She shut the book, put it down, and inclined her head, looking at the film once more.

He made as if to apologise, but that would have been useless, and he felt himself trapped into silence.

'Perhaps the book is different from the film' he said at last, lamely.

She looked at him again and he could have expected her to smile, but there was no flicker. He said he used to like science fiction, heroes on cosmic quests and that.

Nights when Keith was away were the hardest times. She was cold and quiet. Or not really cold. She had warmed to the present, seemed genuinely touched by it. Smiling and holding the black plastic box, staring at it as if she expected it to smile back. The clock-radio had become clumsy in her hands as she tried to thank him. She'd made a performance of showing it to Keith, like a mother anxious to praise, and her husband had joined in the act quietly, like an undemonstrative father. Jack had removed himself quickly, trying to pretend it was nothing, really.

The unassuming, thoughtful etcetera almost-lodger. He had felt himself to be a fraud. It was irrational to feel this. After all, he'd bought the thing on a real impulse. It wasn't as if it had been calculated. Though where the impulse had sprung from he didn't know. Perhaps from the simple need to spend. A small token of my intention to regain control of my destiny.

He winced at having spoilt her book, at her even stare, and they sat frozen watching the film.

At last she got up and walked past him into the kitchen. Not thin, but slimmer about the hips than. You can't help.

He knew that she was changing into her nightie in the kitchen, with a gasjet on the cooker for extra warmth.

The film finished with the hired killer being killed by a hired killer and Jack switched the set off. He checked that the front door was locked, raked down the fire and put up the guard. Judith came in in her dressing gown.

'I'm ready for bed too' he said.

Sod this. Go out next time he's on nights.

She slipped past him, through the hallway and upstairs. He knocked off the lights and followed her. He hung back for a moment to let her go on, but as he mounted the first step he saw her very slowly turning the corner at the landing banister.

He waited, listening to her washing. Waited, having stepped back from the stair in case she stepped out onto the landing and saw him looking up. Finally he heard her padded footsteps on the carpet and the bedroom door being gently shut, and it was safe for him to go up.

* * *

'My crimes' Emlyn said. 'We're going to get we're going to get flipping 'lectrocuted.'

It was quarter to three in the morning. They stared down at the smashed cooling pipe on the reheating furnaces. The gush of water fell away down a wall and through a gap into the cellars.

Keith had gone down into the cellars with the foreman to see the damage. In the large chamber underneath they had seen the water fanning down the wall and rilling over a set of fuseboxes which crackled and blew, shooting sparks.

'I wanted to have a read and get my fucking head down by half past two tonight' Rutter said. 'I'm driving to Swansea tomorrow.'

The foreman disappeared to phone the electricians and left Keith, Rutter and Emlyn alone in the slabyard. The only sound was the unwanted waterfall.

Rutter got some scrap sheet metal. He found a firm footing, straddling the drop into the cellars. The water gushed over his thighs and soaked one boot. Seeing what he was attempting, Emlyn and Keith took corners of the sheet, trying to bend it into shape. Keith could see Em's face redden and the veins straining on his forehead. Faintly in the roar of water, he could hear Rutter rehearsing a large repertoire of curses.

Pulling his gloves off and throwing them away, Rutter had rolled the metal into a makeshift guttering to try to pipe the water away from the wall. As his hands struggled around the metal, Keith saw blood staining the water. Rutter went on struggling and cursing, the skin of one palm deeply slashed.

Keith felt that he was not part of this. Outside it would be freezing and the world was sleeping. He wanted to sleep, on the bench in the cabin, or at home. He looked at Rutter's back bent in obscure labour, the irrelevant blood.

* * *

The mill was down the following morning and they had got a crane to take out some of the rolls on the strip. The lumps of metal slag that collected under the rolls on the mill side of the reheating furnaces were awkward to move. They were fistsized or bigger, gnarled and pocked like meteorites. They were too tightly packed to get a shovel into easily and so were mostly picked out by hand and flung into a skip on the mill floor.

For a while the day gang, except for Ken Francis who had disappeared, worked steadily, bent double, clawing out the metal like cockle gatherers. O noticed Sully and Clarry pacing themselves and Jack and Kelv working at great speed. They would be worn out inside two hours, he thought.

The narrow pit under the strip which the rolls normally covered was very deep in some places, though here it only went down six feet or so. When the mill was rolling, high pressure jets of water sluiced away the scale and slag, but periodically the shallow stretch of pit where the slabs dropped out of the furnaces clogged and the day gang's job was the result.

About three feet down they came to a set of iron bars like railings set sideways across the pit. A lot of slag had come to rest on top of these, but slightly smaller pieces had riddled through. Kelv and Jack managed to lift out a whole section of bars and started to clear the slag underneath them. Kelv was sweating and his face red with bending. Finally they reached the concrete floor, surprisingly clean from the constant blast of water.

'Tell you what, boys' Clarry said, 'we can tunnel under the bars this way, towards the shallower end.'

'I always wanted to be a working class hero' Sully said.

'So did I neither' Kelv said.

'Be all right' Clarry said. 'Just clear a bit this end and loosen it up a bit with a mandrel and then we can blow it through from the other end with a firebag.'

'Oh. There we are, Jack' Kelv said. 'And you thought it'd be difficult, didn' you?'

Clarry produced a pick that he kept hidden in some girderwork along the mill wall, pulled his corduroy cap down tighter, and started levering at the packed slag. O and the others threw the loosened pieces out into the skip. On all fours like a great blue rat, Clarry crawled into the low tunnel he made under the bars. Soon, all they could see was his rubber workboots as he lay on his side, swinging the pick.

He worked in for eight or ten feet and then slowly reversed out. Kelv was down and had shot into the tunnel, snatching up the pick. Clarry got to his feet in slow stages and wiped the condensation off his glasses. He pulled off his gloves and rubbed his knees. O noticed the swollen knuckles.

'Bloody old rheumatic' Clarry said.

They took turns with the pick. O went in and lay quietly for a while, enjoying the dark. It was very hard to shift the slag but he did not think that anyone seriously expected them to move it all. The tunnel was quite long now. Lew Hamer had given them an inspection lamp, and they crouched one behind the other, passing back the nodules of slag. Clarry laughed.

'Bugger me' he said, 'just like working down the pit again.'

Looking back, O saw Kelv, who was immediately behind, pause and look at Clarry.

'Did you work underground, Clarry?' Kelv said.

'Fuck me' Clarry said, 'who didn't? We all had to go down when I was a kid. None of this join the bloody army nonsense.'

'And is it good down there?'

Clarry laughed.

A voice came from the mouth of the tunnel.

'See. I bloody told you.' It was Ken Francis, dark with the light spilling around him. 'They'm just using up the ingots and the slabs to empty the order books. You watch. Rolling like mad and then they'll have you slogging your balls off like this for ten minutes and then' – O could see him, beyond the crouching silhouettes of the gang, jerking a thumb over his shoulder – 'up the fucking road you all go. No bloody point.'

He disappeared again.

Kelv rested his head on his fist. O thought vaguely about September and imagined himself being in the house all day, arguing with his mother. No Wayne.

Kelv raised his head, breathing heavily. He muttered 'Shit' and started clawing the slag back towards Clarry and the others quickly.

'Come on, O, my beaut' he said. 'Get that fucking mandrel swinging.'

* * *

In spite of the slight thaw, it was too cold in the bedroom. Keith had lit the gas oven, leaving its door open, and spread his papers on the kitchen table. He had carefully laid out the token penny and the local book opened to the photograph for encouragement. The hacked page of plans and a couple of tortured pages towards his talk.

Through the closed livingroom door he could hear the early evening news on television. Jack and Judith would be sitting watching it, holding mugs of tea, she on the settee, he in an armchair, with only the light of the fire and the telly.

123

It had been dark all day. The snow had thawed so that it left ugly, dirty white patches on the mountains. They looked piebald, or unfinished, like half-things. So there was no softening light from the snow. And clouds had lidded the valley all day. Occasionally they had lowered, locking everything in murk, but at best they had seemed to be fifty feet overhead, allowing a faint light by which you could see the fronts of houses across the valley, the dark blotches of pine forest, and the mountain shedding its pale grey snowskin.

A couple of miles to the north east of Keith's kitchen, a man standing on the ridge above Moonlow's ironworks in 1800 would have seen, on an evening like this, the glow from the new furnace and in the hollow, the ironmaster's house, being extended on one side. Perhaps the thin light of a candle at a window. There would be the massed bare branches of the forest in the valley to his south. Clearings, made near the furnace by the charcoal burners. Cart tracks through frozen mud. And remotely, on the hills above the treeline or in the fields cleared by the river, a few people scattered on patches of land – there was a name for these small farms in Welsh which he could not remember – living in what conditions? Barely six hundred of them in a huge parish when the furnace was built. How many scores of thousands of people lived in the same area now? The boundaries were all changed. It would be a complicated business to calculate it. The scene would be disintegrating, eaten by the growing dark, and there would be almost no lights. Ridges wouldn't show because there'd be no town lights on the other sides of the mountains. Briefly the swollen clouds, shut across the hills, would tinge a muddy blue before night closed in, and when they were very low the furnaces would make dull, rusty smudges on them.

If you could make a shelter on the hillsides in one night and occupy it, that was your home. On the mountain behind and to the north of the estate where Keith lived there was one tiny farmhouse with some fenced patches of moor above the jumble of grassed old tips. But the house itself could not have been more than a hundred and fifty years or so old. He felt his mind begin to hit against the dark, the lack of detail. The details disintegrating into the dark as he looked into the past, as he looked away from the glare of the furnaces, towards the places where the people lived.

It was dark that allowed you to speculate, left room for endless debate. Others had left more behind. There was the cool accounts book, the photostat of the letter with the bullfrog D.

He picked up the truck shop coin. It was thick and rimmed, the size of a crown. The obverse was blank and on the face was stamped in thick, seriffed letters:

S. M.
1818

Even the fullstops were squares balanced on one corner like diamonds. Ordinary people only appeared momentarily in the gleam of the coin, and then their faces were bored, he thought, as his must have been in the slabyard the night before. The place had been treed wilderness. In eighteen years the man was minting his own money. There was no laurelled profile of someone wanting to be Caesar. Only the letters on the thick coin, confidence unconsciously asserting itself in the weight, the solidity.

The mugs were being swilled at the sink.

'Ommm.'

It was Jack's voice, very close to his ear. The *m* held long in the throat. Keith looked round.

'What?'

'You know, om' Jack said. 'Zen. Remember Hari Krishna and the bells?' He hunched one shoulder for a moment, pulling a face, and said: 'The bells, the bells.' Then, 'I thought you was meditating, the way you were staring at that.'

Keith put the token down, realising, suddenly, how tightly he had been gripping it.

Judith was at the sink. Jack looked over his shoulder at the papers.

Keith felt he should hide his writing, but did not. He moved his arms forward over the papers slightly and then stopped.

'Omm mane padme hum' Jack said. 'My brother had a brass bell and a flowery shirt. I remember thinking he looked a right poof.' He paused and looked into space. 'Then he joined the civil service.'

Jude, who was resting her backside against the sink unit and holding a wet mug, tutted disapproval.

'There's terrible.'

'She speaks' Jack said. 'Do you know your missis is very hard to talk to. You're right though, Judith my love. Terrible. I crossed him off my Christmas card list straight. Or I would have if I had one.'

He hunched one shoulder and, pulling the screweyed face again, he loped in a grotesque stiffarmed limp to her side. He snatched the mug from her and mimed drinking.

'She gave me water!' Slurping. 'Speaking of which' – he straightened, dropping the act – 'let's all go out for a pint.'

He looked at her and she looked inquiry at Keith.

Last time, weeks before, the queasiness had lasted. A few days. Not the three of them together anyway. It would be hard to talk about the preparation with Jude there. He sensed it would be strained.

'Well, I've got to get on with this. I'll never get it done otherwise—'

Eight weeks was it? Jones would introduce him and it would go quiet. He could see their upturned faces. Even old Morgan, author of *The Early Years of The Gwedog Valley* might be there, his bluescarred hands fisting a biro over a notepad. What had he been saying?

'I'll never get it done otherwise.'

Of course, there was already a furnace working in a neighbouring valley to the west in 1800, so if the cloud was just high enough to clear the mountain, the man on the ridge might see a piece of horizon against the ruddled glow.

'Looks like it's me and thee then, lass' Jack said, switching his voice to Coronation Street.

'Go if you like' Keith said.

Judith looked at Keith for a moment.

Jack spoke into the pause. 'We're not worried about gossip are we?' He grinned at her as if he'd caught her out, and he put his arm round her shoulder.

She looked at him and then passively at Keith.

'I don' care what they say, baby' Jack said. 'I don' give a notre dam' for convention.'

He gave a ventriloquist's dummy grin at Keith. She had frozen against the sink unit and Keith could see Jack himself becoming uncomfortable. Finally he removed his arm and sat by Keith at the kitchen table. Keith stopped himself from smiling.

'What's the problem anyway?' Jack looked earnestly over the papers.

Keith found himself saying that there was no problem, that it was just slow work, that was all, and he felt the words slip out of control into a ramble. He stopped and tried to gather his thoughts. Jude was still behind him, but he felt he had to be honest. He needed Jack's simple way of seeing things.

'Look' Keith said. 'See this token.'

He took up the heavy coin.

'This Moonlow bloke came from nowhere, he –' Keith thought of all the processes of extracting, organising, building, making '– he – all this –' waving a hand at the photographs and the papers '– he got it all moving and in the end he, well, him and a couple of other blokes, made a town, and he made his own money. Literally.' He emphasised each word.

After a pause Jack said, 'So what's the problem?'

'Like I said, there en one really. I just can't make him out.'

'I can't make myself out half the time.'

Keith turned the coin over.

'Look. No head. He could have had it done if he'd wanted to. Like Caesar or somebody.'

'The man wanted money. That's simple enough. Wanted it big, that's all.'

'Perhaps so.'

It had crossed his mind a long time ago. It was still hard to believe that that was all.

'Render unto Caesar that which is Caesar's.'

Jude's voice.

'There you are, Jack' Keith said. 'That's what an O level in RE do do for you.'

'Just money. A little empire, that's all' Jack said. He shrugged. 'Like you say, he wasn' the on'y one.'

To Keith this seemed arbitrary and therefore worrying. Either Jack didn't see it that way, or wasn't worried by it. Keith's worries seemed petty now, half-things hauled into the bright kitchen light, and in front of Jude. He turned to look at her, to display his new honesty. But she had gone quickly back into the livingroom, closing the door behind her.

NINE

Judith stood at the window with the cracking view and every morning watched winter turn messily into spring. Frost and thaw and most often rain teeming in grey bars up the valley, blurring the rows of houses opposite. Sometimes she thought of those scenes in old films that showed a window and Hollywood snow fading into Hollywood blossoms and then sunlight and then Hollywood autumn leaves. She felt, sometimes, as if she was only an observer, except that all the seconds were lived through. There was no montage of seasons or animated clock hands.

Beryl had suggested one of the supermarkets in town. On the checkouts you did not have to exchange pleasantries much. Beryl had not mentioned that, of course, though Judith suspected that she had thought about it. They were just inside walking distance too, though uphill coming home.

Keith might enjoy just working at his books and walking, for a while. And Jack. God knew what he would do.

She remembered her mother when she took her first boyfriend home. How she had hoovered the front room that day, and how she had run into the scullery to put her teeth in when they arrived. Keith and Judith had kept up that kind of show for a while when Jack came, but she could see it wearing off like layers of courtesy rubbing away from a courtship. Keith always changed his clothes in front of the fire. After a few days of eating at the kitchen table, they had reverted to plates balanced on knees in the livingroom in front of the television. In any case, because of Keith's shifts and Jack's days regular job, they each tended to eat at a different time on work days. The three of them sitting and eating together was quite rare, and she found it difficult to get the portions right. She did not mind cooking for Jack. He usually ate lightly, sometimes not at all, and frequently did his own food. Not very well, and he scratched the teflon frying pan one day. When the three of them were together Keith and Jack were often quite relaxed. When she was alone with Jack he was quiet and polite, but when Keith was there he told jokes and did impressions, seemed almost to talk down to Keith. Although, she wasn't quite sure about that. He showed more interest in Keith's hobby than she was able to.

One night they were watching television and Jack said, 'Are you enjoying this programme?' and she said, 'Yes' and he said, 'I wouldn' like to play you at poker.'

But that was wrong really, in another sense, because she couldn't bluff about important things. For instance, she couldn't pretend that she was interested in Keith's hobby. She had tried it once, had tried to say something about a pamphlet he was reading, but the words had gagged in her mouth like dry biscuit.

In a way, Keith was the only one who was free. He could be himself in the house with either of them. But she could neither tell him the truth nor lie to him. With Jack she became selfconscious, noticed him looking at her. It was nice, that feeling. She had waited on the stairs for him one night and waggled her bum as she turned the corner on the landing. But the selfconsciousness meant that she felt herself striking poses, was not herself.

He was thin. Thinner than she remembered him when he used to play rugby in school. Much thinner, as well as being shorter, than Keith, and he had the habit of clenching his jaw so that the hollows showed in his cheek. It probably gave him terrible headaches, though he might think it made him look tough. Made his hangovers worse. It made him look tense. She wondered if his whole body was tense like that and thought of Keith's blubber nipped in by the elastic of his Y fronts.

So she didn't see Jack truly relaxing at any time. Neither did she ever relax fully, except when both men were out, so she grew to like being alone, except when she craved sex. Then she felt their presence like a kind of tickling. She wondered if Jack ever relaxed when he was sober. It seemed not, so far as she could tell, and so of the three, he came third, being never quite at his ease. She remembered when she and Keith had moved into the house, three years before, how comfortless it had been with almost no furniture, the bare walls. That must be Jack's condition all the time, to feel as if he was sitting on a packing case. The armchairs and carpets must be a kind of torture to him because he could never be easy among them. That, she thought, was what it meant to be without a home.

In this way she came to feel sorry for him. It induced a kind of motionlessness because she was afraid to offer all the domestic, generous courtesies. It might hurt him. And she could not explain this to him. Apart from being complicated, it too would hurt. There was nothing left but to be quiet and enjoy his looking at her occasionally. When he had bought the clock she had been moved. The black plastic case didn't really suit the bedroom, but it was as if he had offered a feather for somebody else's nest.

Keith had handled the clock clumsily, made a mess of putting the plug on it. She practically had to tell him to say thank you.

If Beryl had been diplomatic about work, she was even more careful about Jack. In fact she had not said a word about him over several visits, even though she had called once when he was there. She and Judith had sat in the kitchen that time while Keith and Jack sat in the livingroom. She had got a good look at him. Judith could imagine some people putting questions straight away and storing the answers for future fatchewing sessions with others. Beryl only brought news of Bron and her son, on remand in Cardiff Prison, and talk about how the local paper was getting it more or less right but was helping to break Bron's heart. This was her major theme, embroidered with shocking jokes, stored from years of factory work, and any small bits of talk.

At last Judith felt she had to say something. The truth,

disseminated through Beryl, would be much better than all the permutations that rumour would put them through.

So she said one day, 'You remember Jack, don' you? He's a friend of Keith's.' And she explained.

Beryl said that she had known his parents, had been at school with the mother, and that that was a tragedy about her too. When she died his father hadn' lasted all that long. Grieved away to nothing. And there she stopped. Said nothing about the two sons.

Judith remembered Jack's father vaguely. Small and thin with hollow cheeks. A lined forehead and his dark hair receded into a long peak. He smoked always and carried his burnt-down cigarette in a cupped hand, burning end towards the palm.

It was that day that Judith learnt from Beryl about Maudie.

'Have you heard about your friend Maudie?' she said.

The fire was lit but the room was not properly warm yet. It was a morning when Jack was in work and Keith was out looking at old cart tracks or something. *Your friend* was Beryl's joke. Maudie, slightly odd, was avoided by nearly everybody.

Her husband, Judith thought.

She passed their house often when she walked down to town. It was a bungalow tucked behind a terrace immediately below the housing estate. She remembered it being built when she was a girl, and Maudie's husband had built it, much of it on his own. She remembered the cement mixer rumbling. Him looking healthy and suncracked in his vest. Ger y Mynydd it was called. In spite of the way Maudie seemed, it always looked spotless, the windows clean. Sometimes, just very occasionally, the car of one of the children would be parked there. Now when she went past she sometimes saw in the darkness of the bedroom window, parked by the low sill, his aluminium walkingframe. She saw him there once in his dressing gown. His skin still suncracked but slack where the fat and muscle had melted underneath.

'No' Judith said. 'I haven't.'

'Dead, gel. Day before yesterday.'

So that was that. How long did they leave it, she wondered, before they sent somebody round to collect the frame.

'Probably a blessing' Judith said.

There would be a lot of such saying, the waste smoothed over like that.

'No.' Beryl's voice was insistent. '*Maudie's* dead. She took his painkillers.'

The tip of Beryl's cigarette glowed through the ash as she sucked on it. Judith could see the paper burning back.

There should be a snatch of theme music now and the adverts. But only her own voice would pierce the quiet.

'Oh Christ' she heard herself saying at last.

Beryl talked about how awful it was and how everybody was shocked and concerned now, although the day before they would have crossed the street to avoid Maudie.

Judith thought about Jack's father grieving away to nothing. Beryl's version of things.

'What about the husband?' she asked. He was a sick man and the children were remote.

'They took him into hospital. He found her. Had to phone and all. It's a wonder that didn' kill him. He won' be around long now, you watch. It's on'y *she've* held him together this last couple of years, running round.' She paused, timing the next comment carefully, punctuating in this way to make it clear that this was only a guess. '*I* think she knew he didn' have long and that she would have gone soon after, and she couldn' –' Beryl hesitated '– she couldn' finish him off like, so she knew that if she –' she gestured towards her own chest to indicate suicide '– that he'd go after.' She stared at Judith. 'You know Doreen Griffiths's eldest daughter do work down the hospital. She said when they took him in he was six stone.'

Judith thought about this on her own at the window. How Maudie's home had been worked at and feathered and was now a shell. The children would sell the house and somebody else would start again, probably never knowing anything about who built it. Their lives had been locked together until one way or another they would be destroyed together. Maudie was the one who had held them together so she had had to make the decision.

Judith had tried to find out about central heating and some firms were going to give estimates. She looked at the front garden, drenched and dirtied with thawed snow and the low cloud fraying into drizzle. There was all of spring and summer to go. A supermarket was the best idea yet. She would find out, too, about that.

* * *

Although the nights were drawing out, he had almost left it too late again. In the waning light he stood on the banking behind the condemned houses of Buchan Row. The bank, which was an old tip long overgrown, fell straight into the backyard of the house with dark green windowframes.

Probably, it had been built before the tip was started. There was no telling what kind of hillside the first crammed tenants would have seen from their backyard a hundred and forty years before.

He put his glasses back on. The roof had been covered with pitched tarpaulin probably by the last occupiers, but the rain had got under it and one corner had come away exposing the slipped and loosened slates. Most of the windows had been smashed.

Ungainly, feeling his gut bouncing inside his coat, he worked his way crabwise down the steep slope into the flagged yard. It was damp and moss followed the joints of the flags. The back door had been boarded, but the planks nailed across had all been torn away or kicked in. He stepped into the semidark of what had been the scullery. There was a smell of urine and the staleness of damp wood, rotting wallpaper. Where the range would have been was a neatly cemented recess. The house had been modernised. A boiler for gas central heating had probably replaced the old fireplace and oven. Now that was gone. The sink too. The floor was strewn with broken laths, glass, bits of slate, pages from women's magazines. He stepped through to the middle room. It was tiny. Seemed smaller, somehow, than it might have been had there been furniture. There was a tiled fireplace. Originally there would have been, perhaps, something in cast iron. A fire had been lit quite recently using the rubbish lying around, not in the hearth but on the floor in front of it. The buff tiles were blackened. Damp had come down the chimney breast and he could see the wallpaper, layer after layer, curling away. The sour smell of paper that had been burnt and then wet.

The rest of the downstairs was very dark, heavily boarded at the front where it faced the street, except for the fanlight above the front door, which the thrown stones had missed. In the splay of light from it he could see the dusty electricity meter, the mould-mottled wall of the passage, and dimly the stairs. Some light came down them, from open bedroom doors on the landing. The stairs were sound. He trod them carefully, aware of his own breathing in the silence. Two doors at the top. Toilet and bathroom downstairs somewhere, then. He had missed them.

The front bedroom had a panelled door, painted brown and combed to affect unconvincing woodgrain. The colours were greyish in the going light. Nothing. Empty space. The floorboards sprang downwards as he moved forward and so he retreated.

In the back bedroom a lampshade still hung on the bulbless wire. A wireframed shade coated with pink plastic. A glassless window, its frames hanging crazy in the sashes, lit the room which was empty except for a cupboard built into a recess.

He knelt before it. The double doors opened easily. There was one shelf on which were a pile of copies of Titbits, rancid and crinkled with damp. One copy of Good Housekeeping. A wet England's Glory box standing on one end so that the ship pointed downward.

On the floor beneath the shelf, a few small, dirtblackened books.

Two. He picked them up eagerly and examined them, tilting them towards the light. One was embossed with faded gold. A picture of a stiffjointed camel bearing a moustached man wearing a fez. An arch of gold letters around these figures said: *With Gordon to Khartoum*. He laid this to one side and looked at the second. It was not easy to see. He took it to the window.

He looked out briefly. Down onto the shadowy backyard and the bank of sour yellow grass. The floorboards near the window were slimy where the snow and rain had blown in.

The book was a commentary on the gospels. He leafed through it. Page after page of useless elucidation that somebody, perhaps at this window, had spent hours poring over.

As he fanned through the damp book with finger and thumb, awkwardly because some pages were stuck, he felt something hard. A piece of stiff card fell from the pages to the floor. He picked it up quickly and held it to the light. White. Slightly bigger than a postcard. Faintly tinged with stains that would turn to ugly brown splotches. It bore a black heading in various types:

ELECTION OF
Urban District Councillors

Two black hands with inward pointing fingers bracketed the words:

VOTE AS BELOW

and the rest of the card was made to resemble a voting slip with a numbered list of names: Evans, Harries, Lewis, Phillips, Williams. Next to number 4, Jonah Phillips of Bakehouse, Twyn Gwedog, Baker, a bold X was printed.

No names of political parties. Only the men's trades were noted after their addresses, except for James Evans, who was simply titled 'Gent'. Hard to put a date to it. The variety of types, the lack of party names, and somehow the thickness of the card, all suggested to him the beginning of the century or earlier. There would be ways of finding out.

He turned the card over.

The back was covered in close handwriting. Urgently he looked more closely, moving nearer to the window and tilting the card further. It was in pencil, very precise and clear. There were occasional crossings out. It was sloping slightly and seemed firm. He noticed some Ds, not quite like Moonlow's, but equally sweeping and positive. A little more ornate. In some places the writing was divided into numbered points. There was no name at the beginning. This was not to anyone. Some personal sorting out, planning. He thought of his own notes for the talk, crabbed and tortured and now almost complete.

He had not felt himself to be any nearer to Moonlow, nor to the men he employed. The changes were too great for the mind to hold. His studies had been making mysteries, not solving them. Now that the work was nearly done, he had come out more to escape the feeling of tension between Judith and Jack. Jack was nervy, he knew, and Jude, although she occasionally seemed to try, could not put him at his ease. Even so, Keith felt in the smashed building the presence of the dead people who had moved through it, treated it as their own briefly.

This could be something like contact. He smiled as he held the card at the darkening window. This Jonah, trawled from the wet darkness was being brought into a fading light, and though he had words, he said nothing. The notes Keith held were in a language that was his own, but that he could not understand.

* * *

'Nice place you've got here' Jack said, shamelessly.

Come up and see my.

He sat on the deep, beige hearthrug which was laid over the thick carpet, classily patterned mock Persian on a red ground. The standard lamp had a beige fringed shade, which gave a soft lustre to the shine on the darkwood upright piano, the brass ornaments.

His mouth, anaesthetised with alcohol, could hardly taste the coffee or the digestive biscuit. Still he drank gratefully, feeling already dehydrated.

Kath, sitting leaning towards him on the tasselled and floral sofa, smiled over her stoneware mug.

'My mother's one for the plush' she said.

It was, Jack thought, the traditional front parlour taken to its logical conclusion. The curtains in the baywindow were velvet and dropped to the floor. It spoke of a lifetime of acquiring and keeping the cellophane on for as long as possible. The result was a room like a luxurious and hardly worn slipper. Kath's impact on this was slight as yet. The stoneware rather than bone china, the brushed steel face of the stereo deck. It had one of those brushes that clean the record as it plays.

Kath, too, was clean and new looking. Like Kelv in his mail order outfit. She had on dark, spotted tights. She had knees too. He stared at them happily. They were at about eye level. Eye level minge, he thought.

'Very nice. Do you mind if I join you on that posh settee?'

She didn't so he did.

Harder now, in every sense. In the pub, with Sully and Lorraine, flirtation had been easy. Alone with Kath in her padded parlour, her parents in bed and only the muted Moody Blues LP to hold out the midnight silence, there was the need to find the way from the innuendo to the clinch. Harder too the erection straining in his trousers, threatening to spoil the wordgame.

They leant against one another as they talked. Occasionally she shut her eyes and swayed her head with some favourite piece of music. He took advantage of these moments to try to arrange himself so that the stonker became invisible, and to look at her more closely. She was plump but definitely haveable. As Wayne would say, I wouldn' mind hanging out of her guts. Tall as me. Slightly flabby under the chin. Well filled out, not fat.

Suddenly she opened her eyes and turned them on him. Her face veiled with sincerity, she said, 'I'm glad I saw you again. I didn' think you'd come into the bank of course. But I hoped you'd come to the pub again. Did you—'

She noticed him looking at her legs and held one straight for him to inspect, tugged the skirt up to give him a better view.

'They're nice, en they?' she said. 'I like patterned tights. They turn me on.'

'Me too' Jack said. His voice almost slipped up to a squeak.

'Did you' she went on, 'did you come to the hotel special?' She looked at him and then looked away.

Jack looked down into his coffee and drained the cup. This, he thought, is it.

He met Sully in the bar of the Gold Dragon. Sully was wearing jeans, an opennecked shirt, and a white jacket with wide lapels.

'I'm on my way to meet the missis' Sully said apologetically when he saw Jack looking at the jacket.

Missis equals girlfriend, Jack thought. Almost forgotten that. Funny.

Sitting on the upholstered bench under the ripely bosomed pinups, they quickly became drunk. Sully smoked nervously and watched men playing cards at a neighbouring table.

'Fuck me, Jack' he said, 'it's just like in work by here.'

Jack looked up at the flattened perspective of bare tits and pouting mouths. 'Oh I 'ouldn' say that' he said. 'The pinups are newer.' He nodded towards the barmaid, indeterminately middle-aged. 'And the chargehand is prettier.'

Sully looked at her. 'I don' know about tha.' He looked at the clock and finished his pint, making as if to get up.

'Woa, woa' Jack said. 'Hang on, boy. Have a wiff. I do owe you a round.'

Sully sat down heavily, proffering the empty glass.

'Listen' he said. 'Come here.' He leant towards Jack. 'I've had a gutsful. Know what I mean, butt. Know what I'm going to do tonight? I'm going to get her to name the day. I'm going to go down on one fucking knee. I'm going to pop the bastard question.'

Jack considered this, weighing the two empty glasses in his hands.

'What?' he said at last. 'You mean you're going to propose like?'

'Sh. Don' tell anybody.'

'I 'ouldn' bother if I was you, butt.'

'There's fuck all else to do. I won' get another contract and there's no bloody building jobs going. I may as well do it while I got a couple of bob to jingle.'

'She working?'

Sully named a factory.

'Bit drastic' Jack said.

'Fuck it. Why not.'

'This is a stag night, then, sort of.'

Sully nodded. Jack hurried to the bar.

One pint later, they left the pub, trying to nestle into their collars out of the cold spring night.

'Why put it off?' Sully said. 'See, Jack, I can see marriage coming towards me like a grinning skull with a scythe in one hand and a bunch of hire purchase agreements in the other. Apart from which, my old gel is getting on my nerves.'

'Live with her' Jack said. 'Your missis I mean. I did that for a bit up north. You never know. It might not work see.'

Sully, like everybody else, was just looking for a bearable way of living. Jack imagined his friend's family turning icy at a liberal arrangement. He thought of Liz and the flat, the evenings stretched on the settee in front of the telly. The old need came back, rising to bay at the remembered pendulous breasts, the pouting mouths.

They had come to the town's one star hotel.

'Look' Jack said. 'You've got a few good years left. Fuck me, you're younger than me, mun. I bet you two grubnotes the next time we do get some overtime, that we could go in here now and pick up a couple of girls' – he clicked his fingers –'like that.'

Sully looked at the pillared porch and the lit windows, considered the two grubnotes.

'We could go in for a last pint anyway' Jack said.

Sully stepped in.

Jack was relieved to see Kath and Lorraine. Any two would have done for the attempt, but he knew that these two would win him the bet.

Kath's eyes lit up when she saw them. Sully gave Jack a thoughtful look when he introduced the girls. The patter was more or less as before. They imitated sober men. Lorraine was quiet as before, though she looked a little more interested in Sully than she had in Keith.

At last, the offered lift and coffee. Sully and Lorraine were dropped off at her house. Sully looked from Jack to Kath and back again as he waved to the going car. His eyes widened as he looked at Jack and, baring his teeth, he made a biting movement of the jaws.

Jack put the empty mug down on the classy Persian-type carpet and looked at Kath, adopted the same veil of sincerity.

'Yes' he said. It was an effort to say this with a definite *s*, rather than 'aye' or 'yeah'.

Easily enough, they pressed their faces together. She seemed quite eager and started counting his fillings with the tip of her tongue.

'I'm glad I saw you again' she said. 'When we were in school I used to fancy you like mad.'

His arm had slid round her shoulders, which seemed square and muscular.

'You don' remember me do you?' she said.

'Who cares about remembering?'

'You kissed me once after a youth club disco.'

Jack could just remember the youth club in the chapel vestry, though not particularly the discos.

'I thought you half knew I fancied you. A lot of girls did, mind.' Her voice almost stroked him. A verbal touch-up, making his erection strain at the roots. 'Some said you were a bit of an ego tripper but I didn' look at it that way. You were walking another girl home. Remember?'

No.

'Cheryl Humphreys.'

Jack could not remember her.

'She's teaching in London now. You came out with your arm round her waist. I was standing holding my bag by the gate, waiting for my friend. Remember we used to put our bags on the floor and dance round them. There were quite a few people about.'

'How long ago was this?'

'It was the year before they landed on the moon. I was about fourteen. You were sixteen or seventeen.'

'Do you remember everything in this detail?'

She rubbed her tongue along the underside of his upper lip.

'Everything.' She kissed him. 'There were people around, I said. And you kissed Cheryl on the nose and came to me and said, "Goodnight, Kathy" and you gave me a luscious kiss. And then you went back to Cheryl and walked off with her. My friend was just coming out. She said you were a cheeky bugger, but I just had wobbly knees.'

Jack remembered none of this and in any case was distracted as she slid her hand up the inside of his thigh and squeezed. He moved his hands into potential groping positions and began to unfasten her many-buttoned blouse.

'Listen' she said. 'Why don' we go up to my room?' Shamelessly.

The pickup arm was shushing gently at the end of the LP.

Jack said something about her parents being in bed.

'My mother's broadminded and my father's a bit deaf.' Too quick an answer, as if she had it ready. 'Otherwise I would have moved out a long time ago. You're not married or something are you? Don' worry. I don' write letters.'

'I'm not' Jack said.

They looked at one another and smiled in relief and recognition.

'Okay' Jack said.

She got up immediately and slid the LP back into its sleeve.

The stoneware was cleared away and she locked the front door.

'Come on. Quiet' she whispered in the hallway, clicking the light off and leading the way up the stairs.

Carrying his shoes, Jack followed, not believing his luck.

Faintly he saw her disappear round the banister on the landing. As he reached the top, a door creaked. He waited. He got used to the dark and could just see three doors, a dark grey where he assumed there'd be white gloss in daylight.

Suddenly the landing flooded with subdued, pink light. Kath's head appeared around the door from which the light was coming.

By the time he'd stepped into the bedroom she was in bed, the duvet drawn to her chin. There was a pinkshaded bedside lamp, a scatter of teddies and a Snoopy poster.

They gasped on whispered laughter as he left his clothes in a heap next to hers and slid under the cover.

Relief. He spread his toes next to the clean cotton. She pulled him to her and he felt her legs winding round the backs of his knees. Clasping her around the middle, he noticed that she had nothing that could be called a waist, and her hair, spread on the pillow, revealed a very thick, short neck. Her eyes were shut and she was mouthing anticipated pleasure. He could feel the coarseness of her pubic hair rubbing against his belly as she angled for the right place. Without opening her eyes she brought a hand down under her thigh and popped the end of his penis into place in a practised way.

Her instinct, oddly, seemed to be the same as his. To ram it home as quickly as possible.

She seemed to grow. Her biceps, he sensed, were larger than his. When he opened an eye her face seemed a yard wide. As she folded herself round him he penetrated her fully.

Nice and tight.

She held his buttocks and pressing the tips of her fingers in, pushed him in a little further. He had the sensation of drowning and felt the coffee and beer shifting in his stomach, his bladder straining, his temples already hurting with the hangover before he was sober.

She dug her fingers in a little harder. His body stiffened and twitched.

Done.

He pulled himself away, imagining his starved body cast up exhausted on some shore, and turning away from her, he went to sleep.

Kath's house was in a superior terrace that led uphill into a cul-de-sac. It was the small front-gardened type, a bit like Connie's or auntie uncle and Viking ship.

After she had shut the front door, having come to it in a kimono dressing gown, Jack paused at the gatepost and pissed out into the street.

Relief.

He hoped that some of the neighbours might see him around curtain edges, though it was unlikely that early in the morning. His penis was still heavy and bloodfilled. Slightly sore. The second time had been better, slightly. He had woken with an erection and had rolled her over and she had taken it in sleepy good humour, even seemed to enjoy it a bit. Nice in the morning. Been stewing all night. Not too fishy.

He had looked at the Snoopy poster and the dressing table cluttered with roll-on bottles, the scatter of soft toys, all sugared under the orange light from the streetlamp filtering dimly through the cotton curtains dotted, like her tights, with some small and delicate pattern. The urgency gone, it had been less frantic, more pleasurable.

The dead end of the street was a mesh fence beyond which were young pines where the Forestry Commission had gradually replanted after the war. Kath's Fiesta, parked on the hill, was blocked with a couple of sandbricks.

He watched the water running away down the sloping pavement.

It struck him that everything sat lightly on the hillside. The cars, the pine trees on their shallow plates of roots. Looking at the stepped roofs of the houses, he could imagine them slipping and fanning down the hill like a tipped shelf of books.

As he zipped up and walked away down the hill, he was surprised that he staggered a little, still lightheaded. He thought that after a long time she had got her own back for something that he had forgotten. He imagined her cutting another notch in the leg of her dressing table with a ladies' razor.

Bitch. Imagine calling Keith a slob.

Keith was days that weekend. The front door was open and the hall light blazing and Keith was leaving with his grub box under his arm when Jack arrived back. They exchanged a few words and Keith left to catch his bus. When Jack stepped into the hallway he was surprised to see Judith in her dressing gown.

'Hello stopout' she said, yawning and closing the door after him.

'What's this?' Jack said. 'You don' normally see your husband off to work on days do you?'

'Well I did today.'

'There's devotion.'

'Look, if you must know, I wondered if you was back. I. We were worried. We wondered where you'd got to.'

He was cold and shaky with the coming hangover. She was standing with her arms folded and her eyes screwed like proverbial pissholes in snow. He put his hand on her neck, sliding his fingers under the tongue of dark hair, and kissed her on the cheek, though the corners of their mouths touched.

'Thanks' he said.

'There's some tea left in the pot' she said, and went upstairs, her arms still folded.

Jack went into the kitchen.

TEN

At the clean and neat desk in the generator room, Ray looked up from his newspaper.

Keith took his hands out of his boilersuit pockets and pushed his safety glasses back into place on the bridge of his nose.

'How be, Ray' he said. 'Sign off the number two roughing mill stand, please.'

Ray turned the hardbound ledger on the desk to face Keith, as if he were the porter at a big hotel, and pointed out the relevant column with the end of his fountain pen.

The first time he had ever signed off a piece of machinery with Ray Keith had tried to borrow the fountain pen, but now he waited a moment. With a smile, Ray produced the smudgy biro from his breast pocket and presented it to Keith. Keith wiped his hands before taking it, signed: 'K. Watkins, Machine Shop, A Rota' and handed the pen back.

'How's the daughter these days, Ray?' he said.

'Oh, much the same, thank you, Keith.' After looking carefully at his old, accurate wristwatch, Ray filled in the other columns, noting the time and the name of the machine. 'Big job on the roughing?'

Keith's mind was elsewhere.

Tonight was the night.

The sheet of paper he had been fingering in his boilersuit pocket was closely covered with notes. The full script of his talk ran to fifteen sides in his small handwriting but with a great struggle he had made a single page of numbered points to check over in work. He had read them over half a dozen times that morning already, in the bus, and then in the bathhouse before changing. The fear and anticipation that had paralysed him for so long had ended in a burst of work, finished just after his visit to Buchan Row. Now, nervousness seized him for minutes at a time so that he became completely preoccupied with some sentence from the talk, trying to get through it in his head, so that he heard and noticed nothing around him. This kind of subdued panic had happened only a couple of times. Mostly he felt apathetic, sick of the furnaces and Moonlow and 1800. He was glad it was Friday and the mill was down so that there was a job on to fill part of his mind.

He told Ray about the spindle change on the mill stand and they went through the responses about why should they bother if it was true about September.

On the mill, Keith joined the eight or nine men round the roughing mill stand. The overhead crane was in position and the two riggers were working with their slings, on the blind side of the stand from the cranedriver in his high cabin. Fitters and mates clutching rags and stilsons clustered around, observing the skill and patience of the riggers' manipulation of the web of oily steel ropes and loads. One rigger was shouting instructions to Emlyn, who was standing well back and signalling to the cranedriver. Keith took Emlyn's place and Emlyn walked over to the stand to spectate and help. In a lull in the cranework, after the old spindles had been taken out, Keith climbed up onto a piece of machinery, a large gearbox, to get a better view of the men working a few dozen yards away, and to make himself more visible to the cranedriver.

This side, the west side of the strip, was choked with machinery, veined with steam and grease pipes and machines passing the drive to the mill and strip rolls. Most of the jumble of cowls and pipes was mantled in a layer of hardened grease, brownish and rubbery, although it was all regularly blasted with steambags. It was the guts of the place and the strip carrying the hot steel on rolling days was like the skin, the bit people saw from the mill floor on the other side of the strip.

He took off his safety glasses for a moment and massaged the bridge of his nose between finger and thumb.

The mill was quiet. The maintenance crew were the only people in sight. Pale spring sun from the skylights washed them in cool light. The knot of men around the darkened end of the mill stand focused on their work, their arms and backs working in obscure struggle. It was a very small patch of movement, like the tiny figures in the foreground of some old painting.

'Keith!'

They reminded him of the time when Emlyn had smashed up a board outside the cabin where Rutter had smashed the windows. He had looked small against the big grass bank.

'Oi!'

The knuckles of his left hand pressed on the page of notes in his pocket, the paper already crumpled and wearing, becoming furry along the edges where it had been folded.

Jack's indifference had helped him to get the work done, and had helped Keith to con himself that the task was a small one. There was no need, after all, to mention Moonlow's motives. There were motiveless things, like that Irish soldier, Rutter smashing the windows. Or if not motiveless as good as. The difference was in the repercussions. In a sense, Moonlow had put him there on the clapped out gearbox watching men struggling with an irrelevant job. It wasn't quite the same industry nor the same valley even, but there was a connection. He remembered the childhood fear of a hand coming from under the bed and grabbing his ankle. He felt unsafe on the machine's slippery back. Moonlow or his descendant might pull him down. The panic eased and as he relaxed he thought that he was worrying about the talk again, getting himself worked up. Greed would do, and anyway he needn't mention motive. The feeling of pointlessness took over again and he thought of the carefully modernised kitchen in Buchan Row, the neat rendering on the fireplace, broken cider bottles, the smell of rotting paper and piss. The face of the election handbill was the skin, advertising the joust for a little power. The pencilled notes were the guts, the machinery, the small dark farms above the treeline, incomprehensible.

Suddenly he felt one of his feet pulled from under him and stuck out his arms to keep his balance. He put on his glasses and looked down at the young machine cleaner.

'Be careful' Keith said. 'I could've broke my bloody neck.'

'I was on'y pulling your leg' the cleaner said. 'What you expect me to do, Sleeping Beauty, kiss you?' He pouted his lips and blew Keith a kiss. Pulling his wool cap forward, he climbed onto the gearbox. 'We can't have you standing here like John fucking Cory's statue when we do want some fucker to direct the crane. Go and help your butty.'

Startled, Keith looked across to the waiting crew. Redfaced, Emlyn motioned him over with his arm.

Keith slid to the ground and said sheepishly, 'It's all a waste of time anyway.'

'Of course it's a waste of bastard time' the machine cleaner said, and he got ready to signal to the cranedriver.

* * *

Perhaps fifteen feet up, a dusty plaque was fixed to the wall. It was a big shield on which was a simplified picture of a finishing mill stand. Through it, cutting the rolls diagonally, was a cartoon yellow lightning bolt. Along the bottom of the shield was a scrolled motto. In the nine or ten years he had been working there, O had glanced up at this no more than four times, and never wondered what the motto, Latin, he assumed, could mean. Beneath it, at eye level, an arrow was chalked pointing to the electricians' shop. Beneath this was chalked:

TO ThePIGGerY

O strolled away from the coiler past these messages and down the strip.

The mill was down and he and Kelv had been given the job of

cleaning the coiler. It was a fair amount of work if you did it properly, as Kelv seemed to like to. O knew, though, that Kelv liked to do the worst bits himself, which made it very easy to work with him. He actually seemed to enjoy crawling under the two coilers to pick up the scraps of chewed sheet steel that somehow collected there, and dragging a steambag through and acting like a hero.

Of course, the job was unnecessary every week, especially now, with the closedown coming. The only useful thing now, O thought, would be to be on production. In the coilpit banding the coils, or on the hilti gun by the transfer boats, or pulpit operator on the slabbing mill. Still, he liked the quiet when the mill was down. There was no steam on the finishing and no cobbled hot slabs to avoid as they were left to cool. No crane sirens going as they dragged cobbled strip metal up the mill to the boneyard, no diving for cover when they got near.

As he passed the roughing he saw some of the maintainers clustered around a stand. On the far side of the strip, a man in a bobble-cap was directing a crane in some delicate job. It whirred and made a loud echoing sort of click when it shut off, the steel winch winding and unwinding as the man directed. Some piece of equipment on the other side of the stand had to be at a very particular height, evidently. The group of men, shadowy on the other side of the mill stand, struggled to angle the load on the cranesling. They reminded O of a television programme he had seen of a calf being born. The farm people had been intent around the back of the cow, focused on it as these men were on the mill stand, and when the two cloven forehooves had appeared they had slung them to a tractor which inched forward to draw the calf.

Kelv had gone to the canteen and would be talking with some of the others. Wayne would be there, which was why O had decided not to go. He wandered on down the strip, seeing it empty, imagining it as Ben and his father had described it and as he himself had seen it, briefly, rolling twenty-four hours a day, making a lot of money, the metal going nose to tail through the stands.

Sully and Jack had been put to work on the squeezer, which pinched the slabs sideways before they went into the roughing stands. It was a squat machine of huge cast steel parts, which crouched over the strip. The process made a lot of metal scale which had to be dug out regularly. As he passed there, O could see their shovels wedged abandoned in the scale and their steambag, shut off but dribbling and twitching a little, hanging over the strip rolls.

He approached quietly and could hear the voices of Sully and Jack. He stepped up onto the squeezer and could see the backs of their heads. Sully fairish and longhaired, Jack dark. They were stupid not wearing helmets as O always did. As far as he could tell they were squatting in a gap in the machinery. They could not be sitting because it would be wet from the bag. The heavy steel parts of the squeezer were running with water. O climbed a little higher so that he could see them better.

'Two o'clock job?' Sully said.

'Yeah' Jack said. 'Whose turn is it? Mine I think. You piss off at two then.'

'You're a gent.'

'I expect Kelv'll want me to do the honours for him and all.'

Sully was smoking nervously, dragging hard on the cigarette so that O could hear the air hissing. If Jack clocked Kelv off that meant he really ought to clock O's card too. About half the day gang would probably leave an hour and a half early that day, with the two o'clock shift.

'You know what Kelv said to me this morning?' Sully said.

'What?'

'He said he's thinking of going down the pit.'

'He's a bloody luny, mun.'

'He's married with a kid.'

'Same thing.'

'The bloke nextdoor to him do work down there. He've been talking to him.'

'I don' think I'd do it' Jack said.

'Fair money see. Better than this place.'

'Would you do it?'

'No fucking fear. I'm a construction worker. As soon as some bastard do start building houses again I'm off.' He paused and there was the hissing sound again, and then he went on: 'Mind, don' tell Kelv I told you. He's on'y thinking of it.'

'How long do he think that'll last then?'

Sully didn't answer. O couldn't tell whether Jack meant that Kelv would go off the idea or the pits would shut.

'He must want to be a fucking working class hero or something' Jack said. 'Remember the song?'

Sully started to sing mutedly, miming the strumming of a guitar. The only words O could pick out – Jack sang them louder than the rest – were: 'You're just a fucking peasant'.

Jack stopped and then said, 'That's my motto.'

Sully paused and said, 'You know you'll have to clock O as well. They're on the coiler together.'

Jack swore.

'He's an odd bugger' Jack said. 'He's very prim and proper, but he don' mind having his fucking card clocked.'

'Can't avoid it in this place, mun. Anyway, it en as if there's a lot to do. Who 'ouldn' take a flyer when the alternative's to sit round in this shitheap?'

They talked on, Sully mildly defending both O and Kelv against what Jack had said. They talked about Kelv's family and the need to have money, and Sully said something about grubnotes.

'Speaking of which' Jack said, 'have you see that Lorraine since?'

'Don' be fucking simple. I wasn' really interested and she wasn' either. I kissed her on the cheek and walked all the fucking way home.' Sully paused. He seemed angry, though the anger was partly put on. 'It was all about you and that other bit of stuff. And I had a row off my missis. Some bastard saw me with Lopissinrraine and told her.'

Sully said he still intended to go ahead, whatever that meant, but that it was all delayed because of their argument.

'And it's all your fucking fault, Priday.'

Jack laughed.

O couldn't understand it. Sully seemed truly upset but could still somehow avoid having a real argument with his friend.

'There you are' Jack said. 'I might not have saved you, but I've got you a reprieve. Think of Kelv. Ten years you might end up down the pit.'

'There's more brains in a frigging blood orange' Sully said as he stubbed out his cigarette in a heap of wet scale. 'Don' you understand? I'm *fond* of the girl.' He stood up and looked at Jack as he said this, bending forward and raising both hands to emphasise the *fond*.

There was a pause.

'Good luck' Jack said quietly.

They both turned and started to climb onto the squeezer towards their shovels. As they saw O, he started and slipped backwards so that he sat on the mill floor, his hard hat slipping over his eyes.

'Aye aye' Sully said. 'A peeping prat. Our secret is out, Jack.'

'You sneaky little twat' Jack said.

O straightened his helmet and stood up. 'I on'y came to see if you was clocking me and Kelv' he said.

Jack had picked up the twitching, dripping steambag. He pointed the nozzle and jerked the valve open. The steam and water mixture flared towards O's legs. He skipped to one side and ran out of range, but from the calves down he was wet and his boots were full of water.

'You flaming rotten pigs' he shouted. 'You bloody rats. You'll have the sack for this.'

Sully and Jack leant against the squeezer, laughing.

O stepped out through a doorless opening in the east side of the mill.

There was a weak sunshine through a film of cloud, but it was cool. He could feel the boilersuit legs and the bottoms of his old trousers inside them clinging already cold around his ankles. His chest felt tight and his eyes stung. It meant that he would have to go to the bathhouse to change into his ordinary shoes, but then he wouldn't be able to crawl about under the coiler. And he didn't want to say anything to Kelv. Sully would be bound to make a story of it though, and then they would all make fun of him and it might happen again.

He walked along the outside of the mill and paused by some of the scale ponds, the deep concrete pits into which loose scale from under the strip was blasted by water under high pressure. The water had been left on though the mill was down, and he could see the place where it swirled into the pond twenty feet or more below. There was no scale visible but he knew that just beneath the surface of the greenbrown water there was the heavy sludge of metal dust and flakes, waiting to be craned out and recycled. When Sully and Jack started shovelling again they would throw the scale between the strip rolls and it would end up in one of the ponds.

He imagined the crane grab smashing through the water and biting up the scale. He imagined the crane loco driver seeing an arm sticking over the edge of the grab as he brought it up. That would teach them to assault him.

The air above the pond was full of dancing moisture and when he turned his head he could see a thin rainbow draped on nothing. He felt very peaceful then and the tightness in his chest eased. For a long time he stood, feeling nothing, until the dim band of colour faded.

He shivered and looked at the sky. Some darker clouds were coming, low and heavy.

He moved quickly towards the bathhouse. Kelv would give him a row if he was much later.

As he changed his boots he decided that he would not phone his mother, as he thought Jack probably wouldn't clock his card for him that day.

* * *

154

'How are you feeling, Carl?'

'Keith.'

'Sorry. Keith. I keep doing that don't I?'

Huw Jones, the physics teacher, rubbed his baleful eyes and drew his hand down his face and his droopy Frank Zappa moustache as if smoothing the wrinkles. He looked tired, but then, striplights always made people's eyes look baggy. He was perhaps forty, brownhaired, thinnish, wore denims and polyvelt shoes that looked too big for him and an upholstered coat that looked as if it might be part of a skiing outfit.

He stretched himself on the old chair of tubular steel, extending his back as if it ached, and, not waiting for Keith to answer, said: 'Christ I'm knackered. It's always the same on Fridays.'

They were sitting in a meeting chamber of what had been the council offices before the Tories reorganised the local authorities. The building, in the middle of the town park, was old and had once belonged to an ironmaster. It was a big room. Keith wondered what it could have been used for in a private house. It had passed into the hands of an aristocratic family whose estate was thirty miles away. They adapted well to industrialisation and even used a corner of the park to build offices, a smithy, and a wheelwrights' shop servicing their iron and coal empire which they acquired piecemeal from the ironmasters who were busily selling off and buying country estates. The aristocrats had never truly lived in the house, and at the beginning of the century it and its grounds were 'given' to the local people. Despite the room having been filled with socialist councillors for many years, a big portrait of one of the family lords still hung over a boarded fireplace. The lord, his upper lip visored in a straight grey moustache which joined his grey sidewhiskers in a carefully shaven right angle, stared blankly through the cracked yellow varnish. Only his head and shirtfront were visible, the rest of him disappearing into the peatcoloured dark of the remainder of the canvas. Keith looked at the dusty moulded plaster ceiling and the dark windows running with rain.

'You know the drill don't you?' Huw Jones said.

Keith had arrived thirty minutes early, had walked round the big hallway with the staircase meant to impress. It was wide enough to lie down on sideways. He had looked at the noticeboard with adverts in felt pen for toddler groups and the photographic club and then had gone into the committee chamber and sat, dripping, on one of the forty or so canvas and tubular steel chairs arranged for the audience.

A middle-aged woman had arrived and sat, sniffing, her handkerchief held folded ready to dab at the droplets. Then Huw Jones, who busied himself for a long time arranging jugs of water and tumblers on the long table in front of the blind fireplace, had sat heavily next to him as the Local History Society faithful began to arrive.

He talked quietly, as if in church.

'There's three speakers' he said. 'I'm MCing, there's the chairman's address, then you, then Professor Prys-Thomas. Old Olly didn' fancy introducing himself as chairman so muggins gets the job. I'll give you a little warm-up and then you do twenty minutes, half an hour. Got a watch? I'll leave mine on the table next to you anyway. I'm between you and Prys-Thomas. Olly's on the other side of him. Should be a nice little evening. He shrugged to indicate that there were no problems, then leant forward so as to see through Keith's glasses, forcing eye contact. 'Okay?' he said.

Keith imagined this was a habit that came from dealing with pouting adolescents, and he became more nervous. His tongue seemed swollen and flabby, his speech slurred. He made some low grunts which he hoped suggested that everything was fine, and shifted the wet yellow plastic shopping bag containing his folder as the rows of seats filled.

At last Huw Jones got up to greet the visiting professor, who had been having tea with Olly Jenkins, the chairman. Keith shook hands with a potbellied man about his own height, with frizzy brown hair, greying, scraped ineffectually over the balding middle. He wore a baggy two piece suit and where his gut strained against his inappropriately smart shirt the links of his string vest showed through. He beamed on everyone through bifocals and had fat cheeks. Keith could imagine him as a schoolboy, tubby and cheeky and enthusiastic.

They moved to the long table and the gathered society members, filling all the seats, became quiet.

Keith, sitting between Jones and Mrs White the treasurer, behind a waterjug and with his back to the blocked fireplace, felt trapped and a fraud. Prys-Thomas had calmly arranged some typed sheets before him and a page or two of handwritten notes, obviously rushed, and was making quiet, smiling exchanges with Olly, who, brylcreemed and rugby club blazered, was going shiny on his balding forehead.

Jones stood up and started to speak. He had taken off his coat and looked very thin. His voice, too, was thin, and the very small piece of paper which he held flapped and then steadied to a rapid flutter as his nerves revved and then throttled back. In the front row, on the other side of the jug, O.G. Morgan sat. No notepad, his arms wrapping his mac tightly to him, the scarred hands hidden under his armpits. He was smiling up at Jones, which, together with the presence of Prys-Thomas, explained the flutter.

And then Olly was on his feet and speaking extempore, repeating 'and on behalf of all of us', his forehead occasionally catching the light. There was some coughing and shuffling that all seemed far away. Behind him, Keith knew, the jaundiced lord was looking over the audience, only his face and shirtfront showing, the rest of the picture disintegrating into the darkness.

And then Jones was talking again. When he saw the paper quivering as before, Keith felt himself beginning to relax.

* * *

'Good luck.'

From the kitchen, Judith heard Jack calling after Keith. The cold air from the open front door found her, and Jack's voice grew fainter as he stepped out into the rain after her husband.

'Eat your heart out, A.J.P. Taylor.'

She heard the door shut and Jack came into the kitchen rubbing his palms as if cold.

'Your husband is a nutcase' he said smiling.

She was glad Keith was gone. Since he had got home just before three he had been odd with nerves, one moment talking almost elatedly, the next abstracted and quiet. She had seen him in the kitchen standing facing the closed backdoor, one hand raised, frozen, perhaps on its way to the doorhandle. She had stood next to him and saw that his eyes were making slight, sharp movements, as if he were reading.

Jack laughed quietly as he slipped some of the dirty dishes past her hip and into the sink.

'What's funny?'

'Sorry. I can't help admiring him. He's bloody mad.'

He made it sound like a compliment.

She swished a cloth round a plate.

You get things dirty and then you clean them. You sleep and then you don't and winter turns messily into – except not quite like in a film because of all the seconds. The crocuses have come and gone and a couple of scraggly daffodils are out and we all go quietly up the wall.

She pulled the plug out.

'Can't you?' she said, and went past him into the livingroom. An angry noise to end the talk.

The anger ebbed in her suddenly. She sat on the settee and looked at the television magazine without seeing it. There was a short silence and then she heard the light click off in the kitchen and Jack came in and sat next to her. He had stood still in the kitchen for a few seconds, registering the snub of his smalltalk, evidently, or letting her know that he registered it, or trying to work out a clever answer.

He looked at her with pursed lips and she looked back at him and then at the page again.

'Anything good on?' he said.

She quickly named the programme, picked up the newspaper and listed the programmes on other channels. Looking up at him as she got near the end she saw the same pursed lips and knew that he wasn't listening.

'You don' want me here do you?' he said.

She was confused suddenly. It was hard to understand how he could be so wrong. Hard to answer too. If she said she didn't want him there it would make it worse and anyway it wasn't true, and if she said she did, he'd think that she meant.

She realised that she was pausing and that he was watching her trying to frame an answer.

'That's an awkward question' she said.

'I thought so' he said, and started to get up.

She put a hand on his arm.

'No wait. I didn' mean it like that.'

He looked at her. As she saw him constructing a meaning on this, her own sense of what she had meant left her.

He sat down again. 'Sorry' he said. 'I thought you were getting irritated with me.'

'Well, irritable, yes. Sorry.'

The confusion receded but she remained tense, as he always was.

'Fancy a game of poker?' he said.

She wondered what he meant for a moment and then remembered his saying something once about her poker face. She laughed uneasily.

'Beginning to see through me are you?' she said.

'I 'ouldn' say that.'

'I think Keith have put me on edge a bit tonight.'

Jack said that he thought it was his own presence that was bothering her and that he was grateful for what she and Keith were doing for him. She felt guilty. Jack's worrying about his effect on them was sort of selfless in a way that made her feel selfish. She thought of the way she wanted to get them out of the house so that she could be on her own. Keith was wrapped in his hobby. She and her husband were the selfish ones.

She told Jack about her worrying about Keith, thinking that she ought to go to the talk.

'I don' think he'd like that' Jack said. 'Make him more selfconscious.'

'I couldn' go anyway. I couldn' sit through it. It would –' how much should she say? '– it would get on my nerves.'

'I got the feeling you weren't too keen on it.'

She switched on the television and, because there were adverts on, turned the sound down before sitting next to him again. All the pretences were going, like the last layers of courtesy from a.

She crooked one leg around on the settee so that she could face him squarely and said, 'I think it's a load of shit.'

He was looking at her leg, doubled with the knee towards him, the sole of her slippered foot resting on the inside of the other knee. She was wearing a loose skirt and no tights. She followed his eyes and felt the hairs on her neck prickle as she saw the down of dark hair on her calf. She rubbed her hand along the shin as if to brush away his stare.

'Oh I don' know.' He looked away. 'I wasn' kidding when I said I admire him. You're a bit harsh I think.'

For a long time they sat without moving, watching the silent television. A double act were going through their patter, two middle-aged men in light suits pausing presumably when the laughs came, looking around at an invisible audience and rehearsing their trademark mannerisms.

She inclined her head towards him and felt that she wanted to lean right over into him, though she didn't. He had leant towards her a little but now she sensed that he was quite still. Obliquely she saw his head begin to turn towards her. She faced him quickly and moved away.

'Shall I turn the sound up?' she said.

* * *

Jack felt sure as soon as she put her hand on his arm.

It was difficult to say 'you don' want me here, do you?' They had never said anything to one another. He'd struggled to say it and hadn't calculated using it as a way of finding out what she thought. It was an unfair question, like all the questions that are worth asking, and though it wasn't calculated, it was revealing.

He had gone to the door with Keith conscious that she pointedly had not and he had gone back to the kitchen to show that he wasn't taking sides.

Crossfire. Invisible, odourless, but paralysing. Worth it for a roof for a while but catch me doing this.

He sat back down, feeling sure.

I read you.

'Fancy a game of poker?'

No pun intended, though the fact intended, lest the fire go out.

And then talking. I thought I was making things difficult for you and Keith – just say if I've overstayed my – I owe you a lot. Hardly hearing himself but fumbling at the truth.

A load of what? Do you hate him? No. I think that too and don't hate him. That fleshway between the knees, the relaxed muscle. The nervous hand over the unshaved lower leg. Christ.

The rain gusted against the windows and she moved away as she saw his head coming. Another punctuation mark, like her leaving the kitchen a bit angry, only this time a different mood.

The burst of truth finished, they sat and watched rubbish on television for a long time.

'No wonder everybody do go out and get pie-eyed on a Friday' he said. Not funny but might lead to something adventurous, like playing a record.

They were sitting closer. Things could not now be as they were before the truth game, the river running only one way.

She smiled at him and tilted her head towards his, the tongue of hair almost licking his cheek. They had slid down on the settee by this time so that although they both had their feet on the ground they were almost lying down. And then the rubbing arms turned into palms sliding over one another. Her hand warmer than his. Washing-up water, he thought, and then their heads were together and they were embracing for a long time, feeling huge relief.

* * *

His hand was cold and sinewy. She felt herself squeezing him as if she wanted to push herself into the space he occupied. The television went on talking and she could hear the wind sometimes. His stubble was a bit harder than Keith's because of the darker hair, she thought, and the bone insistent under taut muscle on the jaw burrowing at her neck.

They were on the floor and lay there for a long time feeling the warmth and laughing sometimes at the bad jokes on the television and shuddering she passed her hands under his shirt along a slim midriff and the belling ribs and the slabs of muscle and the tuft of springy hair on his breastbone.

They were helping each other up like drunks and drunkenly they were opening the door and over her shoulder he clicked on the landing light and the light was falling down the stairwell like a shower. She could see the light glittering on the rain on the frosted frontdoor window and the long window next to it, the curtain not drawn. She went upstairs ahead of him and he had his arms round her waist and near the top step a hand on the inside of her knee and sliding up and then firmly turning her and she sprawled along the stairs and they slid down some steps and she lifted herself a little as he pulled her knickers away though then he didn't touch her, only on the hip, and they slid again.

'This is a bit uncomfortable' she said, too quiet for him to hear, probably, and she pulled herself up and looked over his shoulder down into the darkened hall.

Something pale moved against the black window.

* * *

How did it come to this? We were only mutually interested in the wellbeing of whatsisname. Don't come that with me you bastard, you know perfectly well.

He felt her go tense, suddenly, and, as they were tuned together, he felt his own body stiffen.

'There's somebody at the door' she said.

He slid away from her and tucked his shirt in as a knock came. She stepped astride him where he sat and she rubbed herself on his thighs.

'Relax' she said. 'Relax. Stay where you are. Don' move.'

As the knock came again she went down, pulling her skirt round the right way. She glanced up at him as she reached the door. As she opened it he stared down at her knickers, hanging over the edge of the bottom step.

* * *

A pale face and two white hands she could see through the frosted panel as she opened the door. She could feel the warmth of downstairs after being in the stairway and there was, faintly, the sound of the television and fainter still the aftersmell of the tea she had cooked.

Now, she thought. Murder me. Murder both of us.

She swung the door wide.

His hair plastered with rain and one hand clutching the collar of his blue anorak to his chest, a stranger turned to her. She felt disappointed, relieved. She recognised him then, though she had only seen him occasionally since the schooldays.

'Hello, Rob' she said. 'Good grief. What brings you here?' She felt the cold but still held the door wide, moving slightly to let him get a clear view of the stairs.

* * *

Jack retreated up the stairs backwards a few steps when he saw the caller lean in on the jamb.

He hadn't noticed the. No. Couldn' have.

'Sorry to bother you, Judith' the caller said. 'Is Keith in?'

And Judith was explaining where her husband had gone.

'Hello' the caller said to Jack, catching his eye.

'How be, O' Jack said, looking down from the top step. 'Still wet I see.'

O smiled.

'I'll tell you what it is' he said, turning back to Judith, 'they phoned me up from work. They still had the number because of my father see. I'm the nearest person to you on the phone they do know of. Keith signed a machine off today and he forgot to sign it back on. They're rolling tomorrow. He'll have to go in and sign it back on again. Will you tell him?'

Judith looked at him. Jack, considering her back, guessed her blank expression and thought that she was beautiful.

Get rid of the little twat.

'Righto' Jack called. 'I heard you, O. We'll tell him when he do come in.'

'Well look' O said, 'I'll go down Ty Parc and tell him myself when the talk's finished. He can get straight over on the bus then.'

'Okay' Jack said.

'Thanks, Rob. That's very kind of you' Judith said.

He went, trying to peer up at Jack sitting on the top step as Judith closed the door.

She waited till the shape moved from the frosted glass and then she came back up the stairs. Her hands were cold on his neck and she looked down at him with a smile that turned into a laugh.

* * *

They were drunkenly walking again and without putting the light on they got into bed.

164

They lay still for a long time. So still and in the dark that Judith felt that their bodies seemed to revolve in space. She remembered noticing this as quite a small child, that if you lay still in bed in the dark you could make your body seem to spin any way you wanted and she had forgotten all of this and now she remembered.

She moved her hands over him and he was all bone and small packed groups of muscles. She could feel the sets of muscles in his lips working as they moved slowly on her face. She felt his elbows and hips, squeezed his thigh between hers and she could feel him, too, nervously exploring.

* * *

Like a child, Jack thought. The detached way they examine something new without maps, without assumptions, memories, and completely absorbed. The smoothness and that subtle upholstery of unmuscular flesh. You are gorgeous.

* * *

She became aware of their breathing coming into one rhythm. He was lighter than Keith. Didn' breathe with his mouth open so much.

Now.

* * *

Liz.

Not yet. The pause before the bite is the best taste.

Not so full in the hips as. Not relevant. That's history, or her story.

He slipped into her slowly. Moist and muscular she drew him in. They stayed still for a long time.

No more sweaty thrashes. This is the only. Careful you'll make me.

How can you keep so quiet when.

She held herself to him and away and heard herself laughing and they slid round and the duvet slid to the floor and she almost couldn't keep on him because of coming.

Stupid bloody Friday man you've been a naughty girl you've.

Eggman.

* * *

Home.

* * *

Professor Prys-Thomas took the piece of stiff white card and looked at it through the lower lenses of his bifocals. Keith watched his eyes reading the closely pencilled notes. The Professor was smiling a slight, polite smile amid the groups of smalltalkers remaining in the large room.

'Thanks, Keith. Well done' Huw Jones said, touching Keith's elbow, and he moved away quickly to talk to a hovering committee member.

Keith had started his talk quite confidently. He had decided to be simple and factual. Jones had wanted the perspective of the ordinary working man or something and, partly resisting that, Keith had read lists of statistics and given details of accounts to the last farthing. He was put off when Emlyn stepped in late at the back of the room, and touched by his turning up. The door creaked loudly and heads turned in the back rows. Keith stopped midsentence and then picked up again in the wrong place, realised his mistake and tried to go back, felt his face burning and finally cut a whole section of his talk. He got nervously through to the end and there was polite applause.

As he sat down he saw Emlyn smiling and raising his hands to show he was clapping. Keith pulled off his glasses. This is nothing to do with me, he thought. This is somebody else.

The Professor's talk mostly passed him unnoticed. Not hearing the words, Keith listened to the way he balanced his sentences, spoke quietly, paused in the right places for the laughs his dry humour elicited. His accent was sometimes middle class English but would occasionally swoop into a string of Welsh vowels.

Gradually the shape of the talk seeped through to Keith as he came out of his daze. Prys-Thomas said that the town – our town, he said – was on many frontiers. And he worked through a series of points that developed this: the frontier of rural and industrial; the frontier of farmland and desert; the frontier of moorland and dense forest, and others he produced almost casually, huge ideas. And there was anecdote and detail. Keith could see Jones leaning forward, elbows on table, his hands meshed with only the index fingers pointing forwards, pressed together. He nodded from time to time, signalling alertness. Once he glanced nervously at Keith, and Keith knew that he was thinking that it had been a mistake to put an amateur and a professional on the same platform.

And after, the smalltalking knots of people. Morgan shook his hand. Olly slipped off to the rugby club where Prys-Thomas, accompanied by Huw Jones and Mrs White, would meet him.

'An interesting talk you gave' Keith said to Prys-Thomas.

The Professor smiled his wide smile, the bifocals down on the end of his nose.

'Nothing compared to your scholarship.' His voice was quiet and reasonable. 'You amassed a prodigious amount of detail. I was most impressed by that.'

Keith was pleased, though he felt the tinge of irony. Encouraged, he talked and produced from his yellow plastic bag the brownmottled election handbill.

'You found this locally?' The irony was gone.

Keith told him where he'd found the card.

'My grandmother used to live in Buchan Row' Prys-Thomas said. 'You know what these are don't you? They're notes for a lay-sermon or a discussion at a chapel meeting. See the subheadings: *Dinistr y Deml* – the Destruction of the Temple; *Dinistr Jerusalem* – the Destruction of Jerusalem; and here, *Diwedd y Byd* – the End of the World. Powerful stuff.'

And there was no mockery in his voice. Keith felt that Prys-Thomas was even a little moved by the pencil marks.

Huge ideas, though in a religious mode. It was like a parallel universe in science fiction, Keith thought, though for real, and too complex to find words for, and in another language.

Prys-Thomas quietly handed back the card and was led away by Jones. Keith made his excuses. He would not feel comfortable with Olly and Jones in the bar, smarming around a captive celebrity. He heard Prys-Thomas's voice as they went: '– you see the Welsh consciousness was only partly affected by industrialisation. Town-dwelling, clearly defined working hours and so on were only partly accepted, so we have this extraordinary map in the south of overlapping communities, amazingly heterogeneous which aren't cohesive really, aren't urban quite, but which certainly aren't –'

In the hallway at the foot of the wide stairs on the chessboard tiles, Keith saw O, sniffing and dripping. He dripped hesitantly towards Keith. One whitened hand held the collar of his anorak tight to his neck.

'Hiya butt' Keith said. 'I didn' see you in there.'

'What? Oh no.' O looked a message at Keith, as if he were finding words. Just then a group of people passed through the hallway, pulling on their coats. Keith could see O watching them over his shoulder. O looked down and made as if to speak again. As soon as he said 'roughing mill stand' Keith moved to the door. The stand. There was always something. He couldn't understand why O had such difficulty telling him. He cursed and called a thanks over his shoulder as he stepped out.

On the steps, Emlyn was talking to O.G. Morgan. Em stopped as soon as he saw Keith and came to him.

'I was coming down to the TA for a pint' Em said by way of explanation or apology. 'I thought, damn me, it en far, I thought, I'll pop down the Park and see the boy.'

Keith explained that he had to rush. They walked quickly to the gates that opened into the town. He would just make the half past nine bus that took the nightshift in.

At the door of the Trenewydd Arms he paused to say goodnight to Em.

'That Prys-Thomas bloke's a clever chap.' Em fingered his cap. 'A bit showy with it mind. Hey, and let me tell you this now.' He pointed a finger at Keith. 'Your talk was your talk was b-bloody good.'

Keith went on to the bus stop, not caring about having to go into work. He felt relief and disappointment. He wasn't sure whether it was Em's praise that made him happy, or the picture of himself and Jack pissed on the museum steps, which had so relaxed him earlier when it came into his mind as Jones had introduced him.

ELEVEN

As he walked down the white hill there was the smell first of beer blown from the bar of the Ram by an extractor fan and then of bread baking that made his mouth wet and then he strode immaculate in a suit across the crossroads, past Monnigan's and Mrs Rees's and Mrs Rees in a paisley pinny on the doorstep watched him stride. The door opened on its own and there should have been a fanfare. Home. Keith stood in the passageway, smoking a Woodbine. Behind him was a woman whom he did not recognise standing a little way back. Keith came forward smiling to greet him. Then Keith seemed to sink and his smile disappeared. Jack, in his immaculate suit, looked down and saw that Keith's body was sinking over his legs, the thighs telescoping up into the ribcage, as if he was deflating. Keith's head lolled forward, the flesh of his face gone white and slack, and his hands and forearms settled on the lino as he collapsed.

The red numbers seared like pain through this and Jack became aware of the stiffness of his arm crooked under his head. He could not move and he felt horror and confusion as he stared down at the punctured corpse and across at the numbers.

He managed to lift his head and came fully awake.

Judith lay between him and the red digits of the clock like a long ridge. He moved his stiffened arm down and sighed relief. On his back he felt the comfort of the bed and he felt the horror ebb.

'Are you awake?' Judith said. Her voice was half asleep.

'I dreamt I went home' he said.

She turned and cwtshed to him. She was warm and sleeprelaxed. At first he pressed to her gratefully, then more urgently.

Three-twenty the red numbers said.

Keith was on nights and it was the last of his nightshifts for a while. They were careful. Most days Jack was working and when Keith was afternoons someone might call. Jack made a habit of going out then and Judith often asked her parents round or went to see Beryl or some other neighbour. He thought back over all the weeks and months, the lost time.

'That's a nice dream' she said.

'It was a nightmare. It was all mixed up.'

In the warm nest of the bed he half dreamt snow winding a blanket over the world. Thoughtsnow not really cold, remote outside through the tinted panes of his arctic goggles. They put you in bed with their wives, the Eskimo. Injured but not really injured taken in by these simple folk on his epic trek taking civilised shares in the iceman's Nanook hence nooky while the max factor snow collects in layers and drifts on his sledtracks.

Like a kid's fantasy this. Not since. Like the first time with Judith the exploring like children receptive and unprejudiced and the fantasy unbidden like thoughtplay foreplay. A child will start by loving mud for mudness and then a cardboard box is a cave, a palace. Why, through the furnace goggles, snow, though?

It didn't matter. He kissed her and went to sleep.

* * *

Jack came toadying to O after the business with the steambag, but O knew what he wanted. Jack looked at him thoughtfully at the beginning of one day, and, later, on the slabbing mill, picked a quiet moment, turned to O with one hand resting on a girder and the other holding his sweeping brush. He looked into O's face then away and then back.

'O' he said, 'about that business with' – O felt himself react to the words, stiffening – 'with the steambag the other day. Sorry about that. It was on'y a bit of fun. I didn' mean to catch you with it. A' right?'

Still wet I see. O knew what he wanted.

O just walked away and carried on sweeping up. It was something his mother used to tell him when he was in school. Just walk away. It worked, evidently. Jack seemed impatient with him after that and would keep out of his way.

One day at the end of April, O took stock of himself, alone in the bathhouse after the waiting ritual.

The patches sewn over the fraying boilersuit cuffs were dirty and loose. On the toe of one boot the oilsodden leather was kicked away, revealing the pure steel toecap like a skull through opened flesh. In his pockets he had an old pair of rag gloves which he would reuse so that he could take a new pair home for his mother for knocking the coal up, and his corned beef sandwiches in a Sunblest bag that had lasted three weeks. It might be possible to make it last to the end. He would buy a new pair of boots in work because they were good value, though he would try not to use them in work. He looked at the cuffs and considered. It was hard to tell whether it would be worth having them repaired once more. He would decide later. He would get some works carbolic soap to take home, and another pair of the bathhouse cork sandals. He would see if he could get one of the burners to cut a new bakestone for his mother out of scrap. Oh yes. And he would catch a rat.

* * *

It had been cold in the night although it was the end of April and light snow had fallen on the mountains. It had thawed quickly with the first daylight.

Keith unbuttoned his coat, pushed back the hood and pulled the collar away from his neck as he made his way round the Grib Pond. The water dimpled with the gusting wind and the sky was crowded with fat, fastmoving clouds, but it was still mild.

On a bank above the stone breastwork that edged one side of the pond he looked west and northward. The fat clouds thronged over the horizon and he could see the old view, ridge after ridge, distantly the tip of the big open cast above Merthyr. Nearer to him was the mound of Garn y Gors, below that, the mountain road, and, a few hundred yards away, on the north shore of the pond, the cemeteries. To the south west, an empty cwm, farmed lower down, ran away to join the neighbouring valley, gouged out by the split ends of a glacier in another age. If you turned full circle here you could see only two buildings. One was a ruined farmhouse, the other a small house that stood in the tip of the cwm, just below the curve of the mountain road. You could hear no traffic, even when a bus crawled on the road beneath the Garn.

He shut his eyes and tipped back his head, feeling the mild air flow round him.

Like having a shower.

He opened his eyes. There were clouds. And when he looked down again, there, across a few dozen yards of coarse grass, was the cholera cemetery he had come to see.

It was small and some distance from the other, later mountain cemeteries. The fence and gate were mostly flattened and there were no bushes or flowers. The headstones were mostly broken or laid flat, or hanging at angles.

He had played there as a child, taken Anne there once, courting, and walked there many times since. As he approached, he laid a hand on a fencepost.

The uprights were simply lengths of rail that were pierced in two places to take the one-inch iron rods that made the barrier. The iron was rustpitted, the rods bowed and broken in many places. Would the rollermen in the ironworks have been paid for these rods? He imagined the tongs drawing the iron through the rolls. An act of piety, perhaps, for the dead, for their wives and children, other ironworkers and the colliers they probably looked down on, the fence made of the stuff that had brought them all there in the first place.

He knelt at one lichensplotched stone, still standing, and traced the cut letters with a finger.

ER COF AM
John Williams
o'r lle hwn
Yr hwn a fu farw 18fed Medi 1849
yn 19 mlwydd oed

And there was more lower down, indistinct and lipped over by the wet yellow turf.

Nineteen. That must have been his age. Medi, then. The month. Must be. John. What would they have called him? Sion, wasn't it?

He walked on a few paces. The ground was rutted with settled graves, which were very close together. The next stone was wide, not such a dark grey as John's. Benjamin Davies. A man in his thirties. 7fed Mawrth 1850. How soon after John? Keith imagined John small and dark with curly hair. At nineteen, already working for nine or ten years. Ben was a larger man, looked older than his age.

Nearby was a large stone in English. Anne Butcher who departed this life 13th February 1850 aged 18 years and a verse:

Farewell my mother and sisters all
I must obey my maker's call
But you again I soon shall see
Prepare in time to follow me.

Eighteen. West country of England? Her family hard up, hearing talk of work.

Anne.

He walked beyond the cemetery to a familiar small hollow. How many times there with Anne? Two perhaps. He lay down just within the rim of the hollow, taking care that his coat and hood protected him from the sodden peat turves. He could feel no breeze there, though he could hear it sighing over the mouth of the depression and could see the clouds charging. Twice probably. Seems more. Memory exaggerates. Usually into the pines on the other side of the valley. And once a man with a dog. He couldn't imagine himself having sex outside now.

He imagined John and Anne meeting on the mountain. It would have been much as he saw it now. Some sort of track where the road was. No cemeteries of course. Slipping into the hollow, out of the wind. Talking each in their own language. He saw them foreplaying and at the same time saw the clouds. Jack's back and Anne's face half showing over his shoulder. He realised with a small shock that the John he imagined was Jack Priday with his hair curled.

If anything, the tension between Jack and Jude had got worse. Keith heard them sometimes making stilted conversation. He thought this was to please him. Privately, Jude had gone through a phase of being remote with Keith. He noticed this after his talk, in the days when he had no preoccupations. Then she had been loving and clinging. The last time they had made love she had tried to talk.

'Did you know Maudie Thomas is dead?' she said. She whispered. She'd refused him once because she was afraid Jack in the next bedroom would hear them.

'Who?'

The red glow from the clock just showed her face and he could see her looking wide-eyed, as if the question mattered.

'You know. Maudie from the bungalow just by the estate.'

She told him about Maudie's suicide. He half followed. He remembered the husband, who used to be a surface worker with NCB, had worked with Keith's father underground years before, before Keith was born.

'I think she did it to put him out of his misery' Jude said.

Keith didn't understand this, but said nothing.

'Do you think we ought to have children?' she said suddenly.

He couldn't understand where the question came from.

'I don' know' he said. 'We've already adopted one by the look of it. Not till I'm sure I've got another job. We can't have one of them *and* central heating. Do you want one?'

She was quiet for seconds.

'No' she said at last.

The questions irritated him. They made him feel that he was complacent.

'What would you do if I – popped off?' she said.

'What? Died?'

She said nothing.

'I don' know. What a terrible question. You want to know if I'd pop off after you like Mr Thomas.'

She clung to him. She was muscular and tense. At first he thought that she was crying but when he moved to feel her face it was dry.

Dirty conditions wasn't it? Polluted water and no sewers. He thought of the two teenagers and Benjamin Davies spewing and suffering uncontrollable diarrhoea, becoming sweaty, deflated corpses.

His back began to feel damp. Getting up, he twisted to look inside the back of his coat. The dark wet from the peaty ground was seeping through.

* * *

Mountains drenched in melted April snow.

She had stood at the bedroom window as Keith came home off his last nightshift for a while, watched him lift the latch on the gate as Jack went out not looking back but knowing she would be watching at the corner of the curtain. This while the sprinkled snow still lay and the sun marbled first light through the clouds.

Keith came to bed cool and smelling of work, breathing heavily flumped in beside her and she took his glasses off because he forgot and cwtshed him, still tingling from Jack.

While he slept that morning she went shopping and saw Beryl and Bron, whose son was now in prison. They sat in the cafe and talked about anything but Bron's son, though Judith felt the prison under everything they said. She couldn't help feeling lightheaded, though, thinking of the cafe where Jack had spent every schoolday for a whole year before the school wrote to his father. She imagined him as he'd been then, twitching tensely at the flipper machine.

In the afternoon, from the livingroom window, she looked at the drenched mountains and felt elated. The cloud was high and the air seemed full of colour. She could see below in the valley a flight of starlings catching the light when they turned.

She watched Jack coming home from work, coming up the street with his plastic grub box. When he realised Keith was out he approached her shyly and they necked like adolescents, standing in the kitchen. He smelled of work but was not noisy in his breathing. She put her hands to the sides of his face and felt the clamped jaw slacken.

'Relax' she said.

* * *

When Keith came into the kitchen Jack and Jude were standing close together by the livingroom door. They were talking. She looked up as he came in, flicking a strand of hair from her face. She was still talking quietly and her face was blank as she looked at him. Jack looked round, stepping away from Jude as he did so.

'Hello, Keith' he said. 'Had a good walk?'

He hauled his damp coat off. 'Okay.'

'Where'd you go?'

'Up the pond. Had a look at the cholera graves.'

'You're a morbid bugger, Watkins.'

'No' Keith said. 'It en morbid.' He heard himself sounding irritated and was surprised.

Jack pulled a face as he saw that he'd got a reaction. 'Oh come on, Keith boy. I bet you do love a bit of scab picking, standing by the weathered stones with a glinting drop of glycerine on your cheek.'

He put his arm round Keith and struck an heroic pose like a soviet poster. Keith shrank away.

'Roddy McDowall—' Jack said. He squinted.

'What are you doing?' Jude said.

'Trying to look misty eyed. Roddy McDowall singing *Men of Harlech* on his way to the colliery nextdoor to his eight bedroomed back to back terraced slum with a twenty-foot livingroom at the age of eighteen months to work a twenty-five hour shift in a three inch seam with one two minute break to wash the dust out of his eyes with a thimble of dirty water.'

Keith groaned and broke away, went into the livingroom closely followed by Jude and Jack, who was still talking. Jack had been building up this act for a few weeks.

'Up comes Donald Crisp and Dai Bando on a tandem' Jack said. He slipped his arm round Keith's shoulder again and held Jude under his other arm. ' "Look you boy bach" says blind Dai. "There's been an explosion up at the pit. Hurry you along now begorrah." Roddy leaps on the crossbar. They pedal and reach the scene. Young women in shawls wring their hands. Old women in shawls wail and gnash their gums. Robert Donat bandages Paul Robeson's arm. "Ianto Full Pelt it is" cries lovely Blodwen wringing her shawl. "Stuck he is in the big hole he is look you. Too small is the passage mark you for the big guys." Roddy whips off his bikeclips, dives down the pit, runs down the smokefilled tunnels past sweating men, crawls through a two inch pipe. There's Ianto! Roddy clears the seven tons of rubble from Ianto's forehead. "Are you all right?" he cries. "I guess so" says Ianto. Roddy puts him on his back, runs the thirteen miles to the shaft, swarms up the frayed rope that once hauled the bond and gives Ianto to Robert Donat who has been smiling fondly at Greer Garson. The women throw their shawls and teeth in the air. Dai Bando throws his glass eye in the air. Donald throws his crisps in the air. Everybody cheers. Roddy is carried shoulder high round the little forty yard wide cobbled street. Close-up on Roddy. There is a smear of max factor coal on his face and on his Joseph Cotten shirt but his teeth flash and his eyes shine. Dissolve to the flaking gravestones and the lonely figure with glycerine on his cheek. There's cry will our Mam.'

He stopped and looked at Keith.

'Poignant en it?' Jack said. 'Meanwhile, back in 1977 –' he pressed Keith's shoulder '– tighthead –' he pressed Judith's shoulder '– loosehead. Guess who's the hooker.'

TWELVE

They moved out of the lighted part of the cellars and the pale beam from Lew Hamer's torch flickered across a wet concrete floor oozed over with slime as they walked. He stopped and pointed the torch straight up saying that there ought to be lights in this part somewhere. Jack and Kelv, carrying shovels, followed him.

'Is this where it happened?' Kelv said.

Lew Hamer said nothing but led them further. They came to an opening where some sickly light showed. Jack could see in the lighted place a wall thick with dark pipework. They stepped into a kind of long narrow corridor. The wall of pipes made one side, and the other side was slotted with narrow gaps at intervals like the one they'd just come through. A cable was strung along the wall above their heads and a few bare lightbulbs hung from it. Their weak light seemed bloomed with the dark. The concrete floor, puddled with water here and there, met a deep gutter at the pipe-side and metal plates like sewer inspection covers, but cambered over the gutter, filled the small width of the corridor in places.

'Here' Lew Hamer said. 'We'm under part of the reheating furnaces. These are cooling pipes. Down that end there's a passage that do come out on the other side of the strip.'

'He was taking a shortcut then?' Kelv said.

'Aye. That's what they do reckon. He come up this gully towards us by here and – 'Lew stamped on one of the metal plates '– this one. This cover wa'n' on. There was a narrower cover. The wrong size. His boots must have been a bit slippery and the metal went from under him. He went in by there.'

He pointed to a gap at one side of the cover. Jack could see the surface of a dark liquid.

'How deep is it?' Kelv said.

'I don' know. He went in up to his waist. And it was boiling, which it shouldn' have bastard been.'

Jack felt his stomach tensing, his toes curling inside his boots.

'It's a wonder they found him' Kelv said.

'They fucking didn't. He got out, went the way we came in, got up all them flights of steps and got to a phone before he passed out. Fuck knows how he managed in that state, mind.'

Lew pushed back his cap and led them into the dark place they had passed through moments before. He played the torch over the floor again. A mixture of mud and metal scale had oozed into the space, making a thin, wet layer underfoot.

'The safety officer's coming round this morning' Lew said. 'Give it a good tidy up where he's going to walk through. There's a nice gap over in that corner where you can chuck the spoil. If you do finish you can chip some of the hardened grease off the steps on the way back up. That's a fucking hazard and all. We don' want him going arse over bastard tip before he do get here. I'll see if there's some overtime in it if you like.' He winked and walked away whistling.

'Jesus. Can you imagine that?' Kelv said as they worked.

Jack could see him dimly in the little light from the two openings. The floor was harder to see and they worked by scraping the shovelblades across it, having to judge mainly by touch if they were effective.

'One thing's for certain' Kelv said. 'No fucking flyers for us today.'

Jack asked how this could be. After all, it would be easy for one of them to walk out at two as usual.

Besides, he's afternoons. A bit more time. Perhaps she'll.

'No fucking fear' Kelv said. He jabbed a gloved finger to the lighted corridor. 'That poor bastard in the serious burns unit was down here on his own. He'd no right to be. You're only supposed to come down in pairs, you know. I'm not fucking off and having the blame for you fucking broiling yourself.' The dim light made points in his dark eyes as he stared at Jack.

'Okay' Jack said, bending to his shovel. 'You're the sheriff.'

The time wasted. The time wasted when you sit in buses or wait in a queue. All your life nearly. One third sleeping, one third working, and one third standing in queues, at traffic lights, watching advertisements, washing dishes, digging exhausted earth. She can sit and stare at a wall and not worry about not doing anything.

The metal sludge glimmered as he turned the shovel.

That's the place to be. A fixity, a stillness like the space above an altar. Like a science fiction story. On another limb of the galaxy in a small solar system on a cold planet in a remote cave in an ancient chamber is the mystical prism that makes and explains the coherence of everything. It bathes the finder in its perfected silence. Still and silent and not waiting for anything, like Judith staring at a wall.

Jack stared at the dark, at Kelv slowly pushing back the ooze with his shovel.

Christ, Kelv. Let me go at two to my devotions, away from.

He felt his toes curl again. He saw dimly the dark liquid closing towards his boots like a curtain slowly being drawn as he tried to scrape it back.

He thought of what he had seen on the bus home the previous afternoon, or thought he had.

'Saw a funny thing on the bus yesterday' he said, making words to hold out the silence. A funny thing happened on the way to the. He told Kelv.

The hot mill bus, half full, was waiting in the bus station. The men sat with their grub boxes or plastic bags on their knees. Sully sat next to a man who worked in the roll shop and they were talking quietly. Jack sat next to Wayne. O was further down the bus sitting on his own, unmoving. Through the window, Jack could see, a few bays away, another waiting bus, almost empty. There were two middle-aged women near the front, talking, and halfway along the bus, a man in a cap and mac. Jack rubbed his eyes and breathed deep. The murmur of Sully's talk made him feel sleepy.

When he looked out again, the man in the cap had slipped down a little in his seat and was rolling his head from side to side. His hands moved on his chest and collar and his mouth was open. The movement of the head became quicker and the cap was dislodged, as the man slid down, against the chrome bar along the backrest. This was far away and silent through layers of glass.

Jack tensed and looked around. Sully and the man from the roll shop still talked quietly. Further down, O was unmoving. The conductor and driver had climbed in. The engine was started and left to idle, making a gravelly throb. Jack looked out at the dying man again. A third bus, empty, had slid into one of the intervening bays. Jack leant back and could still see the man, who was clawing the air. One of the women had got up and was approaching him hesitantly, a hand to her mouth. The scene slid past the window as if it were on a slowmoving river. Jack's bus had reversed out and was passing along the backs of the two parked buses. He skewed in his seat to see through the other windows. The back of the dying man's bus was almost opaque with dirt. Briefly, there was an impression of movement through the grime. Two hunched figures and a hand extended. It all slid away around a corner of the shopping centre building.

'What's up?' Wayne said, when he saw Jack turning.

'There was a bloke' Jack said. 'He was having a fit or something. On that bus.'

Wayne turned his head slightly, a token of looking the way Jack was pointing.

'Christ' Wayne said.

'Poor old bastard' Kelv said, still working slowly. 'I'll tell you something. I think I'd rather fall in that boiling sump than go that way.'

If the man was dead it was something new to Jack. Twenty-seven and never seen anybody dead. There's innocence. Not even your own.

He shuddered.

'My Christ' he said. 'Let's talk about something else.'

Like the prismed ice chamber exploring every cranny of Nanook while the world turned in its ice blanket. After the last time, her standing at the wardrobe mirror and her back dimpled on the shoulderblades and above the buttocks. When she lifted her chin the tongue of hair lowered like a curtain on her back. He's afternoons. Judith, this time please, no caution.

* * *

There was a big gap around the place where the pipe entered the wall. A passing fitter who had been eating a toasted bacon sandwich from the canteen had discarded the crusts and the strip of sour grey rind nearby.

O picked up the rind, and, after some thought, one of the sticks of crust, and placed them as offerings near the hole. He moved away and squatted on his haunches, watching the place where he had seen the grey worm disappear.

The mill was rolling, but infrequently, and there were few men about the mill floor. O had used this maze of derelict cabins near the roughing stands as a place for hiding shovels and brushes. It was ideal, too, for ten minutes' quiet.

His shovel was beside him and as he watched the offering, he rested his hand on the place where the haft entered the bladesocket.

After some steel went through the mill outside there was a long silence. He became aware of small sounds. A rustle of paper which came fitfully, a scrutting like a spoon scraped on a saucepan. A pointed snout and a small pink paw startlingly like a human hand appeared in the gap and then went.

O's hand tightened on the haft.

The snout came back, shifting restlessly from side to side. The head appeared and it poured out of the gap, the dark body flowing after it, then the long grey worm.

The rat, with its odd mixture of twitching and smooth movements, explored the food.

O slowly lifted the shovel to his knee and froze.

The rat shifted around the food, stopped occasionally, then came back to the rind, put a pink hand on it, tentatively tried its teeth on it, then shifted to the bread, performing the same actions. Its eyes were bright black and bulged round as wimberries. The fur of the head was exact and clean.

The rat froze with its snout upwards, staring straight at him, sniffing the air. One paw was raised above the crust.

O crouched, one hand holding the shovel up. He was too far away. It would be gone before he could bring the blade down.

The rat half gnawed the crust and patrolled the area again.

Slowly, O leant forward, raising the shovel.

The rat paused again, straddling the bread, its nose dipping and rising towards O.

He brought down the blade as hard as he could.

* * *

Keith sat with his feet tucked up on the bench. It was a good cabin for some peace and quiet, even now the weather was becoming mild. He stared out through the metal frame of the broken window at the bank and the strip of sky.

It was early in the afternoon shift and the mill hadn't finished rolling, but they weren't doing a lot that day. Mostly there was silence except for the hiss from the leaking steampipe outside. The riggers and machine cleaners had gone to their own cabins with crosswords and mugs of tea. The fitters hadn't arrived.

Keith fingered in his pocket the key to the padlock.

Some of the men had been offered jobs in English steel plants. Not the mates and labourers though. The day before, on days, Em had been called into the manager's office to talk about early retirement. You had to be sixty-two to get it and Emlyn would still be too young in September. Aldrich, the manager, had suggested that he should try for a job in the safe, light end of the works, in the cold mill or the new tinning lines, to keep him going till he qualified. 'Qualified' Em had repeated, as if the word cut him. But it was a generous suggestion and he had gone home unsettled but thoughtful.

Keith went into the maintenance shop. As usual it was littered with greasesmeared rags after the previous shift. One of the smirched striplights buzzed and fluttered.

He went to the ramshackle row of works-made lockers and undid the padlock on A Rota's cupboard. Pushing aside the machine cleaners' tin jack of paraffin and their wire brushes, he pulled out two clean mugs, a small teapot, the caddy and sugar.

The tea making ritual.

He placed the cups and the sugar on the cabin table. Spooned tea into the pot. Replaced the caddy in the locker. Walked slowly to the hot water urn in the shop, pot in one hand, lid in the other.

The foreman-fitter walked across the shop on his way to his office.

'Fuck me' he said, catching sight of Keith. 'It's good to see somebody carrying on the essential work of British industry.'

Keith looked at himself, his toe 'tector boots, his greasy boilersuit with a rag sticking out of one pocket, his safety glasses with folding side-panels, and the parts of the dented metal teapot in either hand. He remembered Jack approaching him stripped in the bathhouse. Are you a Man of Steel? Jack had said. His face had loomed towards him, blurred because he had no glasses on and through the veil of water.

The foreman had gone. Keith filled the pot at the urn and went back to the cold cabin.

He waited with the two mugs, the spoon, the sugar and the steaming-spouted teapot. Em would bring milk in an old medicine bottle in his grub box, and his glasses and a paper to do the crossword.

Afternoons were the worst. He looked out through the broken window.

Shut it before it do fall down.

A long time seemed to pass, although it could not be very long. He took off his glasses and his eyes unfocused onto a point in space so that the teapot and the mugs blurred.

Are you a.

He wondered if there were jobs going for mates in the cold mill or on the tinning lines. Or any jobs. They had been standing close together that time and talking quietly and she had flicked a strand of hair, looked blank. He thought of the penny token. However hard you stared, it yielded nothing.

Distantly he heard steel passing through the mill. A metal skin, and here, the innards, purged and collapsed after furious diseases. The lives in shadows away from the glow. The peatcoloured liquid in the dented pot. Or the dampsplotched card printed with the surface goings on of a place, and on the obverse, in the guts, soft tissue preserved like some bog sacrifice, the softpencilled loops and strokes.

When the foreman rapped on the doorjamb Keith felt his own face smiling. Pleased with his thoughts. The man could have been standing there for minutes, looking at his blank, grinning face. Keith wiped the smile and sat forward, feeling caught out.

'Phone message' the foreman said. He was a sleepyeyed man who kept a smallholding on the mountain. He had a stub of pencil over one ear and carried a slip of paper. 'From your butty.'

Keith put on his safety glasses and looked down at the two empty mugs.

* * *

Judith stood before the wardrobe mirror and looked at herself: the too fat thighs and the wedge of dark hair; the bump below her navel where the womb was; the breasts which pleased her – lovely boobs, Jack had said, which she thought restrained of him – and her face, which, when she held her hair back as she did now, seemed to her a little too full in the cheeks. She released her hair and lifted her chin, looking for signs of a dewlap.

Beside her own image, she could see the reflection of Jack sprawled on the bed, watching her back. His head was to one side against the headboard, his knees spread and the partly flaccid penis flopped back against his belly, the brown line showing on its underside. Smaller and hairier than.

She caught his eye in the mirror and turned, slid back onto him.

'You ought to open the curtains' he said. 'Show everybody.'

'You mean that?'

'Why not? Why don' we go and stand in the garden and wait for the ten past nine bus to go past?'

She put a hand to the slack side of his face, felt how the jaw was loose. She pulled the cover over them and they clung together.

'Did you have a house in Accrington?' she said.

He paused for a long time and then said it had been a flat.

'Furnished?'

'Some. We bought some stuff.'

We. She said nothing but sensed that he felt her noting the word. She imagined sparse old furniture. A carpet not fitted, the bought things not quite suiting the rest, dirty curtains fifteen years out of date.

'Was it comfortable?'

'Not as comfortable as this.'

She felt that she was cruel to him, like hypnotising him into thinking he was on an upholstered chair when he was sitting on a packing case.

'Is it true about the closedown?' she said.

'It do look like it.'

'What will we do in September?'

We. She sensed him noting the word.

'Or you' she said.

'Don' know.'

There was quiet for a while and she felt his fingers tugging at the fine hair on her nipple.

188

'Do you think' she said, 'we ought to tell him?'

The tugging continued for a few moments and then he rolled away from her.

'I don' know.'

Because if we tell him it will be *we*. Or am I, she thought, just a nice fuck? Well you are, anyway, so perhaps I ought to be grateful. But no, that would mean afterwards either guilt or being brazen. What she felt was freshness, like swimming, or seeing the mountain suddenly green through snow. Love would justify anything, except its own denial, which meant that if they were cleansed by their feelings, they would have to come clean with Keith. If it was love that would make all the difference.

The ten past nine service bus growled past outside. She got up quickly and standing by the window, yanked the curtains open. He rugby-tackled her back onto the bed so that she could not have been visible for more than a second.

'You wicked bugger' he said. They laughed.

'There you are' she said. 'To you I'm just a good lay. Your private supply.'

'Not true. Anyway, I haven' got you to myself, have I?'

She stretched her arms and legs out on the bed, thought of swimming.

'What do you think of when we're together?' she said.

'Nothing' he said. Then, sheepishly, 'sometimes I think of a cold place. All ice, and then inside it, like in a cave, a place that's just warm enough, and absolutely calm, and everything is clear. That's what I think of sometimes.'

He paused and looked appalled at his own words, as if they were too vulnerable to have been spoken, or as if he wasn't sure that he meant them.

'Shit' he said. 'What do you think?'

'Think of you?'

'No. Think of when we're together.'

She hesitated.

'Nothing really' she said. 'Swimming sometimes. Sometimes I think I love you.' She looked away, ashamed.

He cwtshed to her and they went into a sleepy torpor. He had forgotten, she thought, what she'd said about telling Keith. The furry haze of love feelings that warmed her like cushions only confused her and she dozed.

She jumped when she saw the red figures winking 10.30 and tried to wake Jack.

A quarter of an hour later she was up and dressed and had made a pot of tea.

When Keith came in he dropped his grub box and coat in the kitchen and himself on the settee in the livingroom. She put a mug of tea on the floor near him and sat in an armchair. The television, which was on with the sound low, reflected on his glasses.

Jack might still be sleeping, or having heard Keith come in, he might be moving quietly, straightening the bed and dressing. She listened for the soft bump of his feet through the ceiling but heard nothing. If Keith stepped upstairs that would be the end of it. There would never be a right time to tell him. She sat forward and licked her lips. He slid his fingers under his glasses and rubbed his eyes behind the lenses.

'Keith—' she said. But he sat up suddenly and, reaching for his mug, started to speak at the same moment. They both stopped.

'Aye?' he said.

'No. It's nothing.'

'I was going to say' he went on, 'had some bad news today. Emlyn have had a heart attack. Yesterday apparently.'

She sat back, made conventional responses of shock and concern.

'He's not dead' Keith said. 'Down the hospital. After the dayshift yesterday. He went to do some shopping for his missis. How many blokes can you see doing that? He collapsed on the bus. In the bus station luckily. Think if it had been in the street.'

The plain words made a clear picture. She could feel Keith

experiencing the scenes as he spoke. The ambulance depot was a couple of miles from the bus station, the bus station thirteen miles from the hospital. She imagined the waiting.

'I'll have to see if I can get down there tomorrow' Keith said. 'There's a hospital bus or something I think.'

She could hear Jack coming down. He came in looking bed-tousled. Keith looked at him and then at Judith.

'Hiya' Keith said. 'I assumed you were out.'

'Hiya butt. No, I was having a kip. You know how it is for us Men of Steel.'

She could feel Jack's forced breeziness grating on Keith, who, looking dulleyed through his glasses, sipped his tea.

THIRTEEN

Perhaps because of the diesel fumes from an old forty-five gallon drum, few flies buzzed in the maze of derelict cabins. Hard summer daylight through chinks in the girderframed and steelsheeted walls made the space lighter than usual.

O considered the row of bodies. After some early failures he had perfected his technique and now there were four. The oldest was dry and crisp and flattened. The others were at various stages of decay, lying on their sides with their forepaws held stiffly up as if they were about to tiptoe away on their hind legs. But the newest one was fresh, and big, and showed no damage from the shovel.

Pulling back the edge of his new rag glove, O saw that it was half past one. The rest of the day gang were in the canteen. They would stay there for as long as possible, especially as it was Kelv's last day. O had noticed Keith carrying a bar and sledge into the slabyard for one of the fitters that morning. So he was on days but would go for his shower soon. This was perhaps the only chance O would have.

He stood up, feeling the sweat on the wrinkling of his trousers and boilersuit leggings at the backs of his knees. First he took the Sunblest bag of sandwiches from his pocket and tried putting the large new rat in its place. There was not quite enough room, so he replaced his dinner and unbuttoned his boilersuit. It was loose at the waist which meant the rat would slip down into the leg, so he gently pinned the animal against his ribs with one elbow. He rebuttoned the suit carefully and stepped out onto the mill floor near the roughing stands. There were few people around but he still walked selfconsciously and slowly towards the maintenance shop.

* * *

Clive, the fitter, after swilling and wiping his swarfega-ed hands, touched forward his thinning slickedback hair to give it once more the Elvis shape and illusion of mass. He used a piece of mirror which he kept in his maintenance shop locker and crooned quietly to himself as he turned his head to check his sideburns. Even the collar of his boilersuit was turned up, Keith noticed. Clive discarded his rag on the floor.

'All over for another turn, my beaut' he said to Keith. 'I'm off to the Berni Inn for a slap up feast before scrubbing my nuts and departing.'

He left for the canteen.

Keith washed and wiped his hands and took from the shift locker the plastic bag containing his books. He found a clean patch on the table in the windowless cabin. The dictionary and the notebook. It had been a busy shift, but he would have twenty minutes or so.

Emlyn had been out of hospital for a few weeks but would not be back before the closedown. He might even, he had said to Keith in hospital a month before, be on the sick until he reached early retirement.

Emlyn was gasping, almost naked in the overheated ward, his flimsy pyjamas pulled open and the plastic cups of the electrodes glued to his chest. He lay awkwardly on what looked like dozens of bolsters. His frizz of grey hair hung out, revealing the balding place.

A nurse, looking pressured and hot, came and took his temperature and gave him some capsules in a small plastic tumbler. She left quickly with no glance at Keith, or regard for the sentence she had broken. Keith noticed a pimple on her chin and the pinchmarks where her nails had milked it that morning. He watched her retreating calves, thought of the concrete pounding they did and the varicose veins to come.

There were four beds in this bay of the ward. An old man was leaving the one next to Emlyn's and was sitting with his clothes packed waiting for his family. In the two opposite beds were very ill middle-aged men. One had had a stroke, was moving one arm and making incoherent noises out of one side of his mouth. In the last bed, directly opposite Emlyn, a shuteyed, white, lined face was unmoving on the piled bolsters. The blankets were drawn to the chin, the head turned slightly to the window. He looked dead.

Emlyn and Keith watched the two men.

'That's Mr Collins' Emlyn said. His voice was faint and far down in his throat. 'He was crying all last night. God he's bad aye.' His swelled fingers twitched around the plastic cups. 'These things do itch.'

Keith imagined Emlyn not sleeping, listening to Mr Collins crying. There were lamps down below in the carpark which would show through the ward curtains at night. Outside in the sunlight there was a great billow of mountain and at its foot rich red farmland. It was a different world from home, fifteen miles away, where it was probably still foggy. Irrelevant. Spring blazed like an irony against the windows where the sick people lay.

Keith gave Em a booklet of Welsh placenames and their meanings. It seemed as irrelevant as the world through the window.

When Emlyn's wife arrived, carrying flowers and a wad of letters, Keith backed away clumsily. As he left the bay a nurse was holding down the confused man, who, naked except for a pyjama jacket, had flicked his blanket aside and was trying to get up.

In the corridor there was a waiting room. Its only window opened onto the corridor and it was lit by a single striplight. Keith was surprised at how sordid it seemed. The walls were smirched to shoulder-level by the rubbing of coats. The ashtrays were full and holes had been picked in the cheap upholstery, revealing the grey foam rubber in the chairs.

Emlyn had had a reprieve but would be back. This was where most people came to die. Jack's parents had. Judith's and Keith's parents would, and they themselves one day. What would you do if I popped off? she had said.

*

He put the books back into the bag without having looked at them. After locking the bag away he crossed the maintenance shop towards the door into the mill. The hook and chains of the block and tackle had been slid along their rail in the ceiling close to the door. Keith almost walked into the handsized steel hook, which was hanging at the level of his face.

Squeezed into the hook was the corpse of a rat. The tiny teeth were showing under the long raised snout. There was an opaque white film over each eye, like a cataract.

Keith did not move it but walked on and out.

As he stepped through the door into the great open space of the mill, O approached him. He was suddenly within inches of Keith's face. He beckoned, unnecessarily since he was so close.

'Keith' he said, 'I've been meaning to have a word with you.'

* * *

'I can't bear it with these bastards any longer' the schoolteacher had said to Jack. 'It wears you down in this place.'

That was months before, and he had gone.

At the end of Kelv's last day, some of the gang went with him to a pub. They sat feeling awkward in each other's company in clean clothes, taking the piss out of each other.

'Education is a fucking marvellous thing' Clarry said. 'That teacher went off to work abroad and here's you burrowing into the ground.'

Kelv said little and drank the pints they bought him. Clarry announced that he was going back to being a club steward after the closedown.

'You do all right, education or no' Sully said.

Afterwards Sully, Jack and Wayne waited for the service bus. Kelv drove away remarkably steadily and they did not see him again.

It was June and hard sunlight displayed all the details of the works. It was spread below them on the other side of the railings.

Jack swept his eyes along it south to north, the full two miles from the south gate past the converter shop, the blast furnaces, the open hearth, the scrap bay, the coke ovens, all recently shut and decaying, and then the parts still working; the hot mill, slabyard, galv, pickler, cold mill, tinning lines, and all the other departments servicing these; boiler shop, sling shop, shoe shop, medical centre, garages, offices, railway lines, bridges. He had begun to understand how the place worked or had worked, so that it no longer seemed, as it had at first with its ruddled stacks and rusting cathedrals, like the nightmare version of an utopian city, though a kind of city it was.

'What about us then?' Sully said. 'Who's next to drop down the pit? It's like one of them detective stories where they do get bumped off one by one.'

'Except nobody did it' Jack said.

'They're opening a marshmallow factory on the industrial estate' Wayne said.

'It's the married blokes I do feel sorry for' Sully said.

'Fifty jobs' Wayne said. 'Don' feel sorry. They'll probably on'y take on women. Some of us will live off our wives.'

Jack knew that Sully was engaged, and said nothing.

'We'll just have to con our way into as much overtime as we can' Wayne said.

'There's none going' Sully said.

'The dumper down the cellars is broken down' Wayne said. 'One of the slaggers was telling me. They can't clear the slag quick enough from under the reheating furnaces without it. They're having to barrow it all to the skip. We might get a few turns out of that.'

'You grabbing bastard' Sully said.

There was a long silence. Jack looked up at the upturned keel of the mountain on the other side of the works. It stood between him and home. The mountain was steep and unpeopled. He remembered walking it years before. On this side the wimberries had been coated with a fine red dust from the works. On the far side they were cleaner and the mountain sloped more gently through moorland and pine plantations down eventually to the terraces.

'Fuck this' he said at last. 'I'm walking.'

It was steeper than he remembered it and it was nearly an hour and a half before he reached the ridge. He found no red dust on the leaves. The stuff that did the damage was no longer getting into the air, he supposed, perhaps came from one of the departments now shut.

He felt as if he weighed nothing, as if he could go on walking into the air when he reached the top. It was like bursting through the surface of the water after holding your breath for a long time.

When he looked across the next valley, he could see Keith's estate, the ugly fifties council houses piled near the top of the far ridge with just the rim of the Garn above them, to one side the stunted trees that showed where the cemeteries were. With binoculars he would have been able to see the house, movement in a window. Keith was on days and would be home.

Marvellous fucking thing, education. Don't let school interfere with your.

Even Judith had probed him about the year he missed school, deceived his father. Like a dentist with a probe she stopped when she found the place that hurt. It was part of the exploring, like children, who hurt one another and their parents.

A fine socialist. Your grandfather left school at eleven, I did at fourteen, you'll – et cetera – and through education comes change and not in my time but perhaps in yours, the millennium will come. Halle bloody luiah. And a good company man slogging his balls off would be the first to swell his chest and preen himself if I was, say, a schoolteacher raking it in in Saudi tax free or an index linked civil servant in Reading with double glazing. So who was deceiving who?

Would have been better if we'd had it all out. Mam would have understood. If I'd told him.

And then big brother coming back with a funny accent, looking down his nose, setting things to rights. Bastard.

You broke his

Christ, what if I had told him? A whole year. My whole life, he would have said. Generations sunk into hardened strata like geology all so that you can throw a tantrum and destroy it, or make it meaningless, which is the same thing. The hurt. No.

Tell him.

He descended the rough moorland and arrived at the unmade road through the pines. There were ruined drystone walls on either side. As he remembered them, the trees had been slightly taller than a man. Now they were fifteen or twenty feet high. The strong light, the yellowbrown dirt and the tumbled piles of lichened stones had the intimacy of childhood. But after a few hundred yards of being absorbed in the ground under his feet, the thought came back.

Tell him.

It was Judith who had suggested that, weeks before. The steel probe in the cavity, just finding the hurt. Checking on me. If I'm serious she thinks I'll want to tell. Clear the air. Then what? He moves out?

He imagined Keith running away. Exile, above all things, would hurt him.

Or better if we do the bunk. More like it. Leave him with ancestral voices and hurt pride. No need to tell. The central heating men arriving no longer needed. He only arranged that for her. Eating food cold out of the tin. Coming home off days and lighting the fire. And then laid off. Christ. But better than telling.

It was what made her worth knowing, partly, the steel probe. Like Liz, the Christlike combination of X-ray vision and razor honesty. Before the cock crows thou shalt deny me thrice.

I don' want to make the same mistake twice. Or I've already made it and how to get out? Retrieve what's retrievable. Hint. Taunt. But be honest? Christ.

* * *

198

After she had knocked up enough coal to last several days, Judith padlocked the coalcot and washed and changed into an old Indian cotton dress. They only needed a fire in the evenings and Keith would be in to light it. She put a tinned pie in the oven for him and sat at the kitchen table.

The open back door was alive with sunlight, though she was just in the shade, and a tepid breeze flowed over her through the thin material. She marvelled at how the world somehow cleansed itself by early summer. The smooth concrete of the back steps looked scrubbed, though it wasn't, and the grass of the back garden looked as if it had been wiped blade by blade. What happened to that sticky mess that seemed to cover everything at the end of winter? She had noticed earlier that even the litter along the footpaths through the estate – sweetwrappers, buckled drink cans, and in one place the front fork of a child's bike, seemed purified, made almost venerable by the dry and the light.

When Keith stood in the doorway he was like a disembodied shadow. He wore dark cords and a grey sweater and his hooded coat, which he carried like a talisman almost all the year round, was over one arm. He shut the door and the gallons of marigold air snapped out of existence. In the diluted grey light that replaced it she could see how the climb up the hill had made him sweat in his hairline and there were beads of condensation on his glasses.

He sat down at the table with her for a while, playing with his plastic grub box and not looking at her. She talked about nothing, about the planned central heating and the buckets of coal she had prepared, about shopping, about a bill she wanted him to settle in town the next day. She heard herself talking aimlessly as though to stop his silence forcing itself on her. It was something she had never done before.

Presently he looked up and stared at her. Her eyes flicked away and he took his glasses off. When he looked at her again after rubbing the reddened bridge of his nose she could sense the fuzziness of his vision, his pupils looking blank and unfocused.

'What's the matter?' she said.

He said that there was nothing the matter and got up to hang his coat, which he held across his front like an apron. At the door he stopped.

'Do you feel sexy?' he said.

She saw his eyes move over her and felt unpleasantly naked, like dreaming of being naked in the street.

'What do you mean?' she said. 'No. It's just nice and mild today, that's all. Are you all right?'

'Yes.'

He changed and sat in the shadowy livingroom while his food warmed. She opened the back door once more. He stayed in the livingroom to eat his pie, the plate balanced on his knees. She went in once to fetch a magazine and saw that he was watching his reflection in the grey television screen.

Jack got home late. His usual time was towards twenty past four, unless he had a flyer, but it was well after six. Cold fresh air entered the house with him and his cheeks were flushed. Judith still sat in the kitchen enjoying the last of the warmth while Keith watched *Wales Today* in the livingroom.

She was eating a carton of yoghurt as Jack walked in. Seeing her summery dress he pouted his lips suggestively and made a low growl of appreciation. He put his head into the livingroom.

'Aye aye, butty' he said. 'Master at the hearth, maid in the kitchen. Ataboy.'

Then he came to Judith and kissed her shoulder. She spooned some yoghurt into his mouth and kissed him back.

Later, the three sat in the livingroom. Keith and Judith sat on armchairs, Jack on the settee. It was becoming cool and dark and slowly the daylight grew weaker than the flickering glare of the television. Keith's glasses were blanked with the reflected picture. He seemed absorbed in the programme. Jack talked inconsequentially about someone leaving work that day and Keith, irritated, determinedly ignored him. She watched Keith carefully. He was slumped in the chair, his arms half folded across his rolls of midriff, his head turned slightly to face the television. She wondered what he would do.

Shivering, she got up, pulled on a cardigan and sat on the settee next to Jack. When she leant across him, pressing one hand on his thigh to reach the TV magazine which was on the far armrest, she felt him stiffen and his inconsequential words faltered. He looked at Keith anxiously.

'I'm tired' she said to Jack. 'You don' mind if I lie down do you? I en trying to shift you.'

She lay with her head on the armrest and her legs crooked across his lap. Straightening her legs as if stretching, she yawned showily. He was pinned, absurd and frightened, and he stopped talking. Settling her head down, she half shut her eyes but could still see, blurred through the lashes, the points of light where Keith's glasses were still reflecting the images on the screen.

* * *

Wayne had been right about the dumper truck breaking down. The following day Lew Hamer offered Jack and some of the others a shift of overtime down the cellars. They would come back in with the nightshift at ten and work through to the end of the following dayshift at two the next afternoon, instead of their days regular stint to 3.30. Lew took Clarry, Sully, Wayne, O and Jack down the cellar and showed them the job.

It was in a different area from the place where the man had been scalded. In the striplighted bays beneath the reheating furnaces the slaggers worked. When a furnace was periodically cleaned out with jackhammers, the old inner brickwork and slag was dropped through a trap onto a concrete stage in the bay. The team of slaggers shovelled this onto a dumper which transported it to a skip. The skip was open to the ground at one side and wide enough for the dumper to drive into. It lay at the end of a long unlit alleyway, at the bottom of a shaft up which it could be craned and emptied onto a spoilheap. The ceiling in the bay was quite high but it was still too small a space to keep the dumper's engine running all the time, so it had to be recranked every time it was filled with slag. Jack imagined the blue diesel smoke thumping out of the exhaust in the bright light. The dumper, clapped out, had been craned up in the skip and now there was one builder's wheelbarrow and some planks laid along the potholed earth floor of the unlit alley.

Jack had never been in on a nightshift before. Overtime was rare with the shutdown approaching. The hot mill canteen and the offices were shut and in darkness, the day gang's building locked up. Lamps lit odd corners revealing slimy walls, downpipes, a patch of ground. These scenes hung in unconnected patches on the general dark. The brightly lit bathhouse was silent. Inside, Jack changed and waited for the others. He walked down the central passage, looking down the empty perspectives of the rows of silvered lockers. Like a library, almost.

He found O sitting alone on the narrow steel bench. He had changed and his hands, the fingers doubled into loose fists, rested on his knees.

Probably so as not to get his fingers dirty on his overalls, Jack thought. O stared at a point in space expressionlessly. Above his head the door of his clean clothes locker was open.

Poor bastard. Haven' got the imagination to be bored.

'Fuck me.' Wayne had arrived, and, standing next to Jack, was staring at O. 'There's a picture for you. What do you reckon he's dreaming of?'

Babies. Nothing. Tick tock tick tock.

Jack remembered the LP on the woodcased school mono, the teacher looking bored, the kids baffled by the first week of A levels. As far as he got. One week and then up the cafe for a year. Milk Wood wasn' it? The famous photo of the knobblyfaced pisshead author on the record sleeve. Crap. Better a year on the flipper machine and boot up the arse to end it.

'Nothing' Jack said.

'Aye, I reckon too.' Wayne whistled through the gap in his teeth. 'Oy. Prickless.'

O started and stood up.

Whereas she would dream of – babies, perhaps. Or no. Nothing, like O. He could almost love her for that. Strange. He despised and pitied O by turns for the same thing. Whatever you thought about, the clock still ticked. *Nothing* the most heroic thought then.

O took a short pencil from his pocket and quickly jotted something on the inside of his locker door before shutting it.

'What's that you're doing, O?' Wayne said. 'What do you reckon, Jacko?' He turned his pale, redrimmed eyes on Jack. 'I reckon he's keeping a fucking tally of his lefthanded wanks.'

O locked the door quickly – his was one of the few that could still be locked – and thrust the key into his pocket.

'Come on. Gi's a look' Wayne said.

He moved forward to take the key. O turned his back and hunched against an attack. Wayne wrapped his arms round him, clutching for his pockets and trying to turn him. O squealed and Jack saw the key go spinning across the floor and disappear down a grating. Wayne released O and moved away.

'Now look what you've done, you twat' Wayne said, pre-empting any attempt at anger by O, who, redfaced and near to tears, stood panting.

'Prickless man can't wank, Wayne.' Sully had arrived with Clarry. 'Not even lefthanded. Being an expert on wanking yourself I thought you'd have realised that.'

Jack saw Wayne back away. O crouched on the floor, peering down the grating.

'All right, O' Sully said. 'We'll have to prise your locker open with a bar after.'

Or perhaps she was bored. That little demonstration for Keith yesterday.

The small gang went through the empty mill and down to the row of bays in the cellars.

Their shovels grated in the slag and they took turns to trundle the barrow down the long tunnel. Surprisingly, that was the hardest job. Four of them could fill the barrow very quickly, but the slag was heavy, and only one man could wheel it at a time. Eventually Sully, the strongest of them and fairly sober even though it was a nightshift, took over the barrow and upped the pace. Sitting sweating, he'd urge the others to fill it faster and then take the single wheel along the planks at a run. When he rested, Jack and the others reclined on the heaped slag.

'Hard fucking work' Jack said. 'Nothing like it, boys.'

'You'll be signing up with the NCB next' Sully said.

'Aye. Kelv I was thinking of' Jack said.

Sully looked at him. 'I know.' He looked away and cuffed the sweat from his forehead. 'Fuck me. A good sweat do clean you better than a fucking shower.' He stood up. 'Right then. Two skips up tonight is it?'

When they had filled one skip and had had it slung out to the spoil, they sat in the cellar and discussed plans. Jack noticed Clarry rubbing his back.

'Go on, Cla' he said. 'Go home.'

Clarry said no, he didn't mind staying his time.

'Look' Sully said, 'when we do come down your club for a pint when we're all on the dole, we don' want you with a slipped disc and too ill to pull us a free one. Now piss off, you silly old bugger.'

Clarry laughed. 'I can't argue with that can I?'

He got up and made to go. There was silence as he slipped down off the stage.

'Sure now?' he said, looking back.

Sully threw a lump of slag at him and Clarry, after ducking, retreated. They heard his cackle echoing from the far end of the cellar.

'Who else?' Jack said.

O said nothing. Wayne shrugged.

'No fucking point' Wayne said. 'Clarry's off in his car. There's no buses for us.'

'What's the matter with you, mun?' Sully said. 'I thought you was a big strong territorial soldier. Broke your legs?'

Jack could almost see Sully's mind working. Don' you understand? He'd said. I'm *fond* of the girl.

'How about you, Sully?' Jack said. 'I'm staying anyway.'

Sully looked him in the face. Her parents must be away or something. The rift closed, the ring given.

'We'll need three at least' Jack said. 'Two to shovel, one on the barrow. Us three'll stay. You go.'

'You must be fucking mad' Wayne said, 'if you're going to walk home now and come back in for half seven in the morning.'

It was perhaps five miles to Sully's home.

'Go on, get off to it, Don Juan' Jack said. 'On her own tonight is she?'

Sully looked at him for a moment and then threw his rag gloves into the empty barrow. He went.

The three remaining worked on. Without Sully and Clarry the atmosphere became strained. Wayne cursed them for leaving, though he would have gone himself if he had thought it was worth it. O became quieter than ever.

Jack wheeled the barrow for a while and noticed that the other two worked in silence. Once he saw Wayne lean over to O and say something quietly. O went on working. Finally Jack suggested a swap. His shoulders were stretched and hurting. He meant for Wayne to barrow but O gratefully volunteered.

O took longer and longer to come back down the unlit tunnel with every journey. Eventually the wait became too much for Wayne. He threw down his shovel, jumped off stage and ran down the alleyway. Jack followed, carrying his shovel.

At the far end light fell down the shaft where the opensided skip sat. In the centre, at the end of the last plank stood the wheelbarrow, dramatically lit from straight above like some devotional object. O sat to one side, leaning against one of the concrete pillars of the tunnel. He struggled to his feet as he saw Wayne.

'I couldn' tip the barrow up' he said. 'I was too tired.'

Wayne pushed him into the skip. O fell backwards over the slag. Jack arrived as Wayne hauled him to his feet. The top three buttons of O's boilersuit tore loose and he tried to catch them as they fell. Wayne shoved O towards the barrow.

'Empty it you useless cunt.' He pushed him towards the barrow again.

O struggled with the shafts. Finally he swung them round and tipped the barrow sideways. The slag slid with a scraping sound out onto the earth floor of the tunnel.

'You fucking—'

Jack caught Wayne's forearm as he moved forward. Wayne looked round as if he hadn't realised Jack was there. He hesitated and then pushed past Jack, went back along the tunnel towards the bays.

Jack made to help O to right the barrow but O dragged it away from him.

'A' right, a' right.' Jack backed away, holding up his hands.

From the far end of the alleyway Wayne shouted, 'I'm off up the boiler shop canteen. Either of you fuckers want anything?' He went without waiting for an answer.

Mad bastard. He'll kill somebody one day.

After they had cleared up, Jack shouldered his shovel and walked alongside O as he trundled the barrow. It was the best part of a mile to the boiler shop canteen. They would perhaps go later. O kept stopping and hanging back. Jack didn't realise at first that O was trying to avoid walking with him.

Waiting for O, he said, 'That Wayne's a bit touched I think.'

O said nothing and slowed down. As they emerged into the lighted cellar, Jack could see that his face was cast down and he was sulking like a small child.

'Are you all right, O?' Jack said.

'Leave me alone you.'

O's anger would have made him laugh in daylight. It was twenty past two in the morning and they were in a derelict cave under a doomed city. Just like science fiction, except no crystal to solve everything. Only a skipful of rubbish in the shaft of light in place of the altar. The answer was elsewhere, down mammary valley dreaming of babies. O's playground emphasis on *you* seemed only sad.

O hurled the empty barrow aside, or tried to, but it thumped back on its wheel, refusing to capsize for him.

'I know all about you' – again the playground emphasis – 'don' you worry about that. I know about you crawling and what for when it do suit you.'

He snatched his shoulders away and slouched towards the slagging bay.

Jack assumed an expression of surprise but it was wasted on the hot dry air. He put his shovel in the barrow and pushed it after O, trying to decide on a reaction.

Ignore it and carry on shovelling. Act indignant. Too late for that. Puzzled then. That would be nearer the mark and go better with the pause, though all the engineering of dialogue would be wasted in the cave without a crystal.

'What are you on about?' Jack said.

But O walked on and Jack, stumbling with the barrow, felt absurd.

'O' Jack said. 'What are you on about?'

He took up the shovel, left the barrow, caught up with O and grabbed his shoulder.

'What are you talking about?'

O turned and stuck out his chin still in the small boy manner.

'Get lost you' he said. 'My father's worth ten of you, and your father. I saw you.'

'What?'

'You had no business coming back anyway. Nobody who do get anywhere do.' He paused and Jack could see his fear begin to turn to pleasure. O put his face close to Jack's. '*I* saw you that night. On the stairs with your willie out and your hand up Keith's wife's mwt.' He glanced at Jack's hand on his shoulder and smiled nervously.

A curtain slowly rolled down in front of O.

Willie. Give us a game of conkers. I've got a thirty-two-er.

Jack opened his eyes and the curtain lifted. He tried to laugh.

It was a poor thing, a tightening of the ribs and a hiss of air through the teeth, not convincing in most circumstances, but just enough to freeze the leer on O's face. Jack patted his cheek softly.

'I do feel sorry for you, sunshine' he said.

Well what do you expect at two in the morning in the last, altarless cave under the doomed city?

O's face reddened. He looked down, pouting. Then he thrust his face forward again in a travesty of defiance.

'And I've told him' he said.

'You what?'

Jack's hand tightened on his collar and he pulled him closer.

'You *what*?'

O's face twitched and he pulled himself away, stepping backwards. 'Yesterday' he said.

Jack walked forward, pushing his palm against O's chest.

'Yesterday I told him' O said, retreating another step, 'when you lot was up the canteen.'

Jack hurled him backwards. O fell and Jack raised the shovel as if it was an axe. There was a squealing noise and O lay wriggling, though he didn't try to get away.

'You evil bastard.'

When she lay down on me, touched me up reaching for the magazine, he just sat and watched the box.

He looked down at O, who had thrown up his arms to protect his head and was whimpering. Jack put the shovel down carefully and helped him to his feet.

FOURTEEN

Judith did not mind not having a holiday that year. Keith always resisted holidays anyway and one year when she had got him to go to Spain he had moped and starved for the fortnight. In his last year at the hot mill, he said, he wanted to work right through.

When her work was finished she would sunbathe in the garden or go to her parents' home and sit in the yard with her mother. He had reason enough not to want to bother. She imagined the scruffy works full of shadows and flaring lights, continuing perversely through the summer, and Keith conspiring with it, still wearing dark trousers and shirts, trying to look like a shadow himself. She imagined him getting old, more gross, and she looking after him, a disaffected servant to a failing machine, which was what Keith was, sort of. Except that she wasn't sure how disaffected he was in his service to the useless works.

Jack took a week off at the beginning of July. That Monday afternoon she was in the front garden when a long, bright yellow car slid to a halt by the gate. She craned to look over the wall and saw through the tinted window Jack uncoupling the seatbelt. He grinned at her through the glass, inevitably parped the horn. She was relieved that it didn't play a tune. She went to inspect and, glancing back at the livingroom window, saw Keith, who was home off days, watching.

The driver's door swung open low over the pavement. She could see Jack's thighs compactly designed into the space under the steering wheel, the brown and chrome dashboard looking reliable and solid in the summer light. The radio played mutedly.

'Wadya think, baby?' Jack said. 'I couldn' afford the gold bar and the sunglasses, less I'd have finished the image.'

'You haven' bought it have you?'

'Course.'

Squatting, she placed a hand on the steering wheel, pulled a face of disbelief.

'Did you rob a bank?'

'Not yet. I've got one in mind though.' He stared at her, keeping too straight a face, saw her doubting look.

'No' he said. 'I've hired it for the week. She's a beaut though.'

He gripped the wheel and looked mean through the windscreen. 'Just the job for burning off them twats with the furry dice. I always fancied a Capri. Come on then. Jump in.'

He waved to Keith, who had come to the front door. Keith came to the car slowly, looked along the length of the bonnet, said that it was very nice.

'Shall we go out somewhere?' Jack said.

Keith said no thanks, he was tired. He sat in the driver's seat briefly, ran through the gears, adjusted the mirror, then got out.

'Once you've got one' Keith said, 'you'll never be without one.' And then, smiling, 'Ballocks. If you haven' got the money you got to do without.'

Judith had never heard him say ballocks before. She took a turn in the driver's seat. Jack was in the passenger seat. She took his hand and placed it on hers on the gearstick.

'Show me' she said.

His hand lay a dead weight and he looked down. She looked up but Keith had gone back to the house.

Later, Jack offered jaunts to wherever she wanted. The following day he drove her to the Gower while Keith was at work. She had told Keith about the trip beforehand. He had nodded without looking at her.

Jack was uncomfortable on the beach. His skin was very white and his hairy body looked scrawny in the strong light. Judith basked but noticed him fidgeting. They walked along the lapline of the waves hand in hand like a bad Californian film. The wet sand was chill under her feet. Jack waded in up to his knees and his calves looked even whiter through the water.

Looking along the shore she saw the split grey rock and clumps of rough, salty grasses, the band of beach with its sunbathers laid out like strips of meat. The air was very clear. It must have rained there recently. The sea was crisp and dark to the horizon and glittering with points of light. Keith, had he come, would have been walking among the grass and stone.

Jack kicked the icy water at her.

'Come and paddle.'

She walked in over her ankles but it was very cold.

On the Wednesday he took her to Hereford. She had gently suggested taking her mother, not as a chaperone but because she thought she'd like a shopping session. Jack resisted so she did not press him.

He drove fast and seemed happy. It was sunny again and the town was busy because of the market. Judith had not been there for about five years, and was amazed again at the lushness of the countryside, the huge and orderly fields, the land undulating as if to an instruction to be interesting but easy to manage.

In the market she noticed the burry west English voices and the middle class English placeless accents, occasionally a Welsh voice tanging of home. In the livestock section they stopped at the penned sows, looked at one huge pig, its pink back bristled with blonde hair like a human arm. It lay on one side and she thought that it could never get to its feet. The efficient banks of dugs lay in the litter like repeated features of some machine.

Among the stalls of crockery and mass produced clothes she enjoyed the slowmoving press, the unexpected glimpses, through alleyways of backs and shoulders, of jars of sweets, a row of G clamps, cheap radios. After a lot of thought, she bought from a Sikh a fleecy underblanket for the double bed. Jack followed her dutifully with a plastic bag of small purchases.

Later they sat in the nave of the cathedral. She let her head drop back and stared up through the near solid bars of light to the vault, so dim that it seemed miles away. From outside she thought the building ugly, red and knobbly and small. Inside she felt the huge spaces like unfathomable water. Like the tardis or a theatre, only more so. She laughed at the thought. Looking at Jack, she felt a sudden warmth for him.

'This is like being married' she said.

'The ceremony you mean?'

'No, the day out. The whole day. Like married people spend their time.'

'I suppose this do make it official then' Jack said. 'With this plastic bag I thee wed.'

They walked around the building and discovered on display in a glass case Mappa Mundi, a medieval map of the world. Using the modern diagram and notes posted to one side, they gradually began to understand the old geography. Jerusalem at the centre of the flat disc; the Red Sea literally red like an ox tongue; the pyramids like stepped palaces; Britain small and shapeless on the lower rim. Like a wrinkled foetus, Jack said. The tip of his finger on the glass covered a large part of what they supposed was Wales.

'There you are' Jack said. 'That's what they thought then. Nobody bothered to go and find out what it was really like. They thought god had explained.'

Studious tourists ambled past, pointing things out about carvings and traceries. Once, but only once, she saw a man in clerical robes.

When they went out they sat by the river. She stretched out, watched the sky pass, felt herself relax for the first time in weeks. It was because Jack was beginning to loosen here. For the first time since he had come home and said that Keith knew. Watching the clouds shredding against the blue, she thought that it was not quite guilt.

*

He had come back off his double shift on the same bus as Keith. They had sat together and walked up from the town together.

The three sat in strained quiet and at seven Jack went out. Judith went to bed quite early but Keith stayed up, staring dully at the television. She heard Jack come back and shortly afterwards his foot on the stairs. The bedroom door swung open. She blinked into the light and saw Jack leaning on the jamb. He was not swaying. He walked to her and sat on the bed. There was the smell of beer and smoke in his clothes but he seemed sober.

'He knows' he said quietly.

'Of course. Did you think he was an idiot?'

'Just innocent.' He paused. 'I mean somebody told him.'

'I didn't.'

'I know.'

'Who did?'

He waved his hand and walked back to the door.

'I'm drunk' he said. 'No I'm not. I tried to get drunk but I just went straight to the hangover.' He almost laughed. 'I'll file that one away.'

Later, after Keith had come to bed, she got up. She knew that her husband wasn't sleeping. His breathing wasn't right and he wasn't fully relaxed. She went to Jack, who was asleep at first. His erection came as he woke. She had thought simply to sleep cwtshed to him. His mouth was cold and wet, his bed slightly smelly, but she heard herself saying 'Christ' in the dark as she clutched his small buttocks and it came to its shuddering conclusion. They hung on to each other afterwards, still tense.

In the morning after Jack had gone to work she stayed in his bed for a long time. Keith was going onto afternoons and so would lie in for a while. When she got up she pulled on her nightie and went back to Keith's room. It faced the sun in the morning and was flooded with light tinged by the colours of the thin curtain. Keith lay on his side facing the window, one pyjama-ed arm outside the duvet. He was still, but his breathing was not audible so it was hard to tell if he was awake.

Standing in the doorway she said clearly and without emotion, 'Why don' you do something?'

He rolled onto his back and looked at her. He seemed honeyed with light and she felt mean and shadowy, standing with her arms folded across her breasts. Without his glasses his eyes looked blank.

The shredding continued. A shaving of cloud slowly arched back on the bulk it peeled from. It thinned and disintegrated showing blue through its rents. As the cloud became transparent she felt the huge space behind it. Lying on the bank and looking upwards was like standing in a very high place and feeling vertigo. You could almost detach yourself and tumble away in space.

Stretching, she felt the weight of her body and the illusion disappeared. Not quite guilt.

She rolled onto her side, feeling her belly hanging, to face Jack. He was on his back, eyes shut.

'We'd better go back' she said.

He slowly opened his eyes and looking straight into the sky said, 'Home?'

Her feet hurt after walking round the shops and her leg muscles twitched. The car fitted like a waisted coat. It was nice to relax in the gush of warm afternoon light as they drove back. Jack took a back road part of the way. He wasn't very sure of the route. So far as she could remember his family had not owned a car. She knew vaguely that they had to travel west, into the sun, but the roads switched back and fore. For a long time in the late afternoon they cruised over gentle hills on a quiet, hedged road. Passing over a high place they saw the road drop away and show mile after mile of land turbulent with ridges turning greyblue in the distance. There were hours of daylight left but the sun stood above the place where it would set, softening with yellows the rafts and islands of cloud.

She felt the car bump up onto the narrow verge on her side of the road. He turned the wheel to pull in close to a field gate and stopped.

'Nice view' he said, releasing the seatbelt so that it winched itself back on the inertia coil. He stretched his back and yawned.

She leant her head against the window. The wooden gateposts and the thick hedges seemed unchangeable. Through the tubular steel bars of the gate she could see pasture, clumped lush and green, not like the upland grass at home which turned the colour of lions' manes in this light. In the next field she could see a tractor working, its bright blue paint gleaming.

'I think sometimes I'd like to live in the country' she said.

'Listen.'

She shifted her head so that she could see him. He looked at her and then out through the windscreen at the vista homeward while he talked.

'There's nothing to stop us. If you wanted to we could – we could just drive away. If you wanted to.'

She looked at the distant tractor. The driver was skewed in his seat, looking back at something he was towing. The tractor jerked and stopped as if it had difficulty with the load.

'Where to?' she said.

There was a pause.

'Wherever you like' he said.

'We'd have to go back and collect some stuff.'

'Of course. We wouldn' go today.'

'What about the car?'

'It's a big company. I can arrange to leave it in one of their other places.'

'What about your job?'

He snorted. 'That's all over in a couple of months anyway. They won' mind if I just ring them up and say goodbye.'

The tractor jerked loose as if its burden, snagged somewhere, had suddenly been released. She looked at Jack again. His mouth was slightly open and one hand was on the steering wheel. The thumb moved nervously. She heard the car engine ticking as it cooled.

She looked homeward over the ridges dusted with sunlight,

thought of arriving in some town, taking the car back to the hire firm. He with his nylon rucksack, she with the zipped suitcase bought for holidays. She looked to him again. The thumb still twitched.

'Is it what you do want?' she said.

'If it's what you want. What do you want?'

On the other hand there was being trapped with a failing machine, and no morphine. Neither choice was like anything she wanted.

'Do you want me—'

She was about to say do you want me to do a flit with you, but when she paused she saw Jack shrug. When he looked at her she was reminded of an animal's eyes, eyes in a mask suggesting some presence but offering no contact. It was not quite guilt, she thought, that afflicted the animal, because his tenseness sometimes passed when they were away from Keith. Not fear either. It would be absurd to think of him as afraid of her husband. Humiliation, perhaps. Keith showed none, but Jack did. Sympathetic humiliation, enacting the hurt Keith should have, as Jack's own punishment, which leads back to guilt again – or no – only to another kind of humiliation at being not so good as Keith. She felt a mild pleasure at thinking this through.

'He's pulling a hedge out' Jack said.

He was looking past her head through the window. The tractor was dragging a thicket of earthclogged roots along the top of the field. She watched without seeing and did not look back to him when she spoke.

'You don' want me. I don' want you. So let's forget it.' Then she looked at him.

She had known that he would not be upset, but was still relieved when she saw that he wasn't. He tapped the steering wheel with the palm of his hand, held flat, as if to signal that that was that. She could see him looking for words, choosing a mood.

'I hope you'll be very happy together' he said.

'Neither you or him have got anything to do with me.'

The map of clouds were softer, golder, the ridges hazier, admitting of more possibilities than before. Briefly, as the car started and slid down the hill, she felt only the great space.

* * *

Auntie uncle and Viking ship? Not on your. But then. Briefly things hold together and then like twigs in a stream they get pulled apart by the current and the river only.

He had seen his uncle once in the town. Thinfaced and spectacled, walking quickly. Went straight past. He would probably have mistaken Jack for his brother as he had always done, so Jack was relieved.

The cards on the stand in the dole office promised nothing. There was nothing in the local paper. Except, one week, a story about a man found drunk in charge of a horse – file that one – but no work.

Jack stood by the cold slabbing mill. It had been closed down over a week and slabs were being brought into the works by lorry. That couldn't last long. He imagined them exhausting the stock in the slabyard and then shutting. Wham bam thank you, butty. It had been, as Sully had said, mostly some money for a lot of old rope, though they would have preferred some real work.

The week the slab mill shut some of the day gang had extra cleaning jobs around it. Lew had even given them a couple of bags of grit to soak away the oil and grease spills. They found the reason for this special attention when a film crew arrived. All the men were issued with hard hats, and some ingots were filmed as they were rolled into slabs. Jack laughed at the nervousness of the crew and the way they jumped when an ingot boomed and cracked out sparks as it hit the rolls. Wayne asked one of them what it was for. He was vague about the answer he got, but it was something about archives. Jack stood next to an old rigger wearing huge leather gloves and a metal helmet and they both tried to edge into the shot. But the rigger was watching the mill. He told Jack they were watching history and Jack, trying to look solemn, said nothing.

Disused, the slabbing mill stand looked bigger, seeming to go to the roof. There were no signs of it being dismantled yet.

Hot slabs were still dropping through onto the delivery table of the reheating furnaces. Jack walked past them, noticed the bright green and red paintwork of the cooling pipes, wondered about the scalded man in the cellars. There had been nothing about him in the local paper either.

Imagine, having your balls burnt off in the last rank fart of a spent industry. A mixed metaphor worthy of one who, after the first week, never made it out of the cafe in time for a lesson. Babies. Nothing. Tick tock. Tick tock.

He skirted a blackhot cooling slab on the mill floor and made for Ben's cabin. Unbelievably, though it was August, the radiator was on, the pure water from the leaky valve still distilling itself into the silvered tin. The metal teapot was balanced on top and Norman, alone, sat in the cabin reading by the striplight a battered and dirty paperback. *Seven Years in Tibet* by Heinrich Harrer, price 2/6.

Norman muttered a greeting and Jack sat, watching the turn of a page. The welder's face was expressionless, patient rather than thoughtful.

'What's the matter?' Norman said.

Jack wondered what signal he must have been giving to make Norman think there was anything wrong.

'I don' know. I'm bored.'

'We're witnessing the death of an industry' Norman said, his voice monotonous as always. 'It's sad.'

Jack said nothing and a few more pages turned. Wings flexing. Haydn Luke had walked in on his missis and Ieuan Whatsisname banging it all round the bedroom like everybody did the night Sunderland won the cup and he didn' do anything and she made the move. Except Judith wouldn't, thank god, wouldn't make the move.

The sky that time they were in the Capri had been full of babies, clouds curled like unbearable rosy cherubs in a painting except all too bearable really in a sky the colours of childbirth as the earth slid round. I'm nothing to do with either of you or something like that she'd said. Thank god. The X-ray vision and razor penetrating and flaying but thank god she knew. So she won't make the move and therefore.

He looked at the book's wings flexing.

'What's the matter, butt? You okay?' Norman looked out of his expressionless face. 'Fancy something to read? I got a box full of books in the welders' cabin. Travel books mostly, mind, and quizzes. One of the boys got a couple of detectives I think. Come and have a look.'

He followed Norman to the welders' cabin. He'd never seen it before, though he'd heard others talking about it.

'Fucking welders' Ben had said one day. 'They'm worst than the bastard free masons.'

It opened off a squalid windowless place of homemade lockers and scrap. The cabin was very clean. The floor was not black and for the first time outside the canteen, Jack saw clean, red tiles. The plastic tabletop was white and the walls were decorated with posters and paintings. One poster, he recognised, was a Dali. There was a painting on hardboard by one of the welders of a slightly clumsy white horse in a field.

Norman rummaged in a cardboard box and then noticed Jack looking round. From a corner he produced a few small pieces of sculpture made from welded scrap. One was simply a chain draped artfully, welded into place and painted. Norman talked about the boys who had made them.

'There's one I did' he said, pointing above the door lintel. It was a crucifixion made of scrap, emeried smooth.

'You got to make something of wherever you do find yourself' he said.

All that selfsacrifice crap. Your grandfather at eleven, me at fourteen, he'd say. Sunk under the strata like geology making ourselves the earth under you. This is my beloved son in whom I am bitterly disappointed. In any case, twofaced because he wanted earthly success, socialist millennium or no, whatever happened to the rest of the world.

The sculpture, smooth and stylised, completed the effect of the cabin as a kind of shrine, a side chapel in a large church.

In the labyrinth beneath the doomed city on the small planet at the remote end of the galaxy is the still point, the solving crystal, and when you crawl all the way back against all the solar winds that push you away from the source because the river only runs one way, when you get there, naturally, you drop your spacesuit and shit on the altar.

'Interesting' Jack said.

He avoided borrowing a book, though Norman, saying that travel broadened the mind, urged him. Jack said that he had a science fiction novel in his locker and left the welder still browsing through his own books.

Because home is a place where you can crap with the, but when it's not home you can't because the river.

So flexing my wings which way do I take off? If not auntie uncle and Viking ship, then index linked double glazing in Reading. Bastard. But then, he'll probably be compassionate, understanding, etc. He's that sort of bastard. For a few months at least. Pushing his glasses up. You see, my wife. And perhaps a job, a real job with real work and hence money and who knows, a car. So money can deliver into your own hands the control of your destiny. Worth a try at least. A letter to prime him. Yes.

You broke his

No. Surely he'll be smarmily compassionate. Ask no questions, tolerate me for a while, keep his wife amenable. So long as I stay polite. Make no mention of whirring curtains and their causes.

They got all the coal and ore so they go and rip up the rails, his father had said, maroon us. Well, true, except the place has been kept on longer than is wise, blood and air pumped in after the will is gone, the slabs delivered. And me moving off the exhausted earth.

The sex dried up for a month, she just waiting for me to go, knowing that lack of money, lack of fanny will dislodge the lodger. X-ray vision again, though X-rays forfeit seeing the meat clearly. Leave them then to die of terminal boredom and each other.

Jack sat holding the letter in the coming dusk. Judith watched television. Keith, sitting by a lamp, was studying some pencilled notes and flipping through the red-covered Collins-Spurrell Welsh dictionary that he had been carrying everywhere for some weeks.

'It's from my brother' Jack said.

There was a side and a half of a fair semblance of civility, but then civil was his line, though it seemed like a note from no one Jack knew, written in standard language, not the half elided familiar kitchen tongue that would, if it was written, seem forced anyway.

'He says I'm welcome to go and stay with him while I'm looking for a new job. In Reading.'

'Tidy' Keith said. His finger rested on the page as he looked up. 'You know it's okay to stay if you want to.'

'I don' think' Jack said, 'it would be a good idea in the circumstances.' An almost diplomatic bit of lego language clicking into the circumstance.

Keith looked back to his book and the other two watched him.

Break the tension.

'What are you doing anyway?' Jack said.

Keith laughed apologetically. 'I'm trying to translate some grave inscriptions. It's bloody difficult sometimes.'

'What for?'

'I don' know. Just because.'

Pause.

'I on'y got three weeks left on my contract anyway' Jack said. 'Counting this week, so I'll hand in my notice and finish a week early.'

Keith looked up from his book again as if he was interrupting his own thoughts in midsentence and said, 'Okay.'

Not a wet eye in the head. Goodbye, goodbye, you stinking dugout. Mam have tied all my bits and bobs in a little blue cloth that she used to tie her hair in, or she might have done if she hadn't gone and died years ago, and there's glad I am not to look back at this hole in the earth. And it is holding my thumb out I am by this welshcake shaped roundabout while the small birds twitter in the September dawn and it is hammering past are the articulated lorries, the homely Welsh young executives in their cosy company cars – see you them not? – and their suits of fine flannel hung at their heads tapping at the tinted glass.

His blue rucksack was propped against a post. It contained more clothes than it had when he had arrived: a new pair of shoes, a roll of money, a cheque book for a bank account he had not had before, a battered Michael Moorcock novel fished from the bottom of his locker, trousers that were not baggy crutched.

Distantly, on a hill, some smoke was rising. It was not a coaltip smouldering, but the town rubbish dump, its jumble of smashed sofas and salmonella-filled plastic bags burning spontaneously. The warmth attracted, he remembered from childhood explorations, the mountain ponies gone feral, who duly poisoned themselves on the plastic bags and got their hooves stuck in rusted tins.

The air was the colour of lead. It and the traffic were the right background for his headache, the remnant of yesterday's hangover. He looked away from the road, northward. Beyond a small housing estate, creeping onto the edge of the moorland, were the red-leaded girder skeletons of new advance factories.

Give up. Come with me, boys. How Jack went to seek his fortune. Look, Puss. (He slaps his thigh.) London twenty miles. Except no pussy do travel with me and I was always too intelligent to go to the smoke and become a tramp.

After a few minutes, he gave up looking expectantly at the random drivers who had power over him. Cursing, too, stopped after a few more minutes and he petrified into position, his thumbing arm partly raised, like a bird with a broken wing.

Leave them in their timidity to die of each other and. Or whatever it is they want to do.

He had had to suggest the farewell drink to Keith and Judith on the Saturday, having made his goodbyes to the boys in work the previous day.

'Good for you' Clarry had said. 'If I was a bit younger and unattached I'd be off like a fucking shot.'

Judith had backed down. The idea was evidently too grisly for her, but Keith, although Jack had tried to signal that he had only made the offer for form's sake, agreed.

They went to Cefn Club with the stopped clock and the brass cribbage boards and the cast iron Britannias.

In the street outside they met Sully, dressed in his white jacket and flares, his shirt tail out. He leant against the wall and was swaying.

'Good god mun, Sully' Jack said. 'What are you doing? Pissed up already and it en half past eight.'

'Jack mun, you old bugger' Sully said. 'Ey.' He crooked his finger, for Jack to approach and placed an arm round his shoulder. 'Guess what. Guess what. I'm getting married in three weeks and I've had a bump. I've had a bump.' He whined quietly for a moment, but the maudlin tears did not come. 'Look' he said suddenly, yanking at his trouserleg. 'I've twisted my ankle.'

Jack looked down at the ankle, swollen under the sock to a scarcely believable size.

'Tell you what' Sully said. 'Last week next week. I'll have the bastards. Three fucking years on short contracts. I'll go in on Monday and twist my fucking ankle in work. Slip on a bit of grease. Have comp off the bastards for it.'

Jack and Keith, acting as crutches, slung him Christlike between them and carried him to a bus stop nearby.

'I need the money see' he said. 'It's on'y three weeks.'

In the club, the middle-aged and old men were ignoring the television, playing cards, steadily, quietly drinking. The younger men were beginning to leave for the pubs where girls swigged halves of lager.

Jack and Keith smalltalked for a while, as if nothing had changed.

If I was to stay, Jack thought, eventually we would forget this. But if the river only. This is spent. I have sucked it flat. Still, do the decent.

'Listen, Keith' he said. 'You know this have all been my fault. It was stupid to come back.'

Keith said nothing for some time. He bought Jack a fresh pint, but not one for himself.

'Must be odd to come back' he said as he sat down. 'Especially to go and see your old home have been demolished.'

Monnigan's and Mrs Rees's and our door and Dad or Keith and behind him Mam or Judith and Dad sinking down, his thighs and shins collapsing up into the ribspace, telescoping up, deflating, being sucked flat. No. Wait. On the white hill a blur strangely white, as if there was no street there, just snow, but I did not look up to check. The whole street gone.

He saw Keith observing his reaction.

'Sorry' Keith said. 'Didn' you know?'

Seeing Keith caressing the cast iron belly Jack asked him if they intended having kids.

Keith avoided the question, showed his own kind of X-ray vision, mentioning Liz.

But that can't hurt because it's past, and the river.

The night slid away into alcohol.

Suddenly in the one star hotel, Jack was talking urgently. The tide out and the bloody chartists.

'You're bloody morbid you are, butt' Jack said. 'Stuck in a time warp. Obsessed with the past. I'll tell you what. You're already dead, stuck in this bloody dugout. The historical significance of fucking ballocks.

Tradition. Balls. Your father's a bus driver for Christ's sake.' Over the din of the crush of drinkers he could barely hear his own words.

'He worked underground with your father' Keith said. He still had his coat over his arm. 'And in the works together after, before he got out.'

'Listen' Jack said. 'You like history because it's safe. It's all dead. Why don'*you* fucking get out?'

And a hand tugging the empty glass from his resisting grip. Stoptap ten minutes ago. Dailymailman from the generator room. Ray helpfully helping out, bored and sober, clearing up, asking, 'Is this one dead?' Officious twat.

And outside on the tilting wet pavements people pouring onto the streets from the shutting pubs and queuing outside the Chinese, and Wayne, sober, smiling quietly, saying something, a girl on his arm, flobbing yellow phlegm out through the gap where his front teeth used to be and Keith shouldering Jack, under his arm, taking him not quite home.

Rust of wimberry bushes and bracken the next day, sobering on the mountain.

You can't wish the dead good luck but good luck anyway. I hope you're both.

He picked up his rucksack and ran towards the car which had stopped twenty yards on.

Too intelligent for the smoke, too much of a coward for this. He almost flapped his arms as he ran.

Goodbye you tumbles of wet slated roofs, you faceless new estates, you acres of demolished terraces.

He stowed his bag on the back seat and flung himself in next to the driver who was bleakfaced, in indeterminate middle age. Looking past him, Jack saw the smoking, spent town snatched away by the car's movement.

* * *

Fitters' mates were not in demand. Not in Scunthorpe nor in the new tinning lines at the north end of the works due to start that week. Most of the skilled men were moving to these places. Some, like Clive, the thinning Elvis, were taking redundancy, getting loans and starting their own businesses.

'Front doors, new windows' Clive had said to Keith. 'A lot of graft, my beaut, but you got to make something of yourself. Me and my brother-in-law. He've already got a big shed.'

On the last day, Keith watched the last slab drop out onto the delivery table of the reheating furnaces. He had never seen the mill floor so crowded.

For him there were few possibilities. His redundancy money would cover the new central heating and a small amount to save. There were factories to try. He had written letters. Mostly they took on women for assembly line work. Jude was trying too.

Not dead, Jack. Not quite. First the coke ovens that made the coke then the blast furnaces that burnt the coke to get the iron from the ore then the open hearth and the converter shop that turned the iron and scrap into steel ingots, then the soaking pits, then the slabbing mill, then the hot mill that made the coil. Like some creeping disease that started with the feet. He had almost apologised for living there. Keith had known what was likely. Drunk that night nearly a week before, Jack had not told him anything he didn't already know.

In Cefn Club Jack said, clearing his throat, 'So what now? What's next for you? You and Judith going to have kids?'

Keith took his hand off the cast iron belly of the woman moulded on the table leg. He had been noting again how many casts were needed to make one table. The cast was very common, must have been produced in huge numbers, like a piece plastic injection moulding now. I met a girl up there he had said. Liz. It all got on my nerves and I blew. A word from the past.

Keith looked at Jack.

'This girl' Keith said. 'She was pregnant wasn' she.'

It wasn't a question.

Jack looked into his eyes for a fraction of a second before picking up his glass. 'Of course' he said before putting it to his lips.

'You ought to—' Keith hesitated. 'You could go back there.' Jack smiled and gave a short, unspontaneous laugh.

'I don' want to make the same mistake twice' he said.

Keith didn't follow this, but felt that he should not question it. He had guessed a long time before that O must have told Jack what he, O, had done. He had guessed the morning Jude came in after going to Jack's room openly. It was a pity. If O hadn't said anything, Jack could have left, or perhaps stayed, with no hurt.

Keith kept sober by not drinking on his own round and sometimes leaving nearly full pints when they moved to a different pub. By the time they got to the bar of the hotel Jack was drunk and abusive, though it was too crowded and noisy for anyone to notice.

Still Keith felt his face redden when Jack turned to history.

'It's not something you can escape from' Keith tried to say.

As they spilled out through the double doors with the crowd after stoptap, Jack lunged across the pavement and missed his footing on the kerb.

A young man with closecropped blond hair and pale eyes helped him up.

'Wayne mun' Jack said. 'My old butty on the hot air gun.'

Wayne looked around at the crowd and the girl he was with to show that he was sober. Jack became mock confidential, made as if to whisper in Wayne's ear.

'I escape on Monday' he said. 'Two men vaulting one man tunnelling. "Himmel. The schweinhund ist gone!" Just like in the Victor.'

'Well done, butt' Wayne said, loudly, as if Jack was deaf. 'I know. Me too. I'm going in a couple of weeks. I joined up. I'm going to get to Ulster and shoot Kelv's in-laws.'

He patted Jack's shoulder, leant him against Keith, and moved away with the girl.

Jack raised a fist to indicate an erection. 'She's a cracker. Don' waste yourself on him, love. Come and waste yourself on me.'

He walked up the mill alongside the orange-hot slab as it passed through the rolls of the roughing stands. There were groups of men standing watching. Some, like Keith, were walking towards the top end to see the finished coil. It would be typical if it cobbled now. He smiled at the thought of men scattering if the inch thick metal bent and had to be slung hot onto the mill floor. A pity there was no sun that day. No bars and shafts of light to make known to them the steamfilled space above their heads. Dinistr y deml, though not, of course, diwedd y byd.

Keith ran past the finishing stands as the strip metal accelerated through them. It went faster than any man could run, certainly faster than he could with his gut bouncing inside his boilersuit. He heard the hiss as the waterjets cooled the steel black. It thundered into the coiler. In the distance he could see Aldrich, the manager, in his hard white hat. And by him, talking earnestly, clutching a greasegun presumably for ceremonial purposes only as it now had no other, was Dai Rutter. Breaking his marathon of nightshifts, Rutter, who smashed windows, who once hit a man clean off his feet and over the abrasive wheel. It was like seeing royalty on television, talking aimlessly, out of range of the microphones, to some objectionable bumlicker.

The last slab. It was a non-event. There was no blizzard, no panniered donkeys, no mysteries. The place lost money, that was all. The last coil of the old hot mill would be the first through the new tinning line and memorial tins would be pressed from it. Yet it seemed to Keith that the changes were very big. They were bigger than he had ever suspected and he felt that all he had even then was only a glimmering of the real scale. It was like discovering a huge dark planet that had always been there affecting tides and spasms in the earth and its effects permeated everything and so it was invisible. It was like the people who worked in the piggery who couldn't smell the pigs. Odourless, invisible history would blow them all apart and they would hurtle away from each other through space and never really understand what had shifted them. Except blowing apart was the wrong idea because it was a continuing process, evolving and breaking slowly and then occasionally twitching like this. And it included everything. Emlyn's collapse and Jack's biological imperative. Keith had seen a documentary once which showed a human jaw chewing food. The teeth and the articulating bone and the tongue systematically turned and rendered down the food, pinned it and bit it, pulped it and transformed it. The brain scarcely understood the exactness of the chewing it controlled, and the food, of course, had no consciousness. History was like that. It transformed things without their understanding it and the brain, which seemed in control – Moonlows and managers and governments – it, they, were trapped too. Except history seemed now too thin a word for this.

He took off his safety glasses and squinted, blurring the crowds of men to a dark smudge, trying to hold the glimmering in his mind, seize all the ideas. But the glimmer faded and the darkness melted it out of his grasp.

Replacing his glasses, he saw Rutter, jaw still articulating out of earshot, and the manager, hands clasped at the rear like royalty warding off the lickers.

Rutter would be preparing his story to go with the canon of fishing and army yarns, controlling experience by reducing it to anecdote. What the manager told him personally on That Day to be retold interminably to trapped innocents on nightshifts in some other place. That perhaps, was what historians did, or at least the bad ones. He imagined Rutter telling the story and was surprised to hear himself saying 'Ballocks' aloud.

There was that to thank Jack for, and Jude too. The day after Jack left she had snapped at Keith, was impatient. Keith understood this, he thought, though he didn't know what to do about it. And she had said: 'You know why us two got married don' you? Because when we came round to it we were the on'y people we knew left.' He had thought of Anne, then, on the mountain under shallowrooted pines. He had gone for a walk later that day, saw Ray pushing his daughter in a wheelchair tented with clear plastic to keep the wind off. He had thought of the love lavished on the purplefaced, shrunk child. In a way, the dying girl defined Ray. Jude was right, naturally. A kind of economics or natural selection of the emotions. But that didn't mean it was hopeless.

Climbing the steps to the bathhouse from the mill floor he noticed again the shield on the wall which showed a mill stand, square shouldered like a trilithon, and with a lightning bolt through it. Beneath was a motto:

ARWEINWYR YN Y MAES

He knew now that the last three words were Welsh for 'in the field' but did not know the meaning of the first. Taking the piece of blank paper and pencil from his boilersuit pocket he copied the motto. He would look it up.

* * *

On the last day, O clocked off at exactly half past three. When the second hand jerked up to the twelve, his palm, which had been poised, came down on the punchlever. It was busy around the clocks but the spotter in his glass and brick office seemed busy with paperwork.

Immediately after O, a darkhaired man clocked four cards quickly. O noticed him checking that there were men standing between him and the spotter.

It had, O thought, been a satisfying day and a satisfying week. One of the burners had cut a bakestone for him out of scrap on the Monday. He had taken home his rag gloves unused every day. His hands had got very dirty without them and he had scalded a thumb while using the steambag, but that did not matter and he wasn't sure, but he didn't think a week was long enough to get dermatitis.

That morning he had arrived early and placed his last dead rat in the day gang's cabin. Not near the poison tray. They went away to die. Wayne had picked it up and swung it round by the tail in the faces of the others and nobody turned a hair except for Sully who hopped away because he had a bandaged foot and spoilt it by getting angry and threatening to hit Wayne.

O had cleaned out his locker. It had no lock, but that no longer mattered. Carefully he rubbed the pencilled tally of sandwich bags off the inside of the door. He left his white hard hat hanging on the handle and his toe 'tector boots with the metal showing through the rent leather he placed on the narrow bench.

Outside the gate, O saw a black Viva with a new exhaust left parked, its engine running. The darkhaired man walked past him, got in and drove away.

On the pavement, Clarry, looking odd in his clean clothes and with his shiny pink head revealed, was talking to one of the slaggers. The slagger was near retirement age and had a big pot belly that hung over his belt.

'I got this as a silverneer' the man was saying. He held up his slagging shovel. The blade was worn away to about half its original size. 'Twenty-eight fucking years. Not with the same shovel, mind. It en bad down the cellars. The on'y thing is it do rot your teeth.'

O stood at the bus stop with Wayne, Sully and the others. O stood nearest the litter basket. It was like a normal day except all the men carried bags holding their dirty clothes, the small contents of lockers and private corners.

Before he went to his car, Clarry came to them.

'Listen boys. I'm starting back in the club next month. Come over and have a couple of jars. You too, O.' He looked at O, laying a finger on the zip of his blue anorak. 'It'll be good, mun.'

After he had gone, O looked at the straggly, nearly dead trees on the bank. The slab mill was gone and the pulpit and the rest now. A nice, solving blank space. Perhaps there would be more leaves.

Before he turned to follow the others as they got onto the bus, he took from his pocket the Sunblest bag containing crumbs and flattened bits of corned beef. Smiling, he threw it into the litter basket.

Note on the cover art

The cover is a detail from *Hot Strip Mill*, a painting by Norman Hepple (1908–1994), c.1952, courtesy of Ebbw Vale Works Archival Trust.

Norman Hepple produced a number of paintings commissioned for Richard Thomas & Baldwins Ltd (RTB), including illustrations of the strip mill, and the electric arc furnace. A number of the original illustrations have survived and are held by the Ebbw Vale Works Archival Trust. Hepple was a renowned portrait artist and became President of the Royal Society of Portrait Painters (1979–1983). He was also extremely interested in the architecture of machinery and the combination of these two disciplines is reflected in the natural looking relationship of men and machines.

LIBRARY OF WALES
FUNDED BY

Noddir gan
Lywodraeth Cymru
Sponsored by
Welsh Government

PARTHIAN

CYNGOR LLYFRAU CYMRU
BOOKS COUNCIL of WALES

"No boundaries will limit the ambition of the Library of Wales to open up the borders that have denied some of our best writers a presence in a future Wales. The Library of Wales has been created with that Wales in mind: a young country not afraid to remember what it might yet become."
Dai Smith

"One of the best things we have supported as a government."
Rhodri Morgan

PARTHIAN

In association with Planet Books, a new edition of this seminal book of Welsh literature by Charlotte Williams with an introduction by Professor Hazel V. Carby.

"It is Williams's Welshness that makes the examination of her mixed-race identity distinctive, but it is the humour, candour and facility of her style that make it exceptional... an engaging and perceptive voice describing an engrossing and particular personal story." Gary Younge, *The Guardian*

A mixed-race young woman, the daughter of a white Welsh-speaking mother and black father from Guyana, grows up in a small town on the coast of north Wales. From there she travels to Africa, the Caribbean and finally back to Wales. *Sugar & Slate* is a story of movement and dislocation in which there is a constant pull of to-ing and fro-ing, going away and coming back with always a sense of being 'half home'. This is both a personal memoir and a story that speaks to the wider experience of mixed-race Britons. It is a story of Welshness and a story of Wales and above all a story for those of us who look over our shoulder across the sea to some other place.

WWW.THELIBRARYOFWALES.COM

PARTHIAN

Nigel Heseltine is a long-neglected member of Wales's 'Golden Generation' of English-language short story writers which included Dylan Thomas, Rhys Davies and Glyn Jones. His stories appeared alongside theirs in major magazines such as *English Story* and *Penguin New Writing* in the 1930s and 1940s. This volume collects for the first time since their initial publication the stories published in Heseltine's *Tales of the Squirearchy* (1946), alongside a substantial number of stories never previously collected. Ranging from the starkly surreal to the subtly moving, these tales reveal Nigel Heseltine as a singularly talented writer, the equal of his better-known contemporaries.

"Heseltine is one of the lost voices of modern Welsh writing in English. This new collection of his remarkable stories—by turn farcical, violent, nostalgic and deeply moving—will bring new awareness of his work: it deserves it." Professor Tony Brown, *New Welsh Review*

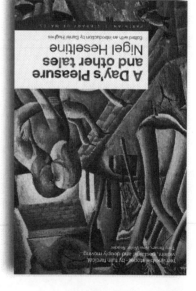

A Day's Pleasure
and other tales
Nigel Heseltine

Edited with an introduction by Daniel Hughes

PARTHIAN | LIBRARY OF WALES

'remarkable stories—by turn farcical,
violent, nostalgic and deeply moving'
Tony Brown, *New Welsh Review*